FUMBLED BEGINNING

S. JONES

Fumbled Beginning

By S. Jones

Cover Designer: Sarah Grim Sentz from Enchanting Romance Designs

Editor: Marla Selkow Espsoito

Proofreader: Virginia Tesi Carey

Formatter: Leanne Clugston from Irish Ink

CHAPTER 1

JP

"We've been spotted," Rhett whispered into my ear as we entered the crowded pub.

"Fucking fantastic," I grumbled, noticing a few cameras pointed our way. I was tired, sore, and in a shitty mood.

The bar was packed, which was no surprise for a Friday night, and I knew the second I stepped inside, we would have to fight for a place to sit. You could feel the stares and hear the hushed conversations about our presence, even though there was a Taylor Swift song playing at an uncomfortable volume. There was nowhere in the state of Georgia where ten Atlanta Arrow players could sneak in unnoticed.

"Am I the only one who thinks this is nuts?" Rhett asked as we edged our way toward the back bar, trying to minimize his six-foot-three tight end body from drawing any further attention.

"No more than the actual marriage itself." I glanced around, my level of irritation spiking because I allowed myself to get dragged into this fiasco in the first place.

Our teammate Beckett's soon-to-be wife insisted that this little bachelor party be low-key.

No strippers and no dance clubs. Just a few cigars and a little booze with the boys. If you thought that was weird, that wasn't even the craziest part. Carrie and Beckett were already married. Tomorrow was their "vow renewal" ceremony, but after the rough patch they went through last year and almost getting divorced, they thought this would be a good way to start fresh.

"At least they scheduled it during our bye-week. Lord knows we need one after that press conference. Rogers really knows how to rattle your cage." Rhett grinned.

"Probably needs to find ways to compensate for his small dick and even smaller brain," I grunted out.

Tristan Rodgers was a hungry sports reporter who was always looking to create a headline for himself. The guy would get a boner anytime he'd get a reaction out of me during our team press conferences. He pretended to ask tough questions about mistakes I'd made on the field. When he brought up the team delaying my contract extension next season, he successfully pissed me off. Instead of giving him a snappy comeback like he expected, I just smiled and gave him a politically correct answer. He wasn't happy with my response, probably because he wouldn't be getting a boner like he had hoped.

We squeezed into an open space at the bar just as a group of girls dispersed. They didn't look old enough to drink and practically had "fake ID" stamped on their foreheads.

"What's your poison?" The female bartender leaned forward, eyeing us impatiently. She had a scowl across her lips, most likely from dealing with assholes like us all night. While my eyes went to the liquor bottles lining the back, Rhett's drifted to her cleavage.

Not wanting to come across as a creep like my buddy next to me, I pretended to look over my choices even though I already knew what I would order. "We'll take two buckets of Corona and a bottle of Patron."

She lifted a brow. "You want the whole bottle?"

"Yes, please." I pulled out my wallet and dug out two crisp one-hundred-dollar bills. "Don't forget the lime."

Rhett slapped me on the back and turned his sly smile on her. "We'll also take a bottle of Jack."

She leaned back, folding her arms along her chest. "What does this look like to you, a liquor store?"

She was a little over five feet tall and weighed maybe one hundred and ten pounds soaking wet. Her size wasn't close to being intimidating, but with her fiery red hair and cunning voice, she came across as a no-nonsense operator.

"No, it looks like a packed bar, and my buddies and I are celebrating tonight, so the fewer trips we have to take to get refills, the easier it will be." I handed her a fifty-dollar tip.

"Suit yourself." She stuffed the bills inside her shirt and walked to the back room. Damn, I sounded like a grump. Probably because I'd been working extra hard in the weight room, pushing myself harder than I ever had in my life. With our season winding down, and playoffs starting, I'd spent all my free time focused on the game. I couldn't even tell you the last time I got laid.

Rhett bit the inside of his cheek. "She's kinda cute." My eyes rolled of their own accord. The guy was a walking, talking stereotype. He grabbed his phone out of his back pocket. "Think she'll give me her number?"

I clapped him on the shoulder. "Easy there, Romeo. We've only been here less than five minutes. You don't need to try to get in the pants of the first woman to speak to you. Let's unwind for a few minutes before you start propositioning the ladies."

He rolled his eyes. "Okay, Grandpa."

The object of his affection strode across the bar, carefully balancing the two trays. "Where are ya'll sittin'?"

I grabbed one of the round trays out of her hands and led the way.

Rhett started rattling out a series of pickup lines, which weren't going over very well. I was pretty sure he was going to crash and burn before he even sat down.

I slid my tall body into one of the four booths we had managed to take over and sprawled my legs out as far as they could go. Let's just say the booth would be better at accommodating a team of horse jockeys than football players.

I listened as the guys complained about the drills Coach put us through today, but I didn't join in. I loved the sport and every minute I got to play. I'd seen too many dreams end before they started, and I learned never to take getting paid to do what I loved for granted.

Our team was young, and we were eager to prove ourselves with our new starting quarterback. But desire didn't always result in a win. We were walking into the playoffs next week as the number two seed. San Diego was favored to win. Getting invited to the dance was just a start; these rookies would have to learn that lesson the hard way.

Rhett downed a shot of tequila and slammed the glass on the wood table. "Anyone else want to set Coach's car on fire for putting us through hell this week. It felt like he was analyzing our every move on the field and acted like we didn't have a chance to win the playoffs."

He wasn't lying. Every missed block, every dropped pass, every mistake was being picked apart and called out.

Mitch Morris, a starting defensive lineman, plucked a beer off the tray. "Stop being a pussy, Rhett."

"Did you not see me puking my brains out in the locker room on Wednesday?" Rhett whined.

"Maybe next year you might want to tell Mommy not to send you home with so many Christmas cookies." Morris smirked. "You're not getting any younger, so your metabolism can't handle all that junk."

We all laughed at the same time Rhett threw up his middle finger. He was always sneaking shit into the locker room that our team's dieticians would have a coronary over.

"You're all just jealous because you can't eat real food and still look like this." The goofball lifted his shirt up, giving us a full view of his abs.

My eyes darted to the TVs over the bar to check the scores of the two NBA games being played. I shook my head and lifted my beer to my lips when I spotted Rylee Cross, my ex-teammate and best friend's sister, occupying one of the stools.

Her black dress was so tight it caused the slit on the side to ride up her thigh. I would know that body anywhere, seeing all the attention I'd paid it over the years. The woman haunted or owned every one of my damn dreams, depending on how you looked at it.

Running a hand across my newly trimmed beard, I debated what to do. I could practically hear her brother's voice in my ear, warning me to stay away from her. But she was right in my line of sight, looking tempting in ways that made me want to forget about every single rule and boundary I set for myself when it came to her.

Mav and I had been friends for years, which was why I'd pushed my attraction to his sister to the back of my mind. There was no way in hell he'd approve. Not that anything would come of it anyway. It was a complication I didn't want or need.

Watching her from afar felt wrong, so I tore my eyes away and focused on a group of women sitting at a table nearby. I'd been so distracted and caught up in my thoughts, I hadn't spotted the guy dressed in a pair of khakis and a bright pink polo that looked like he just came from the country club after playing eighteen holes. My eyes squinted and then bounced between them. The douche was smiling. Rylee was not. She looked furious.

In an instant, I moved in that direction, keeping my eyes on her and the golfer the entire time. I shoved past a few people because I was a large guy, and it wasn't easy to maneuver through a crowded bar without bumping into a shoulder or two.

When I got close enough, I could hear her chewing him out while he stared at her chest.

"You catfished me." She raised her voice to the asshole who was still staring at her tits. Heaven help him if he didn't remove his eyes in the next second.

"Does that mean you're not DTF?"

"Excuse me?"

"You know, down to fuck. My face might not be what you wanted, but my dick sure will be once you feel the size of it." His chuckle was rough, and my blood pressure skyrocketed.

"Hey." I slid up against her back, placing a hand on her shoulder. "Everything okay over here?"

Her head whipped to the side, and those big, brown eyes widened in surprise. I was close enough that her light floral perfume inched up my nose, making my head buzz with awareness. I gave myself a second to allow my eyes to roam over her face and make sure she was okay.

The preppy-dressed guy with slicked-back hair glanced up at me. "Yeah, man, we're good."

"I wasn't talking to you, Tiger Woods."

He puffed his chest out like he was ready to take me on. "This is a private matter."

"I'm going to have to disagree with you there, pal." I crossed my arms over my chest, making my biceps bulge against the fabric of my shirt. I had inches, pounds, and muscle on the man, so the guy had to be smart enough to know that a fight would end badly for him.

"I'm not sure how this is any of your business." A bead of sweat started to edge its way down his temple. "This is between me and my date."

I moved to stand in front of Rylee. The dude looked at her over my shoulder, and after the shitty day I had, my patience was already wearing thin. I widened my legs, doing my best to block her from his view. I was going to handle this, and it would be his choice if it were the hard or easy way.

"Your date is over," I clipped.

"Is it now?" Rylee twisted in her seat and leaned her arm along the bar top; her tone was heavy with sarcasm. She didn't seem too thrilled with me inserting myself into her business.

I was overstepping and out of line, but it was my duty as her brother's best friend to look out for her.

Yeah, right! That was the only reason. You wanted her for yourself, you fucking hypocrite.

"Yes." I tilted my head to the side and fired a look at the guy who was watching us with a mixture of curiosity and panic. "You can go now."

"Wait a second." His eyes widened with recognition. "You're JP Watson. Dude, I just watched that clip of you and that reporter on SportsCenter. That was quite a pass you caught." He snapped his fingers. "Oh, wait, you dropped it three yards short of the end zone. Damn, that was brutal. You might want to get that hand checked out. There must be something they can do." A sneer touched his lips. "Like maybe put super glue on your fingertips."

My brain went back to every NFL training class I had to sit through and tried to remember every technique I was taught to control my temper because I was two seconds away from punching this guy in the nuts.

I looked around the crowded pub. The last thing the team needed was some bar fight footage showing up tonight on the eleven o'clock broadcast before the playoffs even started.

"You don't exactly look like you're in a position to be handing out advice on how to do my job."

"What's that supposed to mean?" He seemed genuinely offended.

I gave him the same condescending laugh he gave me. "Dude, you don't look like you've stepped foot in a weight room in your entire life, and looking at how skinny your arms are, I doubt you could carry my jock strap let alone catch a football moving fifty miles per hour, but I appreciate the laugh," I said with zero humor in my voice.

"Whoa, you don't need to be a prick about it. I was just busting your chops."

A muscle in my jaw ticked as I stared down the little fucker. Although he had a big set of balls on him, I'd give him that.

"Look, dude, if you're half as smart as you think you are, I'd start taking your photoshopped face to the exit. You're done here, now buzz off." I snuck a quick glance over at my teammates, who hadn't even realized I'd ditched them yet. They would give me shit if they knew I was over here pissing all over Maverick Cross's little sister.

He held his hands up and shook his head. "This is way too much work. I'm outta here, but you know what?" He turned as he reached the door. "I meant what I said. You can't catch a ball for shit, bro."

I shoved my hands in my pockets and clenched my fists. I counted to ten and forced myself to calm down.

"Hey, Pinky," I yelled over the noise as he was about to walk out. "If you even think about contacting her again, I'll show you exactly what my hands are capable of."

He flipped me off on his way out the door.

"Asshole," I muttered under my breath.

Rylee leaned back in her seat. Her dainty fingers curved around her martini glass. "You didn't need to scare him off. I am perfectly capable of defending myself."

I trailed my eyes down her exposed skin and composed my face quickly. "Really? Are you sure about that, Sunshine?"

"What are you implying?" She scowled like she always did at her nickname. It started out as a joke because she would always glare when I'd try to say something funny, but over time, it stuck. And I was getting the sense that she liked the fact that I gave her a term of endearment, although it might have been wishful thinking on my part.

I kept my face on hers. "You're only asking for trouble, meeting men on blind dates dressed like that."

My comment seemed to strike a nerve; something about her temper always made things twitch below the waist. "That's a sexist statement. Don't you think you're being a little judgmental?"

Man, I was really messing this up.

"I'm not trying to be insulting. You look gorgeous, as always." I winked, thinking a little charm might do me some good. But judging by her death stare, I was losing credibility quickly. "All I'm saying is, you might want to save the nice dresses for when you know a man well enough to trust him to keep his hands to himself."

It was men like me that she had to worry about.

"You don't seem to mind dating bimbos who wear far less than this."

I've bedded my fair share of women without any regard for how they dressed. I've always been honest and treated them with respect. There were zero expectations involved, so her point was irrelevant.

I leaned in close so she could hear me over the noise in the bar. Her breath hitched when I brought my mouth up to her ear. "I don't date them Rylee, I fuck them. There's a difference."

Her mouth parted open just enough where I could slide my tongue inside. The woman was testing my self-control, and it was the first time I considered this attraction might not be as one-sided as I assumed. "Maybe that's what I was hoping for."

It took me a minute to register what she was implying. I wanted to tell her if she was going to hook up with anyone, it would be me, but I didn't dare say any of that. Hooking up with your friend's sister might not be illegal, but in this case, it might as well be.

"With him?" I pointed over my shoulder where the pink polo shirt had just left. "I doubt it."

Her lips quirked up in a playful smirk. My body remained completely still while my brain fought like hell to rid the vision of all the things I wanted to do with that mouth of hers. I was weak when it came to this woman. Like an overflowing shopping bag, ready to break apart at any second.

"You're right." She darted her tongue out and swiped it along her upper lip. "I actually prefer a gentleman. Do you happen to know one?"

Did she realize she was playing with fire? That we were headed toward dangerous territory? Or was she simply provoking me to see how far she could push me?

Knowing Rylee, it was the latter.

I moved in, putting us at eye level, my mouth hovering over hers. It would have been so damn easy to give in, especially now that I knew she might not resist me. "Just because I don't date, it doesn't mean I'm an asshole."

"Never said you were." Her breathing picked up, and those beautiful brown eyes searched mine. "I guess that just makes you a player then."

"Technically, that's true, but I also have rules that I follow."

She was teasing me instead of fighting me, and I wasn't sure what to make of that. "Let me guess what the rules are. They have to have big tits, long legs, and are an easy lay."

We were close. So close that even I couldn't ignore the heated look in her eyes, or maybe it was mischief; I couldn't tell. Either way, it had disaster written all over it because she was one second away from kissing me.

My smile was big as I stared her down. "Why, Sunshine, you seem awfully curious? Are you interested?"

What the hell was I doing? Guilt squeezed my insides. We were playing with fire, and I was officially going to hell. This woman was off-limits. I shouldn't have been thinking about making a move on her.

"You would like that, wouldn't you?"

She had no idea. It took every ounce of restraint I could muster to hold myself back. Being this close to her and knowing I had to walk away was like being a little kid in an amusement park without any ride tickets.

"You know I would, but I'm not sure Maverick would approve."

"My brother isn't my keeper."

Like a bucket of ice water washing over me, I remembered what was at stake. This little encounter needed to end. Lines were getting blurred, and if I wasn't careful, someone would get burned.

"No, but he is my best friend, and he would kick my ass." I needed to get away from her before I did something stupid.

"What if I said I didn't care?"

I was so fucked.

Instead of kissing her like I wanted to, I brushed my lips along her cheek. "Name the time and place and I'll be there."

Yeah, I was going to hell, and it would be totally worth it.

CHAPTER 2
RYLEE

I spotted JP the second I stepped inside my brother's condo. The room was loud, filled with laughter and conversation, but somehow my eyes immediately went to his.

That almost kiss had been all I thought about. The moment his lips touched my cheek, I knew I was in trouble. I could only imagine what would have happened if we actually followed through with it.

No doubt, it would have been the type of kiss to consume me, but then what? We'd give in to temptation, spend the night together; he would wake up the next day and tell me he regretted it and start avoiding me, leaving me with a broken heart.

Yeah, no thanks! I'll pass. It was better this way. Easier. Safer.

He was gathered in a circle engaged in conversation with his teammates, but it didn't look like he was paying attention to what they were saying. He wasn't even looking at them. His piercing green eyes were fixated on me. My stomach twisted with nerves, and a tingle of awareness crept up my spine.

That swagger was in full effect as his strong legs ate up the distance between us. His thick, no-nonsense black hair was hidden under a ball cap. He was smiling, and those lips I dreamed about last night were formed into a smirk.

He came to a stop in front of me, and I crossed my arms over my chest. Seeing that he was my brother's best friend, I knew there was a good chance that he would be here, and I might have put a little extra effort into my appearance.

"Hey, Sunshine." His gaze raked over my red mini sweater dress and thigh-high boots that I picked out with him in mind.

"My name is Rylee." I scowled, causing him to laugh. Barbs and sarcastic banter had become our thing over the years.

"I know, but it sure is fun ruffling those pretty feathers of yours."

"Really? I couldn't tell." I parked a hand on my hip, doing a terrible job of disguising my annoyance. "What brings you over to my side of the room?"

"Just coming over to say hi. How have you been?"

"You just saw me last night. Not much has changed in the last twenty-four hours."

Another smile slipped out of him. He looked amused. "You don't look very happy to see me."

"Should I be?"

He tilted his head to the side. "Yes, considering I probably saved your parents from finding your dismembered body in the woods this morning."

My eyes rolled. I should have known he couldn't go five seconds without bringing up that bad date. "You'll be happy to know I've sworn off men. No more online dating for me."

The right side of his mouth lifted up. That damn dimple in his cheek was going to be my undoing. "That's good to hear. You don't need those dating apps to find a man anyway."

"You don't think so?" Was he trying to tell me something? I couldn't tell because my brain cells were barely functioning after the liquor-fueled pounding I gave them after he left me last night.

"Nope." He waved a hand up and down his chest. "Everything you could possibly need is right here for the taking. All you have to do is say the word, sweetheart."

I shook my head, trying to fight the smile splitting my cheeks. JP Watson was a huge flirt who could not be taken seriously. It was hard to tell if he was serious or not.

"I'm not touching that comment," I informed him, hoping he didn't notice how I squirmed under his stare. With him being one of the best wide receivers in the NFL, he didn't have to put any effort into finding a date. And there was no shortage of women standing in line. He had more females waiting for him after each game than Bath and Body Works got on candle day. I've had many theories on why he avoided commitment, but all the evidence pointed to his looks and notoriety. Women loved that bad-boy image, and it didn't hurt that he had a fat wallet and was rumored to be very skilled in areas other than football, if you catch my drift.

"Seriously, Rylee. No more swiping right to get a date. It's not safe."

"That's easy for you to say. All you have to do is crook your finger and women collapse at your feet waiting for the next command."

He laughed. "Not all women, apparently. And I can't help it if I like to physically see the person first to gauge if there is any chemistry there."

"You mean before you invite them to share your bed for the night?"

"I'm not as much of a 'ladies' man' as you think I am. I just get bored easily."

That was exactly why I would never be able to take his flirting seriously. It would go absolutely nowhere. And what made matters worse, there would be no avoiding him. He was my brother's best friend, so it would be incredibly foolish of me to entertain any romantic ideas about him.

"It's a good thing I'm not interested in being another notch on your bedpost then," I deadpanned.

"Good, because you deserve better than me."

The casual way he said that didn't settle right with me. His lips turned down as if he were embarrassed about who he was. I didn't like that look on him or how that made me feel. "As you said, just because you do casual, it doesn't make you a bad guy," I said, reminding him of his own words.

His hand went to his heart. "Did you just pay me a compliment?"

"Don't go getting any ideas in that overinflated head of yours." I pointed my finger in warning.

"Go ahead, just admit you're attracted to me."

"You couldn't get me to admit that even if you waterboarded me."

He patted my shoulder. "That's okay, Sunshine, your eyes speak for themselves. I know the truth, no need to say it out loud."

There was a smile on his face, but something else too. I shook my shoulder, effectively knocking his hand away. His close proximity was testing my willpower.

"I feel like we need to set some ground rules," I said with a hell of a lot more confidence than I was feeling.

"It's cute that you think a set of rules will stop me." He crossed his arms. "Don't forget I read playbooks for a living. I know how to intercept rules and turn them to my advantage."

It was an act. It was all an act. It had to be because if it wasn't, then I was in big trouble.

"JP, you are forgetting that we are playing a different game. I'm playing for keeps, you're playing for fun." I tried to keep the waver out of my voice while reminding him we wanted different things. "I'm looking for a relationship, that's why I go on these dates."

"I might not be an expert on relationships, but I know you're not going to find the guy you're looking for through a casual hookup."

"A girl has to start somewhere, right?" I grinned, my eyes shining at the scowl on his face.

"How often do you go on these dates?" he snapped, and I wanted to laugh at the vein popping out of his forehead.

I felt guilty for egging him on, but I would not fall stupid to his charms or handsome face. "Wouldn't you like to know."

He laughed. "I'm not so sure about that."

I was just about to ask him what he meant when I heard my sister-in-law's voice approach from behind me.

"Oh, there you are, Rylee." I tore my eyes away as she shuffled forward with my nephew against her chest.

Zander poked his head up and gave me an adorable smile. He was looking more and more like my brother every day. He was all dark hair, big brown eyes and a ball of energy, just like his daddy. "Look at you, handsome." I pulled on his Atlanta Arrows jersey, noticing his rosy cheeks and toothless grin. The kid was so stinkin' cute. Although when I held my hands out and tried to pull him from his mother's arms, he wasn't having it.

"You know he only does this when you're around, right?" I huffed out at Kinley.

She yanked a piece of hair out of his tiny fist. "Don't take it personally, Auntie. He's ready for a nap."

JP lightly pressed his palm on Zander's head. "He didn't mind hanging out in my lap for the last hour."

Kinley giggled. "You are such a shit stirrer."

"Me?" He took a step back when he noticed my narrowed eyes. "You were just commenting earlier on how well behaved I was at the vow renewal ceremony."

She shook her head. "I take it back. You were in a church, you had to be."

He rolled up the sleeves of his shirt. My eyes went to his muscled forearms and the sleeve of tattoos covering his skin. When I glanced up, he lifted a brow.

"Is there anything you want to add to this conversation, Rylee?" He smirked.

"I was told as a child that if I didn't have anything nice to say, to not say anything at all."

He looked amused. "Hasn't stopped you before."

Kinley's eyes bounced between us. She was smiling from ear to ear.

I shifted on my feet. The tension between us was obvious, and I couldn't have been the only one feeling it. "Well, in that case, the night is still young. Give me time."

The room erupted in laughter. JP inclined his head to his friends. "I'm going to grab a slice of pizza before the guys demolish it all. Can I get either of you anything?" he asked us.

We both shook our heads, letting him know we were all

set. He ruffled Zander's hair, winked at me, and walked away. I couldn't help but stare at his ass as he made his way over to the group. They were all huddled around the kitchen island, fighting over the open pizza boxes on the counter.

There were times I still couldn't believe my brother was one of the greatest quarterbacks of all time. Most women would be starstruck around these men, but I was used to them.

What I wasn't used to was feeling that flock of butterflies in my stomach every time I came in contact with a certain wide receiver.

I was not the type of woman who got swept away by a jock. I was the opposite. I was careful. I was picky. I liked men who had manners. I liked men who used my name instead of a stupid, childish nickname. Sunshine wasn't cute unless you were a toddler. It wasn't sexy, and I wouldn't consider it affectionate. So why did I get all soft and gooey inside whenever he used it?

I watched him laugh at something Rhett said. And when he flipped his hat backward, I felt my knees go weak. Every woman had a weakness; mine was a hot guy wearing a backward ball cap. It screamed confidence and sex appeal.

Once the guys had their plates piled high and beers in hand, they moved into the room to watch a game.

Kinley put my nephew down for a nap, and I walked into the kitchen once it was cleared out to check my work email. I was avoiding the guys in the other room. There were a few wives and girlfriends here, but no one I knew well enough to talk to.

"Hey." Kinley slid a glass of wine my way just as I closed out my email. "What's going on with you tonight?"

"Why do you assume there is something going on with me?" I picked up a piece of fruit from the bowl and popped it in my mouth. Kinley was my oldest friend; she knew me well enough to know something was off.

"Because you've been quiet and acting strange, and"—she pointed to my mouth—"you are eating a green grape, you only like red grapes. So, unless you've grown accustomed to the sour taste, what gives?"

Shit! She was right. My eyes drifted through the kitchen, trying to shake off these weird feelings. It felt like JP and I were playing a game of cat and mouse, only I wasn't sure which role was mine.

"I'm just a little distracted today."

"No shit," she said, placing a napkin in my hand. I wrapped the grape up and threw it away. "I'm guessing this has something to do with your date last night."

It had everything to do with my date last night, just not the "date" itself. "The guy was a loser. I'm officially done with dating and swearing off men for the rest of my life."

"That sounds good to me," Maverick said, making his way to the fridge to grab a beer. I watched as he leaned in and kissed my sister-in-law on the lips. She smiled up at him like she couldn't live without him. I tried not to let the envy get to me.

If you were to tell me ten years ago that my brother and best friend would end up together with a family of their own, I never would have believed you. Now, after seeing them together and how much they love and respect each other, there was no doubt that they were a perfect match.

Plus, he gave up his career in the NFL last year to be a doting husband and raise his newborn son. If that wasn't love, I don't know what was.

Kinley was a lucky lady.

"What happened last night?" she asked, setting the baby monitor down next to her in case Zander woke up.

I turned my head to the boisterous laughter in the other room. "The guy showed up, his face didn't match the picture, JP chased him off, and I went home." I gave her the short version, hoping it would be enough.

"Wait, back up." Her eyebrows shot up. "What do you mean JP chased him off?"

I sighed and took a huge gulp of my wine, practically draining the glass before setting it down. "A few of the Arrows players were at the same bar. JP overheard the guy being a jerk and thought I needed him to step in and save the day."

Kinley picked up a piece of pepperoni pizza and handed me a plate. "I think he likes you," she said a little too loudly.

I looked over my shoulder to make sure no one was listening. "Will you keep it down," I warned. "He is Maverick's best friend, so I'm sure he felt morally obligated. Nothing more."

"Yeah, I'm sure that's what it was." She dabbed the corner of her mouth before looking at JP and then back at me.

"Don't even go there," I gritted out. Kinley and I have been friends forever, long before she and my brother became a thing. Having a friend who knew you so well was both a blessing and a curse.

"He is hot and it was hard not to notice the spark between you two." She smiled smugly.

"Wipe that smile off your face." I scoffed, not liking how observant she was being. "You know as well as I do that he's nothing but a skirt chaser." I stared down at my plate, feeling my cheeks heat.

"He's more than that and you know it."

She was right, but I would never admit it. Saying it out loud would change everything, and I wasn't ready to tell her all the things that made him stand out to me. He was fun, gorgeous, highly successful, a good friend, and had a big heart. As much as I would have loved to confide in her, I didn't want to put her in a bad position. So, my crush on my brother's best friend would remain my own little secret.

"Kinley, his flirting doesn't mean anything." I sighed, trying to keep my face even. "Besides, most men are slimy and you can't trust them, so I am done forever."

It was unfair to lump all men in the same category, but after a steady string of bad dates, my insecurities were kicking in. All my friends were settling down, and I was convinced that I was meant to be single forever. I wanted what my parents had and what Kinley and Maverick had. I wanted love and marriage and the baby carriage. The older I got, the more I doubted it would ever happen for me.

She leaned across the table, her face filled with sympathy. "Maybe you should consider a more traditional route. Like meeting someone at a bar or a coffee shop. Avoiding men forever isn't very practical."

"Why not?" I asked, finishing off the rest of my wine.

"First off, it would cost you a fortune in double-A batteries. Second, you would only have your job to keep you company. And third, it sounds lonely and boring."

"I have Oakley."

"He's a dog."

I leveled her with a look. "So are most men. They hump anything that moves. The main difference is, dogs are loyal, men are not."

She giggled and held up her ring finger, displaying the jewels my brother put there. "Not all men are like that."

"Maverick and my dad are exceptions."

She could try her damnedest to convince me otherwise, but I wasn't budging. I deleted the app, and I was done wasting my time on random guys who weren't worth a second of it.

"You'll meet someone, Rylee. I promise."

"I'm not so sure about that anymore." It was hard to meet someone who didn't expect me to sacrifice my goals or use me to get to my brother.

Her eyes narrowed. "Are you sure this isn't about Dominick?"

I sat back in my chair and groaned whenever I thought about my ex. "Dominick and I are strictly coworkers. Whatever we had is over."

I still had to deal with him on occasion, especially if there was a contract issue. We were cordial at best, and I was pretty sure he wanted me back, but I was done. Sometimes, it felt like he made up compliance issues as an excuse to meet with me. Thankfully, his legal duties and travel schedule kept him out of the office most of the time because I needed the space.

"I don't know how you could be so friendly with that snake after what he did to you."

"His drinking problem isn't my problem anymore."

My ex liked to hit the bottle a little too hard at night. When I asked him to stop, he refused, so I ended it. To say the breakup had been messy would be an understatement.

"I wasn't just talking about the alcohol. I was referring to him cheating on you."

"We were technically broken up, but it doesn't matter," I said, bringing my glass to my lips, but frowned when I realized it was empty. "We were over long before I left him. I'd rather be single than waste my time on another relationship that ends up going nowhere."

"I wouldn't give up on finding love just yet. They say it happens when you least expect it."

Her eyes darted across the room, and, of course, mine followed. I needed to remind myself why I was so intent on staying single. I shouldn't even have been thinking about my brother's friend, but it was getting harder and harder by the minute.

CHAPTER 3

JP

THERE WAS SOMETHING SERIOUSLY WRONG WITH ME. A beautiful woman was sitting on my lap; she was blond, gorgeous, and had a body that most men would kill for. Yet, all I could think about was how everything about her felt wrong. The color of her hair, the way she laughed, even her height was an issue for me.

It was official; I preferred short brunettes with brown eyes who gave me sass and challenged me. This chick was too easy, and I was pretty sure she'd do anything I asked.

I shifted her onto my lap and brushed the curtain of long hair off her shoulder. Her blue eyes sparkled as she trailed her long, painted fingernails along my arm. My gaze dropped to her chest, which didn't leave much to the imagination, and I waited and waited to feel something. I felt nothing. It must have been something in the air tonight.

"I like your place." She was doing her best to get my attention, but I don't think a dozen Viagra pills would have tempted me. She'd been clingy all night and refused to leave my side when all I wanted to do was unwind.

"Thanks. Would you like another drink?" I was looking for an excuse to get up and move around. Even her perfume was starting to annoy me.

"As long as it's a *stiff* one," she cooed as her hands moved toward my zipper.

Could this chick be any more cliché? I wasn't kidding when I told Rylee I got bored easily, and situations like this were getting old.

The drinking, parties, and random women all left me feeling unsatisfied. These interactions didn't hold the same appeal as they used to; they felt more like a chore than a good time.

I scanned the crowd, feeling bored, and noticed all the people gathered in my living room. Normally, I'd be all in, but spying all the Solo cups, carpet crumbs, and empty beer bottles scattered around, all I could focus on was all the cleaning we would be doing later. I was getting too old for this scene.

I looked over at Rhett, who was acting as the host of the party while making drinks at *my* kitchen counter. A harem of chicks giggled at his side, eating up whatever bullshit he was spitting out. I wasn't one to judge because I had my own reputation to worry about, but the guy rotated through more women than a NASCAR pit crew did with tires.

My eyes went to the commotion at the front door, and when I looked up, I started thinking of all the ways I could get this fangirl off my lap without causing a scene.

She was chatting away, but I wasn't listening to a word she was saying. My sole focus was on Rylee and the way her hips swayed in the denim jeans that were a little too tight for my liking.

A little smile was curled on her lips as she strode my way.

"Well, I'll be damned. Look what the cat dragged in. I didn't know you were stopping by tonight?"

Rylee looked between me and the woman parked on my lap.

"I heard you were having a party and thought I'd stop by for a drink." She glanced around. "There is a pretty big crowd here for a Sunday night."

This was the third straight day in a row where we've run into each other. Did she come here tonight to see me? It would make my night if she did.

"It's our last night of freedom before our playoff game this weekend." I leaned forward like I was getting ready to tell her a secret. "Just don't tell Coach." I gave her a teasing wink.

"About the party or the lap dance?" She angled her head to the woman on my lap.

I was about to dump Blondie off my leg, but Rylee waved me off. "Don't let the fun stop on my account."

Was that jealousy in her tone? My entire body lit up inside at the thought.

"I'm sorry, but who are you?" the blonde on my lap snapped. Her tone was a little aggressive, something I didn't appreciate.

Rylee's brows lifted. "I could ask you the same thing." She smiled sweetly and turned her gaze to me. "Who is your friend, JP?"

I wanted to laugh at how sweet she sounded because there was nothing about her smile that was sweet.

I winced when the girl tightened her hold on my neck. "I'm Shayla, JP's girlfriend."

"You are my what?" I blinked a few times, trying to process what I just heard. Did she say what I thought she said? She's had a few drinks tonight, but we both knew she wasn't my girlfriend. I didn't even know her damn name.

"I'm your girl, JP." She gave me a pouty look. "At least for tonight. I've been waiting forever to get my chance with you. I don't want to share. I want you all for myself."

"I think we need to get a few things straight." I grabbed her hands and attempted to remove them, but the next part happened so fast that I didn't have time to react.

She flicked her hair over her shoulder and pulled her shirt up, exposing her boob. "But look what I did for you." My eyes nearly bugged out of my head at the tattoo of my jersey with my name and number on her skin with little hearts and footballs surrounding it.

Jesus Christ! I raked a hand through my hair. We needed to rent a "crazy" detector before letting any more women into the parties.

Scrubbing a hand over my stubbled chin, I sent Rylee a pleading look, begging for a little help. Instead of coming to my rescue, the little shit turned her head to the side and bit the inside of her cheek to keep herself from laughing. If I wasn't concerned about this chick being a psychopath, I might have found this whole thing amusing.

"I think it's time for you to go." I pushed her shirt down and covered up the tattoo before the guys caught wind of this. After playing ball for almost a decade, you would think I would be used to this madness.

Blondie gawked. "What do you mean, it's time to go? You invited me. You can't just throw me out."

The fuck, I can't, I wanted to shout.

"If this is about her"—she pointed to Rylee—"then I'll reconsider a threesome, but I get to have you first, she gets what's left."

Rylee snorted. "Well, some might consider that a tempting offer. I'm going to have to pass. You two kids have fun."

She strolled away, and I wanted to follow her like a lost

puppy. Instead, I turned my attention to the woman taking up space on my lap.

Despite what Rylee thought, I didn't invite this woman. I didn't know this woman, and what little I did know, I didn't like. I was so damned tired of this nonsense.

I pushed to my feet and untangled her body from mine. "I'm going to ask you nicely to leave without causing a scene. You have no right to lay a claim on me and I won't tolerate the way you were talking to my friend."

She pulled on the hem of her short skirt. "Why are you being such a jerk about this?"

"I don't play games, and I don't do drama."

She rolled her shoulders back, batted her eyes, and gave it one last-ditch effort. "You don't need to get so worked up. Besides, I thought you'd like the ink?"

No, I didn't like the ink. She knew nothing about me. She only got that tattoo because she was hoping to get something out of this. She was a cleat chaser who fucked for bragging rights.

I folded my arms across my chest. "Did you drive or do you need someone to call you an Uber?"

She eyed me up and down, debating whether to keep pushing or cut her losses. For her sake, I hoped she chose the latter.

"I can call my own damn ride. This party sucks anyway." She pushed past the mass of people, huffing and puffing the entire way. If this wasn't a wake-up call that this party life wasn't for me anymore, I didn't know what was. I had officially reached my limit, and it was time for a change.

My eyes searched for Rylee across the room. I walked outside and scanned the yard when I didn't see her. Where the hell was she, and who invited her tonight? It sure as heck wasn't me.

She was no stranger to the guys on the team. Most of them looked at her like she was a little sister or didn't look at her at all. It was something Maverick drilled into the guys early on.

My mind started wandering, and I had to push down the possessive feelings prickling my skin. I had no claim to her whatsoever, but man, did I want to change that.

A streak of giggles and rowdy laughter came from my garage. I jogged across the yard, like a man on a mission, ignoring the people calling out my name, trying to suck me into meaningless conversation.

I wasn't wasting any more time. I wanted her and wasn't giving up until I had her.

My feet came to a sudden stop once I reached my garage. Rylee was bent over my pool table, cue stick in hand, trying to focus on her next move. She laughed at one of the rookies like he was the funniest guy in the room. I found myself smiling at her laugh until I noticed the back of her sweater was open, exposing tanned, smooth skin. I marched over when I caught a flock of my teammates making their way around the pool table.

"Would you like a little help?" I whispered into her left ear.

Her eyes flashed to mine. "Trying to distract me?"

"Nope." I threw her a shit-eating grin. "Just trying to be a good friend."

"Oh, so we're friends now, huh?" Her eyes moved across the room as if she were searching for someone. "Speaking of friends, where's your 'new' girlfriend?"

"What's she talking about?" Rhett asked, striding toward us with a groupie under each arm.

"You"—I pointed to the little shit—"need to start doing a little vetting before you go giving out my address and inviting random cleat chasers into my home."

Rhett's arms fell from the girls' shoulders. He took a swig of his beer, looking like he didn't have the first clue what I was talking about. "Was there some type of problem?"

"There's going to be a big problem if you don't knock that shit off?"

Rylee's eyes were twinkling in humor. "He's upset because one of your guests was hoping for a marriage proposal."

Rhett quirked a brow. "Which one?"

"The blonde on his lap earlier." She grinned, clearly enjoying this too much.

I gave Rylee the evil eyes as she chalked up her pool stick. My eyes went to her tight jeans as she bent that sexy little ass of hers over my pool table. I loved my teammates like brothers and would have their back any day in a fight, but if they didn't tear their eyes off her in the next second, no one could protect them from me.

I was unhinged when it came to that woman, and it was so unlike me. I wasn't possessive. I wasn't an asshole; I was just a man who was sick and tired of denying himself.

Rylee leaned back, sinking her teeth into that bottom lip as she watched the cue ball sink into the pocket right after the eight ball. Her shoulders slumped forward in defeat. She might have been good at many things, but she was horrible at playing pool. Maybe I should offer her private lessons.

"Better luck next time," I said, standing at her back, blocking my teammate's view.

Rylee picked up the red Solo cup and swallowed the blueberry-flavored vodka mixed with Sprite. "Not sure there will be a next time. I'd much rather play beer pong."

"A girl after my own heart." I moved her out of the way so Morris could rack the balls for the next game.

I placed a hand on her shoulder. "Would you like to go out back and get some fresh air?" She creased her brows, and I barked out a laugh. "I promise I don't bite." I leaned into her ear. "Unless you ask me to."

She rolled her eyes. "You need to come up with new material."

I guided her out the door, ignoring the look my teammates were sending my way. "Are you saying I'm washed up?"

"Are you seriously fishing for compliments?"

"Sunshine, when it comes to you, my ego could always use a little boost."

We walked along the back of the house, and I snagged a few things out of the storage shed as we made our way along the paved sidewalk that led to the lake out back. This was my sanctuary. It was where I came to relax and get away from all the noise. I bought this plot of land with my signing bonus. Over the years, I've added on to the property, and now it was exactly as I wanted it.

Most guys had beach houses in Miami or vacation homes in Montana, but not me. This place was all I had and more than I could ever need. Atlanta was officially my home.

"So, why did you bring me out here?" she asked as I laid the blanket over her lap and tucked her in like a child. A slight breeze came across the lake, making the nighttime air feel cool and crisp.

"I needed a break from all the noise," I said, taking the spot next to her on the dock while the party continued back inside the house. I could still hear the music and faint laughter coming through the windows.

She tilted her head to the side. "A break from the noise, or a break from the groupies?"

"A break from all of it."

I had a sudden urge to scoot closer. Close enough to put my arm around her and pull her into my side. The need to press my lips to hers was growing by the second, and that was concerning, because I never thought about just kissing. Sex was usually what I thought about, and although I wouldn't mind having sex with Rylee, that wasn't the driving force of my feelings.

"Why did you have a party if you weren't in the mood to entertain?"

"Because that's what the guys wanted to do."

And I hated being alone because I got too far into my head, and having people around was a distraction.

"So, this is all about making your friends happy?" she asked as I pressed my body against hers. She fit perfectly against my side. And it didn't go unnoticed by me that our faces were inches apart.

"What can I say? I'm a good friend," I said, inhaling the smell of her strawberry-scented shampoo. I wasn't sure how much longer I'd be able to keep up with this charade. I wanted her, and I was pretty sure I was at the end of my rope.

"If you keep letting your soft side slip out, then I'm going to have to start being nice to you."

"Then I guess my plan is working," I said, inhaling deeply through my nose.

She leaned back and looked up at me. "Were you just smelling my hair?"

"Your smell is addicting."

Her body tensed. "Are you drunk?"

Jesus, I was losing my touch. When was the last time I got laid? Weeks. Months? It was obviously long enough for me to forget.

"Not even close. Unless you can get drunk off of your scent."

She lifted her eyebrows playfully. "That was a terrible attempt at reciting a Luke Bryan song."

Normally, I would laugh at her joke, but tonight, I was in a mood. I was on edge and feeling off balance. I closed my eyes in embarrassment at how desperate I was coming across.

"I know you think I'm playing games and just trying to get you in my bed, but I like spending time with you, Rylee. Do you think one day you could give me a chance and take me seriously?"

She swung her legs back and forth while staring out into the darkness. "Isn't that against the rules?"

"What rules?"

"Dating a teammate's sister." She wet her lips like she was trying to convince herself that it was somehow prohibited.

"Your brother isn't my teammate anymore." I smiled, not mentioning that there was still a bro code, one I took seriously, but one step at a time. "So, what's your next excuse?"

She shook her head. "Aren't you the one always telling me that I shouldn't go on anymore dates."

"Let me clarify." I paused and debated how far I wanted to push her on this. "I meant anyone but me."

She laughed. "I can't figure you out."

"Ask me anything. I'm an open book."

"I can't tell if you're joking or serious."

"I'm dead serious, Rylee," I answered immediately. "We are both attracted to each other and even you can't deny that we have chemistry."

I so desperately wanted to move past this conversation and finally make my move, but I didn't want to push her. I wanted her to know where I stood, break down these damn walls, and convince her to give me a chance.

She shifted her body. "Who says I'm attracted to you?"

This woman wasn't giving me an inch, but I was calling her on her bullshit.

My gaze dropped to her lips. "Are you seriously going to pretend that you've never wondered what I kiss like? Never curious about what it would be like if we spent the night together?" I asked softly, noticing the rise and fall of her chest.

"I don't know what you are talking about."

"I don't believe you." My eyes tracked over her features, and I cupped her cheek. "Just so we are clear, I would worship those lips and spend every waking minute getting lost in them."

Rylee leaned into my touch, and I had to mentally tell myself to calm down. Never in my life had I ever felt this type of yearning. We were one second away from crossing a line, but I couldn't think of anything that would stop me.

Her lips parted, and my heart pounded in my chest, hoping she was finally going to put me out of my misery and fucking kiss me.

"Yo, JP, you back there?"

Worst fucking timing ever!

Rylee pushed away from me just as Rhett came into view.

He stood at the foot of the dock with a shit-eating grin. We probably both looked guilty as hell, even though we did nothing wrong—unfortunately.

"What's up?"

"Am I interrupting something?" the cockblocker asked.

Rylee turned her head, unable to meet his eyes. She kept her gaze on the water.

"Rhett, did you need something?" I snapped, hating that things were now awkward.

"Yeah." He scratched the side of his jaw. "One of the

girls got sick in the kitchen. We cleaned it up but I was wondering if you had an old T-shirt or something she could change into."

"Jesus," I muttered under my breath and was about to stand up, but he held his hand out.

"I got it. I wanted to make sure you are cool with it."

"There should be something in the guest room at the other end of the hall."

"I'm on it and I'll start clearing out the house." His eyes bounced between us. He looked like he wanted to say more, but when he saw the murderous look on my face, he retreated back to the house.

My house. The guy had as much money as I did; he could afford his own damn house. He loved to host parties, and it was past time he started looking for his own plot of land. I was done.

Rylee removed the blanket from her shoulders and stood up. "I should get going."

Damn, my friend and his shitty timing.

"You don't have to leave," I said, trying not to come across as a pleading idiot.

"You have guests and I'm taking up too much of your time." She faked a yawn. "Besides, I'm beat and I have work in the morning and Mondays are always the worst."

She started walking up the dock, and I followed her, keeping a respectful distance. I shouldn't have been so drawn to her. I shouldn't have wanted her as badly as I did. Things would never work between us, no matter how badly I wanted them to. My friendship with her brother was too important to me, but that wasn't the only reason things would never work.

I had nothing to offer her, and a woman like that deserved it all.

CHAPTER 4

JP

"Are we chasing an axe murderer or something?" Rhett panted out, running on the treadmill next to mine. I lowered my pace and wiped the sweat sliding down the back of my neck.

"Just pissed that we're stuck hitting these machines instead of doing drills outside."

I preferred the fresh air with the sun beating down on my back, but the weather was shitty outside, so the coach made us do our workout indoors.

"Are you sure that's the only thing that has you all hot and bothered, big guy?" he teased, taking a long chug of his water bottle.

"What's that supposed to mean?"

"You and Rylee looked pretty cozy at the end of the dock the other night."

"Nothing happened. We were just talking." I hopped off the treadmill and walked over to one of the padded mats in the weight room.

He laughed and followed me. "I also saw you chase off that golfer in the pink shirt on Friday night."

"What's your point?" I stretched my right arm out over my head.

His eyes met mine in the mirror. "Something's going on between you two."

"No, there's not." I switched to my other arm, and he laughed again. "Is something funny?" I asked, narrowing my eyes at the instigator.

"It's hysterical that you're trying to act like you're not into her."

"I would really appreciate it if you would shut the fuck up."

"I'm sure you would." He grinned. "But as your friend, I think we should talk about this and that little 'almost' smooch I interrupted."

I was waiting for him to bring that up. This was the last thing I wanted to get into, but I had a feeling we were going to talk about it anyway. "I think we are way past the middle school years, don't you agree?"

"I see you're not denying it." He smirked.

No, I wasn't because I was using all my energy to chase away these feelings that were consuming my every waking thought. There was something brewing, even though I tried to deny it. That seed of attraction was growing into something much bigger. Something I couldn't control. As much as I wanted a chance with her, I couldn't go there. Hell, I shouldn't have even been thinking of her.

"It wouldn't matter how I feel, she's Mav's sister and that makes her off-limits to all of us."

He rolled his lips together. "I mean, yeah, if you were just looking to get in her pants, that would be shitty, but if it's more than that, then I wouldn't worry about breaking some bro code. Mav is one of your best friends. He respects you; I don't think he would have an issue with it."

I wasn't so sure about that. If I started something with

her and things ended badly, he would have to choose a side. And I wasn't an idiot. He would choose his sister.

"It would be awkward and I don't want to risk it."

"You keep using Mav as an excuse, but I have a feeling there is more to the story and you don't want anyone to know about it."

Rhett might have acted like a goofball most of the time, but the guy was also insightful. It was a quality that served him well on the field, but I didn't need him trying to analyze something I didn't fully grasp myself.

I grabbed the hand towel and wiped my face. "Let's drop it, okay?"

I was already frustrated and fired up about the whole situation, and we both needed to focus on the playoff game.

"Okay, but just a heads-up, the boys were wondering why you were a no-show last night?"

When the team plane touched down in San Diego last night, most of the guys went straight to the lobby bar after checking into their rooms. A few of them gave me a hard time when I told them I wanted to stay in and relax.

I hated away games, the travel time, the crappy beds, and lousy food. Not to mention, a lot was riding on this game. But as it turned out, I wasn't good at relaxing. There was nothing on the television to hold my attention, and I got bored scrolling through my phone.

For a hot minute, I debated calling a random girl from my contact list to help take the edge off. I started gathering numbers in every city early on in my career, but with the last game of the season approaching this weekend, I needed my focus to be on the field. At least, that was the excuse I was telling myself. It had nothing to do with Rylee.

"Tell them we've got bigger problems to focus on. Let's not waste our time on ones that don't exist."

He clapped my shoulder. "Don't worry, big guy, we're going to kick San Diego's ass on Sunday."

"That's wishful thinking, but I hope you're right."

———

The entire team was assembled in the locker room the next day. The flight back to Atlanta last night was long. The coach was pissed, and I couldn't blame him. The final score was 31-28. San Diego was advancing to the next round in the playoffs; we were out.

We all racked our brains, wondering what we could have done differently. Aside from the interception, there wasn't much we could have done. A fumble in the first half cost us a touchdown. We slowly came back but never managed to get ahead. I hated playing from behind.

"You guys were so close," Coach shouted while pacing the locker room. "But you weren't hungry enough for that championship. You can't win if you don't want it. You should all be embarrassed. One bad play, that's all it took."

He was wrong, but I wasn't stupid enough to call him out. One play didn't cost us the game; we blew it because San Diego outplayed us. We, as a team, lost. It didn't matter how hard he ran us at practice or how many hours we spent reviewing film; we walked in knowing we were the underdogs.

"You had the score tied up with less than two minutes left. You had possession of the ball. All you had to do was run the clock down and kick for a field goal, not get hit with a holding penalty." He pointed to Rosa. "Your job was to hold on to the goddamned ball so we could get another play. Instead, you carried it on your outside hip where anyone in the city of San Diego could have ripped it away. Fuck, their mascot could have knocked it out of your arms. You might as well just have handed it to their safety."

Rosa sank in his seat, embarrassed by the ass-chewing he was receiving. The coach didn't usually get all fired up and jump all over his players; he allowed his emotions to get the best of him. I've been in the league long enough to know why we win and lose some. It was never just one play.

We played poorly, and we lost. We needed time to process and learn from our mistakes so that we could come back better next season.

"And you." He pointed to our team's number one hothead, Derrick Howes. "You might have laughed the first time you got fined and had to fork up six grand for throwing a football into the crowd. Let's see if you're still laughing from your little stunt today when you have to pay twelve." He shook his head. "I wish I had your kind of cash to just throw away."

You could tell it was taking everything in Derrick to honor the code of conduct that the NFL made every player sign. If Derrick wasn't careful, he was going to find himself in the unemployment line. He was young and full of himself. He was bringing negative attention to the team, and the front office has taken notice. It didn't matter how good of a player you were; everyone in this business was replaceable.

"Now," Coach put his hands on his hips and looked around, "I know I'm being hard on you. I don't want one bad game to take away all the good you've done all season. But if you continue to play the way you did today, odds are, you'll get the same results. So, before you leave, I want you to type these questions into your phone and share your answers with me during our one-on-one meeting." He walked over to the whiteboard, where he usually drew up plays, and scribbled out his questions.

1. List five things we did well this season.
2. List five things we didn't do well this season.
3. What do we need to do to get better?
4. What do we need to STOP doing to get better?

He set the dry-erase marker down and glanced across the room. "Before you leave, remember that bad plays don't make you a bad player. Failure and setbacks are part of the process, and not a reason to quit or give up. Don't get lost in your loss. There's work to be done, room to get better, and games to be won." He tapped the table. "You're dismissed. Enjoy the off-season."

I cleaned out my locker and said goodbye to the guys who were flying home to wherever they lived during the off-season. I loaded up my car and backed out of the parking spot. It was always an odd feeling driving away once the season was over. It felt like I was leaving all the weight and stress behind. My body was tired, and I was ready to mentally relax.

But I knew from experience, after going off a schedule for the past nine months, it would feel weird after the first week of having nothing to do.

My only worry was, with so much time on my hands, I wouldn't be able to stop thinking of a certain brunette whose brother was ringing up my phone right now.

"What's up, Mav?"

"Dude, that game was brutal."

I blew out a breath. "At least you only had to watch it once. You know Coach is going to make us watch it so many times, my eyes are going to catch fire."

He laughed. "I don't miss those losses."

When my friend retired last season to raise his family, I was bummed. We'd played together for years. We had undeniable chemistry and were always on the same page. The tabloids used to say we had a bromance going on because we just clicked, both on and off the field. Between his good arm and my good hands, we made a damn good passing tandem.

"I bet you don't." I flicked my blinker to switch lanes. "At least now I can sleep in all day like you for the next few months."

"Bitch, please. My kid gets up at the butt crack of dawn. There is no sleeping in around here."

"And you wouldn't have it any other way."

"Damn right. Listen," he cleared his throat, "Kinley has a friend coming into town next weekend. Her name is Taylor, they used to work together. Any chance you're available to go out to dinner with us? My sister offered to babysit."

My body tensed. Did Rylee know he was asking me? Was she trying to set me up with someone else? I stared straight ahead, thankful that my friend couldn't see me. It was taking everything I had not to pound my fist on the steering wheel. I had no idea where I stood with that woman.

Irritation licked its way up my spine. If these feelings I had for her were reciprocated, she wouldn't be offering to babysit her nephew. She wouldn't want me on a double date with another woman. It was well past time I accepted the fact that she didn't want me at all.

I heard her loud and clear.

"Sure, let me know when."

CHAPTER 5
RYLEE

I was bouncing Zander on my lap and swiping through my Instagram to see if there were any updates to JP's story.

I hated everything about this and was questioning my sanity at this point. When I offered to babysit, so Maverick and Kinley could go out to dinner with her friend, I had no idea they would turn it into a double date. Actually, it was my sister-in-law that suggested it. I had a feeling she did it on purpose.

She was pushing me to admit my true feelings. Instead, I called her bluff. Now, I regretted it.

Taylor was nice, but watching her get ready, asking a million questions about my brother's friend, and seeing the excitement in her eyes when he showed up made me want to rip her little head off.

I faked my way through an entire conversation when he got here. He stayed for a full ten minutes before they left, but it was the longest ten minutes of my life. I told them I hoped they had a good time, which was a big fat lie.

After a bath, a bottle, and two more books, Zander was

passed out in his crib, and I was snuggled up under a blanket on a Friday night on my brother's couch.

I was flipping between *Stranger Things* and *The Walking Dead* when the front door swung open. I switched on the lamp and sat up, noticing three figures instead of four.

Maverick unzipped his coat and hung it on the rack, and Kinley dropped her purse on the side table. JP stood in the doorway with his hands shoved in his pockets, looking annoyed.

"Hey." I kept my gaze trained on the door to see if Taylor was behind them. "You guys are back early."

Kinley sidestepped the guys and walked down the hall toward Zander's bedroom. "The meal took forever, and we were all tired, so we didn't end up going out for drinks after."

I could feel JP's gaze burning into my skin from the corner of my eye. What was his problem? Did his date not go well, and he somehow blamed me?

"Where's Taylor?" I asked, pushing the blanket off my lap.

"She went back to her hotel," my brother answered as he walked into the kitchen to grab some beers from the fridge. He popped the caps off and handed one to JP. "How's my little guy?"

"He was a perfect angel."

I took a sip of my water, trying to buy some time before I had to acknowledge the man who seemed to melt my brain cells with a simple look. I lifted my gaze to see him standing there, watching me with an expression I couldn't quite read.

When he strode over and sat beside me, I had to force myself to stay calm and collected. There was plenty of space for him to stretch out on the other end, so what the hell was he doing? My mind was racing, and I hated the way he made me feel all out of sorts. I don't ever recall having a problem being around him like this before.

"I'm going to change into sweats." My brother put his beer down and quickly left the room.

Then there were two.

A heavy silence fell over us, unless you counted the deafening sound of my heart hammering away in my chest. My eyes darted to the TV. I pretended to be fascinated with the screen.

"How was your date?" I asked, making small talk because I was unsure what to say at this point.

"Isn't it obvious?" He took a long pull of his beer.

"I take it things didn't go well." I could feel his eyes on me, but I was too much of a coward to look at him.

He shrugged. "Wasn't interested."

Do. Not. Smile. Do. Not. Smile.

Damn it. A slight grin peeked out and spread across my lips. I kept my face away from his, hoping he didn't see it. "I'm sorry to hear that."

"Are you enjoying yourself?" He flung his arm along the back of the cushion.

"What do you mean?" I had a good idea of what he was implying but didn't want to make any assumptions. And there was no way I was admitting how relieved I felt that he was here with me instead of with her.

"Did you set up that date, Rylee?"

I swung my head in his direction and blinked. "I only offered to babysit. I had no idea they were trying to set you up."

He tilted his head to the side like he was trying to determine whether he should believe me or not. "Just checking."

"Did I do something wrong?" I asked, trying to make sense of his little attitude.

"I don't know, did you?" His eyes held mine like he was searching for something, but I had no clue what he could have been looking for.

"I don't think I did." My eyes drifted across his face, hoping to find a clue to what was going on in that head of his. "You just seemed a little worked up tonight."

He was trying to be casual about it, but his face was hard as stone. "Why would I be worked up?"

All I could manage was another blink because I was clearly having difficulty keeping up with him tonight. Why did it feel like I messed up somehow?

"Rylee." My brother's voice had JP jumping back and thankfully getting me out of a very painful conversation. "Are you going to stay and have a glass of wine?" He rounded the corner and picked his beer up off the table. "I feel like I owe you."

I ran my hands down over my leggings, thankful to now have a little wiggle room. "Um…" I looked at my watch. "I should probably get going." I stood from the couch and walked over to put my shoes on by the door. I couldn't get out of the apartment fast enough.

"Don't run off on my account." JP's tone was heavy with sarcasm.

I sliced him with a look, wishing I knew why his anger was directed at me, but I worried if I stayed that Maverick and Kinley would be able to pick up on things I wasn't ready for them to know yet.

I gave my head a shake because I wasn't sure if I should have been annoyed or concerned with how he was acting.

I had work in the morning. I needed sleep. I needed to clear my head. I didn't understand what was happening between us. He was under my skin. I was under his skin. I had no idea what we were doing. It's been a weird night, and I was in a strange mood. I didn't trust myself to act normal around him.

Decision made; I was going home.

"I have an early morning," I said just as Kinley rounded the corner.

"We are all pretty tired. It's just one drink." Her smile was devious.

I was definitely getting her back for this.

"Sorry, I can't." I arched my eyebrow at the little matchmaker, letting her know we would have words later.

Maverick craned his neck from his spot on the couch where he was checking the scores of tonight's games. "You're really taking off?"

"Yeah." I grabbed my coat and purse off the hook.

Maverick paused the TV and came over to say goodbye. "Thanks for taking care of Zander tonight."

"Of course." I gave him a hug and walked toward the door.

I gave JP an awkward wave and shot Kinley a look.

She reached for my elbow as I was walking through the door. "I'm sorry," she said into my ear.

"I'm going to get you back for this," I whispered low enough to where only she could hear me.

She winced. "Just trying to give you a little nudge." She looked over her shoulder at where JP had joined my brother on the couch. "For what it's worth, he was not into Taylor at all and she tried."

"What if he was interested in Taylor?" I asked.

"Then I guess I would have been wrong about how he feels about you."

"I'll call you tomorrow," I said, taking one last look over her shoulder. I expected JP to be facing the TV. Instead, his eyes were on mine. Like a chickenshit, I hurried out the door.

I had my key in the lock and was ready to push my front door in when I heard, "Whatcha doin' home early on a Friday night?"

"Jesus, Tilly." My hand flew to my heart. "You scared the crap out of me."

I pushed the door forward, and my neighbor followed me inside.

"I need to let Oakley out," I said, reaching for his leash.

"Already did," she said, sliding into the recliner and kicking the footrest out to get comfortable.

I paused and turned around. "When?" I asked, eyeing her suspiciously. Oakley was at her feet, waiting for one of the treats she carried in her pocket.

"While you were out." She tipped her glass toward me.

I tilted my head to the side and contemplated how to handle this. Tilly was an older woman who needed to learn some things about boundaries. She was Oakley's dog sitter occasionally and had a key to my condo. However, she had a habit of using that key anytime she felt like it. I couldn't even begin to count how many times she would walk right in without knocking; sometimes, she was bringing me leftovers, so I didn't complain, but there were other times I'd come home after work and find her napping on my couch.

"Tilly." I placed a hand on my hip. "You need to stop letting yourself in without my permission. What if I have a man over?"

"Ha, real funny."

Now I was getting annoyed, and after the night I had, I wasn't in the mood to deal with her. "It's a possibility."

"You haven't had a man over since you broke up with

that jerk who liked to hit the sauce a little too hard." She stretched out and kicked her shoes off.

"I've gone on dates." Tilly wasn't a fan of my ex, Dom. Now that I thought about it, no one was.

"Doesn't matter; you're not getting any action. I probably get laid more than you."

I rolled my eyes and plopped down on the couch. "Thanks for the reminder."

Now I knew why her bar went out of business, and it had nothing to do with her selling so she could retire and move closer to her kids. The woman had no filter. People went to a bar to relax and unwind, not to be insulted by the meddling older woman serving them drinks.

She raised her eyebrow. "What's got you so flustered tonight? Is it sexual frustration?"

More like sexual tension with a particular wide receiver who I couldn't figure out. "Whatever I tell you stays between us," I warned.

"Your secret is safe with me," she said, taking a sip of her wine. It was filled to the rim and close to spilling on my floor.

"You spill it, you clean it." I pointed to the glass.

She rolled her eyes. "I ran a bar for twenty-five years, remember? Now tell me who this mystery man is."

Inhaling deeply, I leaned back in my seat. "He played football with my brother, so he's pretty well-known."

Hell, his picture was basically on every billboard in the Atlanta area.

"Oh, I wasn't expecting something so juicy." She set her glass down and rubbed her hands together. "Which player is it?"

I had no idea what possessed me to even bring this up, but there was no way to avoid this conversation now that I opened my big mouth. I sighed and prayed that I wouldn't regret this. "JP Watson."

She was smiling so big that I felt the need to help myself to a drink. I walked into the kitchen and grabbed the bottle of pinot I already had opened. I didn't even bother with a glass; I pulled the cork out and brought it back to the couch.

"All right," she said, downing the rest of her glass. "Let's talk about this because I gotta be honest, that man is easy on the eyes, especially for an older lady like me."

She was right, but he had so much more going for him than that. "I'm ninety-nine percent sure he's attracted to me."

She nodded. "I'm assuming the feeling is mutual, because hello, who wouldn't be attracted to that man. So, what's the problem?" Her forehead wrinkled in confusion.

I set the bottle on the table and folded my legs underneath me. "For starters, he's Maverick's friend, which complicates things. And I'm not sure what to do."

"What do you want to do?"

I ran a hand through my hair. "I want to *not* be so affected by him. He's not the relationship type, and I'm done with casual hookups. I'm not getting any younger, so the next guy I decide to spend time with will be with someone who wants the same things."

She leaned forward with a look of understanding. "Ahh, I see what this is about. You don't want to waste your time if it's not going to go anywhere."

"Exactly! I've been brushing off his flirting, so he doesn't catch onto the fact that I actually like him. He's a no-strings kinda guy and I'm afraid I'd still get tangled up somehow."

"What if he's not the man you think he is? What if he's more?"

My eyes popped open. "That thought scares me even more because I'd probably end up with a broken heart."

She flattened her thin lips. "Only one way to find out."

I narrowed my eyes. "I don't like the sound of that."

I never should have let her follow me into my house tonight. And tomorrow, I was going to Home Depot to buy a new lock for my front door.

"Rylee, he probably doesn't know where he stands with you either. Let him sweat it out a little bit longer. Men like him get handed things way too easy, they need to be challenged."

"I don't like playing games," I said automatically, letting her know that I didn't agree with her suggestion.

"This isn't a game. This is real life. There is no harm in playing it cool. Do you want to keep wondering if he's just playing with you, or do you want to find out if he's being genuine?"

I hopped off the couch and made my way into the kitchen. I placed the bottle back in the wine rack and pushed away whatever thoughts she put in my head away.

I would not allow myself to get giddy over a man I didn't see a future with.

CHAPTER 6

JP

THIS FUCKING SUCKED. I TURNED SIDEWAYS SO THE photographer could get a better angle. My dress shoes pressed into the green turf, and the stadium I'd called home for the past eight years was all around me, but at that moment, it didn't feel like anything close to home.

"Lift your chin up," the photographer said, pointing to the sky like I was an idiot who didn't know what direction he meant. "Put your hand on your hip so we can see the watch," he said in between clicks of his camera.

I did as I was told because I wanted the damn thing over with. Normally, these endorsement deals were fun, and I typically didn't mind doing them, but knowing I would meet with the team management after this wrapped up, had me on edge.

I shifted uncomfortably as the guy kept clicking away at the camera. My agent, Robin, beamed from the sidelines. She'd flown in from New York last night, and we spent most of it going through every scenario possible. The team had expressed an interest in extending my contract for two more years, but nothing was a done deal until my name was signed at the bottom of the page. There were a couple of trade options on the table, neither of which interested me, but I had to prepare to walk away if it came to that.

"You looked great." Robin smiled and handed me a coffee.

"Thanks." I adjusted my tie and took the hot cup from her hands. "I'm glad to be done with it."

"At least you get to keep the cool-looking watch," she teased, bumping her shoulder into mine.

Robin had been my agent for the past five years. The guy I first started with retired, and Robin came highly recommended. As the daughter of one of the most sought-after sports agents in the country and the wife of a hall-of-fame running back, she knew the ins and outs of this business better than anyone. And the best part of all was I trusted her.

"Are you ready for this?"

"No."

"Well, too bad, it's showtime." Her tone held a level of authority that shouldn't have made a guy my size flinch, but damn, the woman was scary. I might be the one signing her paychecks, but she was the one running the show.

"Your husband is a lucky man," I said, my voice heavy with sarcasm.

She rolled her eyes and handed me her coffee so she could set her iPad in her bag. Her big-ass diamond ring took up half of her left finger and was sparkling in the sunlight. "So, do you have any last minute questions for me?" she asked as we stepped inside and headed toward the elevator.

I pushed the button for the top floor. "It's been a while for me, so I'm a little out of my element."

"Like I said, the tone of the meeting will be more about the financial impact. Cash flow, salary cap, and things like that."

"Can't wait." I ran a hand through my hair and straightened my suit as we stepped off the elevator. I knew their focus was building the roster for next season, but if they wanted to resign me, I wasn't taking a pay cut, even though I knew I would be a big hit on their salary cap. My entire career was on the line, and there wasn't a damn thing I could do about it.

"How are you feeling walking into this meeting?" Robin asked, leading me down the long hallway to the reception area.

"I'll feel better once I know my fate," I said, giving her a practiced smile and rubbing my sweaty palms together.

The coaches and upper management had been in meetings all week, discussing contract renewals, trades, and budget cuts. The draft was next month, so they wanted to get the team roster in order as quickly as possible. I was taking it as a good sign that they wanted to meet earlier rather than later, unless they wanted to cut me in order to free up their budget for a younger player.

"They are ready for you." One of the assistants smiled while holding the door open for us.

Robin and I walked into the conference room and were greeted by the entire management staff. Beau Landers, the owner of The Arrows, sat at the front of the sleek glass table. The Atlanta skyline could be seen through the wall of windows directly behind him. Jerry Fields, the GM, Coach Ludden, and head legal counsel, Max Kasmerick, stood as we shook hands and exchanged pleasantries. Laptops, water bottles, and notepads lined the table. A large projector screen was on the far end of the wall.

"Gentlemen." I smiled and pulled out Robin's chair before I got settled in my own.

Max pulled out a folder and passed it to our end of the table. "Let's get started and get down to business."

Anxiously, I flipped through the paperwork and forced myself to sit and listen as they went through each page, discussing terms and conditions.

As the minutes ticked by, I had to give Robin credit. She was a good listener and didn't interrupt once. She asked questions, took notes, and didn't allow words to get twisted around. I knew firsthand that negotiations could turn quickly. You had to be patient and not let your emotions get the better of you.

"As I'm sure Robin has already mentioned, Baltimore and Denver have expressed an interest." I nodded as Max continued. I had no interest in going to either team, but they didn't know that. "We would like to get this deal locked in before your other offers come in. Based on the team's physician report, and reviewing your current salary, we would like to extend your contract for two more seasons."

I blew out a sigh of relief and looked at Robin. Her face showed nothing.

They went through benchmarks, incentives, and a bunch of legal mumbo-jumbo that I couldn't care less about.

Jerry folded his hands on the table and leaned forward. "With Maverick retiring last year, we've invested a lot of money in rebuilding our team. We understand the importance of keeping a few veteran players, that's why we came up with an offer that we think you'll be happy with."

Everyone around the table went quiet as I thumbed through the paperwork. The number was more than we predicted. I snuck a glance at Robin, whose eyebrows were bent in concentration. I twisted in my seat because the woman was known to be a tough negotiator.

Robin leaned forward, folding her hands in front of her. "I understand you have a spending cap to abide by. But it is my job to put my client in a position to ensure that he is getting the value and compensation he deserves. I would like to negotiate the terms of this contract."

I took in a long, deep breath and blew it out slowly. I loved my teammates, my home, the fans, the city of Atlanta. I didn't want to leave yet, so I prayed and hoped Robin knew what she was doing.

———

"Holy Shit! You did it," I said, clinking my glass with Robin's.

"*We* did it, but you're welcome." Her smile was victorious. A couple of guys walked by doing a double take. The second we stepped inside the restaurant, the whispers and stares started. I usually avoided public places, but today was an exception because we were celebrating.

"For a minute there, I was sweating bullets. I thought for sure they were going to kick my old ass to the curb when you showed them that dollar amount."

"They spent a lot of money last year bringing in a new quarterback who you've done well with. Their focus this year is the defensive line. They had too many on the injured reserved status, they need their guys young and healthy. And you, my friend, might not be the youngest guy on the team, but you're healthy and know how to get the job done."

It had been a long day, filled with highs and lows. I was glad to put the bullshit behind me now that I knew I was returning to the team next season.

Robin pulled out her iPad, and we quickly scanned the contract, ensuring the base salary and all other guaranteed money added up. I made a note to schedule an appointment with my financial advisor next week once the contract was finalized.

I started investing my money and planning for retirement early in my career. A lot of the younger players were under the assumption that once they started making money, that meant they would always have money. Nothing could be further from the truth. Everyone was one play away from being cut or injured. It was a quick fall from making millions of dollars a year to making zero.

"JP?" My head flew up at the sound of that voice.

Damn, Rylee was a sight for my sore eyes. She was in a black power suit, her hair was pinned back, and she wore a pair of pumps that made her look like a fucking boss. It was my first time seeing her in her business attire, and I liked it—a lot! Especially the silk blouse with the pearl buttons that I wanted to pop open with my teeth.

"Hey, Sunshine? This is a pleasant surprise."

She took a timid step forward. "I was on my way out the door and thought that was you."

"It's good to see you." I tried to compose myself, but my grin grew wider by the second. "What are you doing here?"

Her brows creased when she spotted the woman at my side. I could see the question in Rylee's eyes, wondering what Robin was to me.

"I had a business meeting." She glanced over her shoulder at the small group getting ready to leave.

"What are the odds of us running into each other?" I scratched my jaw.

She pursed her lips. "Seems to be happening a lot lately."

"Are you sure you're not stalking me?" I teased, leaning back in my seat and crossing my feet at the ankles.

"I don't have any tattoos with your name and number on my breast yet, so you're safe for now."

I threw my head back in laughter. I should have been more excited over the contract I had just signed instead of being so giddy over seeing my friend's sister.

"Ahem." Robin cleared her throat. Shit! I forgot she was sitting right next to me.

"Oh, sorry." I stood up and allowed my feet to carry me to Rylee.

"Rylee, this is Robin. Robin, meet Rylee Cross."

"Cross?" She leaned forward, resting her arms on the table. "Any relation to Maverick Cross?"

"Yes, he's my brother." Rylee's eyes bounced between the two of us. "I'm assuming you've heard of him."

Robin chuckled while dipping a shrimp into the cocktail sauce. "Who doesn't know your brother?"

Rylee went quiet for a minute. "Right." Her smile was tight, and unless I was mistaken, there was a glare in her eyes directed at my agent. "I didn't mean to interrupt. I'll let you two get on with your date."

"Date?" Robin sputtered, and I couldn't help but snort out loud.

"Yes, you are here together, correct?"

I scrubbed a hand over my jaw and stared at the woman who had driven me to the brink of insanity since the moment I met her. Something was going on in her head, and I wished I knew what it was. Because I wouldn't allow myself to believe it was jealousy. Not that I would mind it one bit.

She hiked her purse up over her shoulder and was about to leave. I grabbed her by the elbow, halting her in place. "Robin is my agent," I explained as she blinked slowly. "My very married agent."

Her eyes closed, and her head tipped back. "I am so sorry, I assumed…"

"Please." Robin waved a hand in the air, cutting her off. "It's totally fine. Just don't mention any of this to my husband. He's a bit of a caveman, and I kinda need JP to keep his limbs attached to his body. My husband is retired, so I'm the breadwinner now, and I've got kids to put through college soon."

I wanted to laugh because Robin and Nick were worth millions. Nick made more money off his investments than when he played in the NFL.

"Would you like to join us?" I asked, hoping the offer didn't reek of desperation.

She smoothed a hand along the front of her skirt and shifted on her feet. "I wish I could, but I have to get back to work."

"Can't you stay for one glass to help us celebrate?" This begging and pleading were so unlike me. Women typically came running in my direction, not the other way around. The irony wasn't lost on me; it was probably best to stop trying so hard. A challenge was one thing, but at this point, I was questioning my abilities.

"Celebrate?"

"Yep." I pointed in Robin's direction. "My shark of an agent just secured me a two-year extension to my contract and got me a nice raise in the process."

"JP, that's great." Without thinking, she flung her body at mine. It was hard not to grin at how hard she squeezed me. Her skin was warm, she smelled good, and she felt too right wrapped up in my arms, so I made zero effort to pull away. I've had chemistry with other women before, but nothing like this.

"So, what do you say?" I lifted my chin to the empty seat at our table.

"I'm sorry." She stepped back. "I'm running to another meeting or I would."

"A raincheck then?" I stared down at her, feeling my stomach twist in disappointment.

"Sure." She peered up into my eyes. "I should head back."

I gave her a crooked smile because, honestly, I was having a hard time keeping it together. "I can walk you out."

"That's not necessary." She moved around me, putting a halt to my attempts to see her out the door. "Stay and celebrate. And congratulations again. I'm glad they decided to keep you. You are a huge asset to the team and a great leader to the younger guys. I can't wait to watch you play next season."

Pride swelled in my chest. She had no idea how much those words meant to me.

"Thank you, Rylee."

She nodded and started moving toward the exit. "It was nice meeting you, Robin."

"You as well. Tell your brother I said hello."

I stood and watched her walk out the door. A huge part of me wanted to follow her outside and beg her to give me a shot, but I resigned myself to the fact that wasn't what she wanted.

Robin must have sensed something because she leaned forward and studied me. "Can I give you a friendly piece of advice?"

I slumped back down in my seat, feeling a lecture coming on. "I have a feeling you're going to give it to me whether I want it or not."

"It's obvious there is something there between you two."

Christ, I shoved a hand through my hair. She sounded just like Rhett. "You came to that conclusion just from that little exchange?"

"I mean, I'm not blind, but I'm pretty sure even Stevie Wonder could see it."

"Put your matchmaking hat away," I grumbled and took a hefty sip of my drink.

"How long before her brother detects something?"

I glanced at her quickly and pushed my flute glass aside. "There is nothing going on between us."

"But you want there to be."

Clearing my throat, I played with the corner of my napkin. "It doesn't matter what I want. She doesn't see me that way."

She tilted her head to the side. "I'm not so sure about that. I am a woman and let me tell you something." She leaned forward and rested her arms on the table. "When she saw us together, before she knew who I was," she picked up her utensil and held it in the air, "she looked like she wanted to stab me with this salad fork."

I eyed her skeptically. "I know she's attracted to me, but I'm not sure she wants *me*. She doesn't take me seriously. She sees me as just a player."

Rylee had no idea how bad I had it for her. The woman was all I thought about. There wasn't a single person on the planet that affected me the way Rylee Cross did. I wanted to get to know her on a deeper level. I wanted us to be on the same page and quit playing these fucking games. It seemed like every time I'd get close enough, something would get in the way. I was sick of her being within my reach and not being able to pull her in.

"Well," Robin lifted her glass in the air, "convince her

otherwise. You're JP Watson for Pete's sake. It's time to step up your game and get the girl. You and I both know that you are more than just a player in every sense of the word. You need to show her the real you and let her know how serious you are."

"And if she shoots me down?"

"Then you move on."

CHAPTER 7
RYLEE

My eyes closed, and I slammed my head on the steering wheel. It was just my luck that I took the next exit off the highway to avoid construction, only to have my freaking car die in the middle of nowhere. It was late; I was cranky, tired, and hungry. According to the last message from AAA, the tow truck was two hours away. What a joke. I wasn't sure why I even paid for the service.

There was nothing nearby for at least another three to five miles. If it were daylight, I would walk, but it was pitch-black out, and I was in heels. I had just come from another lousy date; no, it wasn't from the online app; a coworker set it up.

Max was handsome and nice enough, but it felt more like a job interview than a date.

Where do you see yourself in five years?
Tell me something about yourself?
What is your greatest strength?

I knew after the third question there wouldn't be a second date.

I picked up my phone from the cupholder and called my brother.

"Rylee?" His voice was a whisper.

"Hey, I didn't wake up Zander, did I?" It was weird thinking about my brother home on a Friday night at ten p.m.

"He's resting on my chest, drinking a bottle, but Kinley's sleeping next to me. What's up?"

"Oh, never mind." Kinley hasn't been feeling great and has been complaining about a lack of sleep. The last thing I wanted to do was disturb her. I'd figure something else out.

"What's going on?" he asked. I could hear him getting out of bed and shuffling across the room.

"My car broke down off of I-75, I'm on some side street near Piedmont Heights and the tow truck is two hours away."

"Shit. Let me wake up Kinley and I'll come get you."

"No, don't do that." I glanced down at my phone and started scrolling through my contacts. "I'll call Dad."

"Rylee, it will take him forever to get there. Let me call JP. He'll be awake and he's not too far from there."

"No," I barked into the phone. "I'll wait." The line went quiet, and I already regretted my outburst. "I don't want to bother your friend."

"He won't mind, and he owes me a few favors. Send me your location, and I'll text you when he's on his way."

For a quick second, I considered hitchhiking, but after watching one too many crime shows, that didn't sound like the best idea.

The last few times JP and I have run into each other, things were awkward. The streak of jealousy over his date with Taylor and my reaction from the restaurant only proved my point; I couldn't do casual with him. I was glad we didn't end up kissing that night on the dock, even though that's exactly what I wanted to do. I probably would have let him do more than that if he wanted to.

I was scrolling through my phone in an attempt to distract myself when I spied the taillights pull up behind me. It was actually hilarious that I was more nervous about seeing him than potentially being abducted.

I unrolled my window, and the sight of him made me wish I had walked or called my dad instead. His playful green eyes smiled down at me.

"Thank you for coming. I hope I didn't tear you away from anything too important, like a date or something like that."

His brow raised, and I suddenly felt the urge to pound my head against the steering wheel. Maybe it would reset my brain and get it to start working right again.

I felt like Baby in *Dirty Dancing* when she blurted out, "I carried a watermelon."

"You didn't tear me away from anything. I was up watching ESPN." His face broke out into a full-blown grin. "Would it bother you if I was on a date?"

"Of course not. It's none of my business what or who you do." I huffed, feeling a tiny bit of rage at the thought.

He snorted. "Yeah, I can tell."

"Whatever." I sighed in irritation because it was painfully obvious that I was lying. "How much do you know about cars?" I asked, leaning back slightly. His large frame was taking up so much room it was hard for me to think clearly.

"What seems to be the problem?" he asked, sticking his head farther into my personal space. I could practically feel the heat coming off his body, and with the smell of his cologne, that was a dangerous combination for me.

When I looked up to answer him, I swallowed, and my

attention immediately went to his tattooed arms, gripping the end of my door. Every tiny movement would cause the hem of his shirt to ride up his perfectly cut stomach. I averted my eyes up to his sharp jawline and noticed his newly trimmed beard, it was short, and I liked it—a lot. It made his lips more noticeable, and I wanted to kiss him so badly that I practically tingled everywhere. I envisioned what it would feel like to run my hands through his hair while he devoured my mouth. No doubt I would savor every second because a man as confident as him had to be skilled in that area.

He cleared his throat, pulling me from my thoughts. "Rylee?"

"Yeah?" I blinked up at him, trying to remember what we were talking about before I slipped into fantasy land.

"Your car?"

"What about it?" I was confused and distracted and making a complete fool of myself.

His eyes were sparkling. "You mentioned something about overheating."

"Yes, right, that would be me." My eyes flashed to his in mortification. "I mean my car! My car is overheating. Not me!"

Jesus Christ, Rylee. Shut up and stop talking.

His lips twitched. "Why don't you pop the hood and I'll take a look."

I reached to the left and pushed the button. JP rounded my car and looked under the hood. His tight green T-shirt looked ready to rip open if he moved another inch.

Glancing up at the sky, I silently wondered what I did to piss God off so much. Clearly, I was being punished for something.

As much as I wanted to sit in my car and avoid him, I

didn't want to be rude. I fixed a few strands of hair and stepped out of the vehicle.

"Hey." I strode over to his side. "Any idea what it could be?" He was bent over, twisting a few caps, and checking the oil. Why was that such a turn-on?

"I'm not a mechanic, but my guess is it's either a leak with the coolant system or something with the radiator."

I pulled my white sweater tighter around my shoulders. "My Jeep is only two years old. I shouldn't be having this kind of problem with a new car, should I?"

He closed the hood and wiped his hands off on a towel. "Probably not, but because it's newer, any major repairs should be covered under your manufacturer's warranty."

"Great." I sighed. "Now what?"

"Text your brother and let him know that I'm bringing you home."

"What about my car? I can't just leave it alongside the road, I'll get a ticket."

"I'll call my mechanic; he has a tow service."

"You just have a mechanic on speed dial?"

"Yep." He rounded the car and looked inside. "Make sure you don't leave anything valuable in there. I'll give my guy a call while you grab your stuff."

We were in a quiet area, but plenty of cars were still driving by. JP stayed close to me, keeping his body near the road. I grabbed my purse and made sure I wasn't leaving anything behind.

I hopped inside his truck and pulled my phone out of my purse when we merged onto the pavement. I was just about to call my brother when my phone buzzed in my hand with a new text.

"Speak of the devil," I said as JP side-eyed me.

Maverick
Any update on the car?

JP called his mechanic; he's having it towed
to his garage and bringing me home now.

Maverick
Glad to hear it. You're safe with JP. Tell him I
owe him. I'll call you in the morning to figure
out your car situation.

Sounds good. Now go back to bed.

Maverick:
Call me when you wake up. Night!

"Where were you coming back from?" JP asked,
glancing in his side mirror.

"I had a date tonight?"

His jaw tightened. "I thought you said you were done
with those stupid dating apps."

"Relax, it was set up by a mutual friend."

He pressed his hand firmly on the steering wheel. "You
said you were done, I assumed you meant with dates in
general."

"My friend Stephanie thought it would be a good idea
to set me up with her neighbor."

"How did it go?" His temple pulsed, and I had to
unroll my window to let some of the tension out of the car.

"I've had better," I said, trying to make light of the
situation. The date was terrible, and JP was clearly agitated
about it. Just thinking about it made me realize how
hungry I was, so I wasn't surprised when my stomach
protested by making an embarrassing noise.

"Please tell me you didn't hear that."

"I didn't need to hear it. I could feel the vibration all

the way over here." I playfully smacked his shoulder. "Hey, why are you taking your frustration out on me? Did your date not feed you?"

"We went to a sushi house."

He made a look of disgust. "You hate sushi."

I loved that he remembered that. "I don't hate all sushi. I just don't care for raw seafood. I'll eat cooked sushi."

"Wait a hot fucking second. Did your date sit across the table from you and not notice that you weren't eating?" He shifted in his seat. "Where the hell do you find these guys?"

"The appetizer was cooked," I said a little defensively, but I wasn't sure why. "He ordered the love boat for two special, which came with assorted uncooked sushi and sashimi."

JP broke out in laughter. "The love boat for two, huh?"

"Yeah, I sat through dinner, sipping my martini while he talked about his kids."

"Sounds like the guy was a real winner. Maybe that's another sign that you need to stop going on these dumb dates with people you don't know."

I turned in my seat and folded my arms. "How am I supposed to meet anyone, genius?"

"Who is to say you haven't met him yet?" He winked.

"Speaking of dates, why were you so agitated with me the night I babysat Zander?"

The muscle in his jaw ticked. "Because I assumed you set it up."

That's exactly what I thought. "Well, I told you I didn't, and that doesn't explain your attitude toward me that night."

He scrubbed a hand over his jaw. "Because, Rylee, you've been shooting me down left and right and it felt like you were shoving someone else in my face."

Oh, I sat back in my seat. His blunt honesty threw me off, and I wasn't sure what to make of it.

"Where are we going?" I asked, noticing we were headed in the opposite direction of my condo.

"Seeing that your date didn't feed you, I'm going to rectify that situation."

I folded my arms and twisted in my seat. "Is that so?"

"Yep. His loss is my gain."

———

"You didn't get anything?" I asked, opening the cardboard box. The pizza looked amazing, and I noticed he got me exactly what I liked without even asking.

"I already ate."

"Do you mind if I eat in your truck, because I'm starving?"

He reached over to the glove box and pulled out a pile of napkins. "Dig in."

I placed the pizza in my mouth and moaned when the flavors hit my tongue. It was a huge slice, so I folded it in half and ate it like I hadn't had a carb in years. I was so hungry that I didn't even care that I was eating like a starved animal in front of him.

JP handed me a napkin once I was finished with my second piece.

"That hit the spot. Thank you."

He glanced at me and back to the road. "Did you save room for dessert?"

I patted my stomach and let out a long sigh. "I always have room for dessert."

"Good, because there is a food truck that serves the best apple fritter donuts and cider you'll ever have."

"You had me at donut."

He winked and pulled off the highway. He kept one hand on the steering wheel and the other rested along the center console between our two seats. I couldn't help but notice how muscular his forearms were. He had a sleeve of black tattoos along each arm. I've seen enough pictures of him to know that the tattoos covered the top half of his chest. They were beautiful works of art, and all seemed to have some type of spiritual meaning.

I was so caught up in trying to decipher what they meant that I didn't notice where we were until we pulled into a little park overlooking a small lake. There was a block with food trucks shutting down for the night.

He turned off the engine and looked across the parking lot. "Do you want me to get the desserts to go or eat here?"

There were heat lamps lining the picnic area, and it was a nice night out. I also wasn't ready to have him bring me home yet. "I wouldn't mind eating here."

JP nodded his head, seeming pleased with that answer. He hurried out of the truck and tried to race around to my side to help me out, but I beat him to it.

We walked side by side as I followed him up to a pink truck with pictures of sprinkled donuts across the front. It had a big sign over the top that said, Glazed & Confused.

After placing our order, we walked along the pier to a small bench at the end. JP handed me my cider and unwrapped my donut for me.

"Thank you," I said, taking a bite. It was hot and tasted absolutely delicious.

"Not bad, huh?" He smirked while taking a bite of his own.

I patted his leg. "You did good. How did you discover this place?"

He finished chewing and took a sip from his water bottle. "The team participated in an event here for kids with physical disabilities. I was paired with a little kid named Mattie. He used to play hockey and wrestle, but one day during one of his matches, he landed wrong and ended up paralyzed from the waist down."

"Ugh! Those stories always tear my heart open. How old is he?"

"Fifteen now, but thirteen when it happened." He cleared his throat. "Anyway, I could tell he didn't want to get pushed around the park in his wheelchair, so I rented a tricycle with a seat on the back. We spent the day riding around the lake and discussed everything except his disability. He appreciated the fact that I was treating him like a normal kid. Meeting people like Mattie inspires me and challenges my thinking. No matter how often they get knocked down, they get right back up and keep pushing through. So, that's why it irritates me when people look up to me like I'm some type of hero. It's kids like Mattie that should be admired. We could all learn a lot from them."

"That's got to be hard, but I know how much those kids love the attention. I went with Maverick to a children's hospital once. It was an eye-opener."

"Yeah, but it's especially hard when you have to watch someone you love slowly fade away right before your eyes, without any control of the outcome." He stared up at the night sky.

JP lost his brother when he was a teenager. He was known to have the biggest philanthropic heart in the league. Not only was he notorious for giving back, but his charity, the Justin Watson Foundation, was heavily backed by the NFL. There was also a youth sports complex in Atlanta with his name on the building.

"I'm sure it meant a lot to Mattie." I met his eyes, not bringing up all the other charities he was involved in. I was getting the impression that he didn't want to take credit for all the good work he did.

"It probably meant more to me than it did to him. Some guys just want to write a check and pose for the camera. They don't know what they're missing."

"So, between the charitable work, the games, and practices, what do you like to do for fun?"

"I'll tell you what," he said with a glint in his eye that I was familiar with, "I'll show you what I like to do for fun if you agree to one date with me."

"JP, I'm not looking for a one-night stand," I said, reminding myself who he really was. I might have gotten to know his softer side tonight, but we were at different places in our lives. I wanted commitment, and he wanted freedom—two complete opposites.

"I don't think you'll have to worry about that."

"You don't think so, huh?" My lips twisted together in an attempt to hide my smile. It would be so easy just to give in. God, did I want to give in. He was wearing me down, and I had a feeling he knew it too.

"Nope." He shook his head. "Trust me, you'll want more than one night with me." He winked.

I poked him in the chest playfully. "You really want to take me on a date? Do you even date? I mean, I know you hook up, but when was the last time you actually tried to woo a woman?"

"Woo?" His shoulders shook with laughter. "Is that what I would be doing?"

"This is pointless." I sighed, staring out at the water. His playfulness was making it difficult to say no.

"I agree, so Friday night? I'll pick you up." He poked me back. "I promise the flirting and the charm is included in the date. I'll woo the hell out of you."

I laughed at how ridiculous this was. For the life of me,

I would never understand why he was pushing this. He didn't need to beg, plead, or do any favors. All he had to do was smile and crook his finger.

"Come on." He bumped my shoulder. "I'll even bring you a donut." He pointed to the empty bag. I shamelessly ate two.

"Oh, man, you really know how to tempt a girl." I twisted my lips in an attempt to hold back my smile.

He lifted my chin. "One date."

His eyes softened with emotion that I wasn't prepared for. Turning him down was getting harder and harder. I convinced myself he wasn't my type from the moment we met. I tried to keep him at bay, but with every interaction, my feelings for him just seemed to build and build. I didn't know what was keeping me from giving in, but I was still hesitant. "I'm not sure that's a good idea."

He tried to hide his disappointment, but I could still see it. "Why? Afraid you won't be able to keep your hands off me?"

I held his gaze, looking for a weakness or a chink in his armor. I was grasping at straws, trying to find a reason to stick to my guns. He has implied many times that he wanted me. He might not check all my boxes, but maybe it was time I started thinking outside the box.

God, was I seriously considering this?

"How about this," he said, breaking through my thoughts. "Let's not call it a date. Think of it as a dinner. It's the least you can do since I came to your rescue—again. Plus, I want to prove to you that I'm not just the player you think I am."

"Okay," I whispered, decision made. I could do this. I could guard myself, have a good time, and keep my emotions locked up.

"Really?" His eyes grew big. I smiled at how excited he looked.

"You have worn me down." I stood up and started collecting our things. "One dinner." I pointed. "Don't make me regret it."

He took my hand. "I'll do my best."

That's what I was afraid of.

CHAPTER 8

RYLEE

Every date outfit I owned was spread across my bed. Maybe I was overthinking things, but none of them seemed right. Not the black blazer with my leather pants or the one-shoulder jumper; even my slinky red dress screamed hard no.

"This is impossible," I said to my golden retriever, Oakley. He popped his head up from where he was resting across the room. "You men have it easy." I waited for him to respond, but he just ignored me and laid his head down on my carpet.

My shoulders slumped because I had officially lost my mind. It didn't help that I didn't know where we were going. JP thought surprising a woman who always needed to be in control sounded like a fun time. I begged him to give me a hint, and the only breadcrumb he threw my way was to dress warm and comfortably, hence, why none of my outfits would work.

Nibbling on my bottom lip, I glanced at my closet. I grabbed my best-fitting jeans, a simple white top, and a dark green blazer. I slipped on a pair of brown boots that offset the look completely. My hair fell in long, loose waves down my back. He seemed to like it that way, and I thought, why not apply an extra coat of that red lip gloss he was a fan of too.

When the knock sounded on the door, I gave myself one final twirl in the mirror, grabbed my bag, and took the steps I needed to get to my date.

Oakley trotted across the room, eager to greet our visitor. I swung the door open and held my eighty-five-pound golden retriever back by the collar.

JP leaned against the doorjamb in a charcoal gray sweater with dark jeans that molded perfectly against his muscular legs. Jesus, was he hot. His hair was styled in a way that showed he put extra effort into it, which made me smile. The man could be a cover model if he decided to switch professions.

"You look gorgeous." He handed me a box, and I immediately recognized the label. I tried not to swoon, but JP Watson didn't seem like the type of man that needed to go out of his way and stop by a food truck to bring his date a donut. All because he made a little joke about it the last time they were together.

"Wow!" I stepped back. "A man of his word. This night is off to a good start."

Oakley lifted his nose and started sniffing the box. "Back away, you little mooch; this isn't for you," I said, holding it out of his reach.

JP pulled something out of his pocket, and it took me a second to realize it was a dog bone. "Oh, my God. Are you trying to win my dog over too? Is that part of your big plan to woo us both?"

He laughed when Oakley made a beeline for his legs. "Oakley here is going to be my wingman. Isn't that right, old man?" He scratched my dog behind his head; the fur ball lapped up the attention.

"If you want to be his new BFF, you might want to call him something other than old man."

"Noted." He laughed and took off the plastic so he could feed it to him. "He's gotten so big."

Everyone on the team knew who Oakley was. I used to bring him to the practice field during the preseason to visit my brother.

"He's been slowing down a bit, so I've been shortening his walks, but other than that, he's doing pretty good."

"How old is he now?"

"He just turned eight last month."

"That's what? Fifty-six in dog years?" He bent down to give Oakley more attention.

"You're going to have hair all over you," I told him as I made my way into the kitchen.

"It doesn't bother me. It will come off." He got down on the floor and started rubbing Oakley's belly. "I hope I'm lucky enough to have as much hair as you do when I'm your age."

I started stuffing my things into my purse. "Are you sure I'm dressed okay? I can change or better yet, you could give me a hint on where we are going?"

"Nice try." JP stood up and started moving around; his new friend was hot on his heels. "You look perfect, no need to change."

My shoulders deflated. "It was worth a shot."

"So, this is your place, huh?"

I made a decent income and lived in a good area, but it was nothing like his massive estate or my brother's penthouse. Suddenly, I was feeling self-conscious. "I know it's small, but it's only me, and it does what I need it to do."

"Maybe next time you can give me the full tour."

"You mean all eleven hundred square feet of it, sure."

He held his arm out for me to loop mine in his. "Ready?"

"If we don't leave now, I might back out," I teased, but I knew before we even left my condo that this date would be the best date I ever had. Right off the bat, it felt different. Maybe because we already knew each other, there would be no forced conversation or random questions. Or perhaps it was the intense chemistry I could feel deep in my bones; whatever it was had me smiling all the way out the door.

JP reached for my hand, which I thought was sweet, and led me to the parking lot. "Is Oakley going to be okay if you're gone for a while?"

"Yeah, my neighbor Tilly is going to let him out later. She is a nosy little old lady who loves to help take care of him."

"Don't you mean 'lonely' little old lady?"

"Nope." I shook my head. "If you look over your shoulder, up to the third-floor balcony just to the right of the lamppost, you'll see her peeking through the blinds."

JP turned his head and chuckled. "What's her story?"

"She and her husband, Hank, used to run a biker bar outside of Nashville. When Hank passed away, she sold the business and moved to be closer to her son and grandkids."

"A biker bar, huh? That's pretty badass."

"Tilly is a character, that's for sure." I was surprised when we stopped at a sporty-looking white car. "Where is your truck?"

"Home." He opened the door, and I hopped in and buckled my seat belt. The black seats were soft, almost like suede.

"How many cars do you own?" I asked as he slid into the driver's seat.

He shrugged. "A few."

That was vague. Was he afraid he would come across as a show-off? "What kind of car is this?"

"Dodge Hellcat." He started the engine and pulled out of the parking lot.

"I don't know much about sports cars," I said, glancing around at the roomy interior. "But I'm surprised by how much space is in this car. I could probably fit the contents of my walk-in closet in here."

He laughed. "Technically, it's considered a muscle car."

I rolled my eyes. "Of course it is."

He pushed his foot down on the accelerator; my body jolted back against the seat. "It has great horsepower and handles better than you'd expect."

"I can see that," I said, keeping my hand on the dashboard. "We don't need to set any speed records, so get your lead foot under control."

"You've got to live a little, Rylee." He smirked but thankfully slowed down.

"You're right. I do, so stop trying to kill me," I said, flopping back in my seat once I was convinced he was slowing down.

He laughed. "I can't wait to take you out on my bike for the first time."

I winced. "You're not talking about a ten-speed bicycle, are you?"

He smirked. "I haven't had one of those since high school." He took one hand off the steering wheel and rubbed it along his thigh. "Lots of memories on that ten-speed though."

"I probably don't want to know." I shook my head and picked up his phone from the cup holder. "Let's see what kind of music you have on here." I squinted at the screen, wishing I had brought my glasses. "I see you like a little bit of everything."

"Doesn't every man?"

"Cute." I poked him in the arm.

"That's what the ladies call me."

"Oh, my God."

"They say that a lot too."

"Shut up," I said, clicking on a Morgan Wallen song. I immediately started singing and dancing in my seat.

JP reached over and turned the volume up.

"Is this one of your favorite songs?" I asked, unrolling the window for some fresh air.

"No, I just can't concentrate with your horrible singing."

I swatted his leg. "That's not very nice and my singing isn't that bad."

"Has no one ever told you that before?"

I rolled my eyes. "It's not like I go singing in public every day. I mostly sing in the shower."

He smirked. "Now that I would like to see."

I shook my head, trying to fight my smile. "I'm sure you would."

The rest of the drive was filled with fun banter and critiquing each other on our music tastes. When we pulled onto the familiar street, I bent my head in confusion.

"You brought me to your house for our first date?" I gave him a sideways glance.

"Trust me, okay." He winked and stepped out of the car.

"Let me guess," I teased as he reached for my hand. "We're going straight to your bedroom?"

He laughed and linked our fingers together. "In your dreams."

Now it was my turn to laugh. He led me around the

back of the house, and my mouth dropped open. String lights wrapped around the trees, a small fire burned in the middle of the yard, and tiki lights lined a small table with two chairs.

I did not expect this. I assumed he would take me to a fancy restaurant with overpriced food and small portions. He would flash his smile at everyone who approached him and spend the entire night trying to impress me.

"You did all this?" I asked, spinning around to take it all in.

For the first time since I met JP, I saw a shy smile creep onto his handsome face. "I didn't want our first date to be in a restaurant where there would be a noisy bar and there wouldn't be any privacy." He looked away, unsure, and I had a sudden urge to kiss him. "I guess you could say I'm selfish and I wanted you all to myself tonight."

Do not fall for this man, I repeated over and over in my head.

"I love it." I smiled, putting him at ease. "It's perfect."

"Hold on, I'll be right back." He rushed into the house and emerged a few minutes later, carrying something in his hands.

I stared at the charcuterie board with olives, assorted cheeses, meats, nuts, and fruit. JP pulled out my chair, and I smiled up at him. "Pulling out all the stops tonight, huh?"

"I have to win you over somehow." His eyes met mine, and I tried not to lean too far into his touch as his fingers caressed my back.

"So far, you're doing pretty good." I crossed my legs while he poured me a glass of wine. "This is pretty romantic. I'm impressed."

"Then I guess my plan is working. And just so we are clear, you are the only woman I'd go to all this trouble for."

I swallowed my wine, not knowing what to say to that.

My willpower was slipping fast, so I purposely steered the conversation in another direction. The man made me more nervous than a cat in a room filled with rocking chairs.

"I've been here a few times, but I've never appreciated how nice it is."

JP had a few sitting areas, a fire pit, a beautiful in-ground pool, and a hot tub. There were trails with a lake out back, making it feel like a secluded paradise.

"It's one of the few things I've spent my money on. Unlike a lot of the other guys, this is the only home I own. I made it exactly as I wanted it."

"What about the home where you grew up? Does your family still live there?"

He peered up at me from beneath his thick lashes. His eyes were the prettiest blueish-green I'd ever seen. I could get lost in those eyes.

"A few do."

I laughed. "That's pretty vague."

He slowly sipped his wine. "Not much to talk about. I grew up in a small town in Upstate New York where everyone knew your business." He sat back in his seat. "The winters suck and the sun probably shines about five days a year."

"Sounds like you miss it." My tone was heavy with sarcasm.

"I miss the summers and the fall. There are a few people I miss, but not enough to make me want to move back. There isn't anything left for me. My life is here now."

Okay. I knew how to take a hint. That topic was off-limits. "Tell me about college. Did you like playing for Penn State?"

"Ahh…Google me, did you?"

I laughed. "No, I've seen you wearing a lot of Penn State gear and it's not a very well-kept secret."

"Are you sure you never crushed on me?" he teased, popping a cracker into his mouth.

"I hate to bruise that big ego of yours, but no."

"Really?" His hand went to his chest. "Not even a small one?"

A laugh bubbled out of me. "Sorry, but I only had eyes for Rhett."

His jaw popped open. "There is no fucking way."

"Oh, come on. You know all the girls love Rhett." He shot me a scowl, and I felt bad for teasing him. "He's got that swagger; the right amount of confidence and he isn't bad to look at either."

"I think it's best if you stop talking now."

"I'm just teasing you." I lifted my gaze to the night sky and swallowed hard. "If you want the honest truth, I never allowed myself to think of you as anything other than Maverick's friend. It wasn't because I wasn't attracted to you, it was the exact opposite. I always felt that there was something between us, but I convinced myself it was safer to keep you at a distance."

His eyes softened in understanding. "I'm really glad you decided to give me a chance."

"Me too." I smiled.

JP and I talked and laughed throughout our entire meal. Going into this date, I had no idea what to expect. One thing was for certain, though: I liked him a lot. He was unlike any guy I've dated, and I could see myself becoming completely consumed by him.

He held out his hand. "Are you ready for dessert?"

I followed him over to the table next to the fire pit, where he had all the fixings for s'mores set up.

He handed me a marshmallow, and I lowered my

skewer over the open flame. I was one of those people who was impatient. I liked to cook mine fast and preferred it burnt. JP, on the other hand, held his stick high over the fire and was constantly rotating his stick with a focus that made me laugh.

"What's so funny?"

"You look very serious over there," I said, licking the gooey goodness off my fingers. I've already roasted three marshmallows, and he was still on his first one with the level of patience of a brain surgeon.

"Sorry, I like my s'mores enjoyable, I'm not a fan of the burnt charcoal taste."

"It's the best," I said, handing him a piece of chocolate and a graham cracker so he could make his sandwich. "I can see why this is your happy place."

"It's my sanctuary." He stretched out a bit.

"Can I ask you something?"

"I told you before you can ask me anything," he said, pressing the chocolate and marshmallow together before bringing it to his mouth.

I tilted my head and waved my hand around. "If you feel that way, why do you allow all those random people to invade your personal space? Why all the parties with random groupies?"

He looked up at the night sky. "There aren't as many parties as you think, but sometimes it's easier to host here where I can control the crowd, especially with the younger players. They tend to find trouble pretty easily. It's my subtle way of keeping them from doing something stupid. Although between you and me, I'm getting sick of that scene and always having to be their gatekeeper."

I was not expecting that. "Are you really saying that you're sick of the cleat chasers and the endless parties?"

Could we possibly be on the same page after all? I held

my breath, waiting for his answer, and tried not to get my hopes up.

He set his stick aside and scratched the back of his neck. "I have been for a while. Maybe it's my age and because I'm starting to take life more seriously. I'm not getting any younger, and I know I need to make some changes in my life."

"What kind of changes?"

"Good ones, I hope." He winked, and my gaze went back to the fire. All the reasons I conjured up about why things would never work were slowly fading from my mind. There was no humor in his voice, no laughter in his tone, just complete sincerity. This may not be a dead-end road after all.

———

"What do you think?" he asked as the credits rolled across the screen.

I rolled my lips together like I was giving it some deep thought. "I think you need to stop feeding me donuts and s'mores if I want to look as good as Jennifer Lopez does when I'm her age."

We just finished watching *Shotgun Wedding*. I assumed it was a typical romantic comedy. I wasn't expecting all the grenades, explosions, or the pirate-kidnapping-terrorist, but it was pretty funny.

"I think you're perfect just the way you are."

We were lying side by side on his oversized sectional. JP had been the perfect gentleman all night. I kept expecting him to cop a feel or, at the very least, let his hands roam a little, but the only movement he would make was to tug me closer against his chest when I would shift in position.

"I think you need to get your eyes checked." I laughed

and stood up to bring my empty wineglass into the kitchen. "You obviously haven't noticed the little scar right here on my jaw." I pointed to the little white line that most people barely noticed, but I always knew it was there.

"What happened?" he asked, wrapping his arms around my waist from behind.

I set the glass in the sink and turned in his arms. My fingers shamelessly crawled up onto his strong shoulders. We were so close I could feel his heart beating in his chest. "Maverick was six and I was three. He was pulling me down the driveway in a little red wagon, and we went over a bump and out I went."

He flinched. "Ouch."

"Yeah, thankfully, I don't remember, but from what I've been told, it required four stitches."

He dragged his soft lips along the faded white line. My eyes slid shut when he moved to the corner of my mouth. He was treating me like glass, but I wanted to crawl into him and beg him to ruin me.

I pushed up on my toes and tightened my arms around his neck. His eyes held mine, searching for permission or reassurance. I couldn't tell.

His hands slid up my back. "What do you want, beautiful?"

I arched my body into his. "I want your mouth on mine."

He tilted my face, positioning me where he wanted me. "I will never deny you of anything." His tongue dipped inside, and his hand splayed along the curve of my ass. The kiss was slow, and it was going to be my undoing.

It was tender, soft, sweet, and not what I expected. I expected him to tear my clothes off, push his arousal inside me and take what he wanted.

Everything ached. My body was on fire, and with every

lick of his tongue, a hot, searing intensity burned through my veins.

I lifted and tightened my leg around his and rolled my hips. He was hard and obviously just as sexually frustrated as I was.

"Rylee." He pulled away and peered down at me. "I didn't bring you here for this."

I blinked slowly and took a minute to respond because, if he was telling the truth, I needed to find a way to change his mind. "Why did you bring me here then?"

"Because I wanted to prove to you that I'm not the guy that you think I am. You're my best friend's sister, not a quick fuck. I wouldn't do that to you or disrespect my friendship." He shoved a frustrated hand through his hair. "But it feels like no matter what I do, I'm going to mess this up somehow."

"The last time I checked, I was a consenting adult," I said firmly, letting him know Maverick didn't get a say in this. "I don't need my brother's permission to sleep with someone."

His eyes turned stormy. He looked pissed, and that flutter in my stomach kicked up a notch. "This isn't just about sex."

I blinked, stunned at what I just heard. "C'mon, JP, you expect me to believe that? Just because I'm Maverick's sister doesn't mean you have to treat me differently or pretend to suddenly have feelings for me."

"Suddenly? Have you not noticed what an idiot I sound like whenever I open my mouth around you? How I can't peel my eyes off of you." He pinched the bridge of his nose, and I thought he would stop there, but he kept on going. "I've sat back and watched you date stupid men who weren't good enough and didn't deserve you. I had never touched you before because I was convinced I could never give you more. But I want to go on record and make it crystal clear that I thought about touching you so many times that I lost count. My head would explode whenever I saw you with some asshole that wasn't me. I accepted the fact that we would never be anything more than what we were. And I was okay with that until recently. When I realized this attraction I have for you wasn't going away."

He said all that without taking a breath.

How could I have been so blind? Misread things so badly? "You've had feelings for me all this time and never once tried to make a move on me? Why?"

"Because I knew once I touched you, it would change everything."

"What does that even mean?" I was afraid to ask but had to know. And goddamn it, why did I like the sound of that so much?

"Rylee, I don't trust myself to answer that now." He kept his body rooted in place. "I'm trying to keep my hands to myself. To keep my addiction to you under control. But a man only has so much restraint, sweetheart, so don't go asking questions you're not prepared to handle."

The only thing I could focus on was the way his chest rose and fell. The clenched fists at his sides. The way my name sounded like a plea coming from his lips. JP stared me down like he was two seconds away from ripping my clothes off. And I was here for it.

Screw common sense—screw responsibility.

"I'm more than ready, JP. I'm done pretending that this chemistry between us doesn't exist. So, let's solve the mystery once and for all and see what kind of magic we can make together."

CHAPTER 9
RYLEE

HIS EYES FLARED, AND MY BODY FLOODED WITH WARMTH. JP leaned forward and pressed his lips to mine. His mouth was just the right amount of pressure as he kissed me with a passion I'd never felt before. The strokes of his tongue were controlled and calculated, which only made me want more. I gripped the back of his neck tightly, drawing him closer. Electricity raced down my spine as he took control of my mouth.

"Is this what you want?" Strong fingers slipped into my scalp and twisted my hair. His voice was strained, borderline frustrated.

"Yes."

His jaw clenched as he stared at me. I could see the conflict in his gaze. He was at war with his loyalty to my brother and his attraction to me. We both knew once we did this, it would change everything. My eyes pleaded with his to choose me. Choose us. Even though there wasn't an "us' yet, I wanted there to be.

He tipped my head back, forcing me to meet his gaze.

"You've been driving me insane, Rylee. I haven't been able to think about anyone but you."

A little moan popped out of my mouth before I could stop it. "The feeling has been mutual," I confessed, feeling my throat grow thick with emotion.

He gripped my chin; his eyes had a wild look to them. "What did you just say?"

I know I've been sending him mixed signals, but couldn't he see how much he's affected me? Maybe I hadn't been as honest with him as I should have been, and it was time to make my intentions clear. "I've dreamed of this moment and now I'm kicking myself for all the time we've wasted."

JP emitted the hottest growl I'd ever heard. "Why the fuck didn't you say something sooner?"

"Because I didn't think my attraction to you would turn into anything."

I saw the moment it dawned on him. "My reputation scared you away?"

"Yes."

He brushed the tip of his nose against mine. "No more assumptions and no more doubting me, okay?"

The smile on my lips was playful. "Sounds good to me. Now kiss me, we have a lot of lost time to make up for."

"You are a demanding little thing, aren't you?" he murmured before slanting his mouth back over mine, where it belonged.

Our tongues moved against each other in small circles. The single taste of him had me hanging on by a thread. His hard cock pressed against me, and I knew I would feel it long after this was over.

"Rylee." He spun me around, pressing me against the wall. "You have no idea what you do to me."

I arched into him. "I think I have a pretty good idea."

He reached out, lightly gliding his palm over my leg. I let out a whimper, shocked at how easily a simple touch could send me swimming with pleasure. "I can't believe I'm actually touching you." His hands went to the buttons of my jeans. He didn't push them off or shove them down my legs. Instead, he paused and looked into my eyes. "How far do you want to go?" he asked, sliding his hand up my shirt to pull on the cups of my bra.

"All the way." I moaned in approval when his thumb brushed along the peak of my nipple.

"Can I take this off?" He pulled on the lace straps of my bra. "So, I can suck on these?" He moved his mouth to my chest, bringing a nipple into his mouth.

"Yes." I whimpered at the soft feel of his hands running along my skin. Now I knew why they were his biggest asset.

He moved his mouth to my other breast to give that one equal attention. "This feels like a dream—almost too good to be true."

The scruffiness from his cheek was foreign to me and felt better than I imagined. "You're going to drive me crazy with this, aren't you?" I teased, dragging my fingers through the short stubble peppering his jaw.

He pulled on my leg, wrapping it around his waist. "You have no idea. Wait until it's between your legs. I'm going to have you withering underneath me so bad, you'll never want anyone else there but me."

I dug my heels into his back. "Good, because that's exactly where I want you."

He slipped his hand into the zipper of my jeans and placed his palm against my center. My hips jumped forward when he shoved the lace fabric aside and dragged his pointer finger along my slit. "Is there anything else you want?"

"All I want is you," I said, leaning into his touch.

"I'm all yours." He dragged his mouth to the shell of my ear. "But I have a feeling once I have you, it won't be enough. I'm going to want more. Are you going to give me whatever I want, Rylee?"

"It depends." I withered and arched as he curled his fingers into my flesh.

"On what?" He paused his movements with questions in his eyes.

JP was skilled, and I had no doubt he knew that, but I still felt the need to tease him. "I will give you anything as long as you've got the skills to back up those words." I was egging him on, trying to hold on to what little control I had left. He was used to women bending at his will, and I wanted to be different.

He gripped my hip and shoved his fingers in and out. A gasp left my mouth, letting him know he was hitting all the right spots. "You were saying?" He smiled.

I clawed at his back, encouraging him to keep going. "I can't remember." I was too busy getting swept away by the building sensation to recall what we were talking about.

"You were questioning my skills." He smirked as his fingers continued their steady movement. Everything tightened, and a feeling that I couldn't describe but wish it could last forever came rushing out of me.

It took me a minute to float back down to earth, and when I did, he pressed a light kiss to my lips. "You good?" I nodded as he gently unfolded my leg and made sure I could stand on my own. I didn't know what to say, words would not flow from my mouth, and if I was honest, I didn't trust myself to talk. I just had the most mind-blowing orgasm of my life and was already craving the next one.

And we hadn't even had sex yet.

His hands went to his belt, and I watched in pure fascination while he stripped off his clothes. I always knew he was in great shape, thanks to his training schedule and working out, but seeing his body up close was more than I expected. He was hard everywhere, and there wasn't a muscle on his body that wasn't defined.

My eyes traced the black ink covering his shoulders, chest, and arms. Normally, I could give or take tattoos, but with JP, they added to his appeal.

Once he was completely naked, I had to squeeze my legs and pray to God not to embarrass myself. My gaze was stuck on his erection. It was big and thick, and I was completely captivated by it.

JP groaned. "Rylee, you've got five seconds to shed the rest of your clothes." He started stroking himself aggressively. "Or this is going to be a one-man show. So, unless you want to sit and watch, you better start stripping."

I pushed my shirt over my head in a rush, and he laughed when my pants got stuck at my feet.

"Let me help you."

He stepped between my legs and lifted my calf. His eyes never left mine as he pushed the material past the arch of my foot. I whimpered when he brought his nose up to my core and inhaled. JP closed his eyes, and a look of sheer bliss shone across his handsome face.

"You're soaked," he said, and I bit down on my bottom lip to keep my mouth shut. "And you smell just like I knew you would. Absolutely incredible." He sniffed deeply, and holy shit! Where did this man come from?

I wanted to give him everything, and I wanted him to take whatever he needed from me, but I was seriously questioning whether I would ever be enough for him.

He backed me up to the kitchen counter. With one arm

along my waist, his other swiped the empty wine bottle and glasses across the room. A loud clatter sounded across the quiet kitchen.

"You just made a mess." I smirked.

"I don't give a fuck." He wrapped my leg around his middle. "The only thing that matters right now is you."

I slid my hands along his carved shoulders, loving that I could touch him that way. "I've dreamed of this moment."

"Yeah?" he asked, peering up at me with a boyish grin that I didn't know he was capable of.

"More than I care to admit," I whispered as he laid me down on the cold granite.

"I wish you would have said something sooner." He pressed his lips to mine and kissed me. It was soft, sweet, and possessive. Nothing about him was predictable.

"You would have lost interest in me quickly if I had."

His hand cupped my breast. "Never." He squeezed and brought his mouth down to my nipple.

My back arched off the kitchen island when he gave it one long pull. I was sensitive everywhere.

I squirmed and moaned as he took his time, dragging his teeth, mouth, and hands across every inch of my body. I dug my nails into his back and looked up. He was watching every move I made and seemed fascinated with every little sound.

He spread my legs open, keeping his gaze on mine the entire time. The intensity was too much, so I closed my eyes and tried to shut my brain off. We were strictly casual, and I needed to remember that.

He dragged his thumb along my inner thighs before brushing it along my slit. I pushed my hips forward, searching for friction and trying to prepare myself for what was to come. He dropped his head and flicked his tongue along my center. I wasn't expecting that, but I wasn't going to complain one bit. The heels of my feet dug into his back as he took long, languid strokes with his tongue. Everything ached and throbbed. Never in my life had I ever been so turned on. Just seeing his face disappearing between my legs was enough to send me over the edge for a second time. He sucked hard and licked forcefully. It was unfair how experienced he was, and if I didn't think it would go to his head, I would ask him if he was trying to set a world record.

As if he could read my mind, he shoved a finger inside and curled it against that bundle of nerves. I pulled on his hair, needing something to hold on to. "Oh, God!" I screamed loud enough to where his neighbors could probably hear a mile away. I closed my eyes as his fingers and tongue sent every nerve firing off. He sucked hard and twisted his fingers until I came apart. His name was on my lips as my orgasm spilled out of me. If I weren't completely boneless and could get my brain to work, I'd ask him how he got so damn good at this. It was as if he knew my body better than I did.

He wiped a hand over his mouth and smiled down at me. He looked pretty damned pleased with himself. "I finally got you right where I want you."

"I think I need a minute," I rasped between heavy breaths.

He chuckled, and I looked off to the side, trying to get my body to relax. My eyelids felt heavy, and a part of me wanted to surrender to sleep, but when I saw the look in his gaze, I knew that wasn't going to happen.

JP licked his lips. His gaze was hard. He looked untamed, and I had a feeling he was done taking things slow.

There was no way I could refuse him, no matter how

tired I was. Who the hell was I kidding? I wanted him inside me just as much as he did.

"You good?" he asked, his fingers tracing over my hip.

"I think so." I nodded, feeling my heart flop in my chest. I can't believe that just happened.

"I need a yes, Rylee."

I swallowed while looking down at his thick erection. "Yeah, I'm ready."

"You deserve better than to be fucked on my kitchen counter, but I can't wait another second to be inside you. I promise to make it up to you. Are you on birth control?"

I paused for a moment. "I'm on the pill."

"Do you trust me?" His eyes held mine, and I didn't have to think twice.

"I do."

"Then you've got to believe me when I tell you that it's been a while for me, and I swear on everything I own that I've always been cautious. I'll use protection if you want me to..."

"Wait a minute." I blinked in disbelief. "What do you mean, it's been a while?"

The pads of his fingers brushed along my jawline. "You are all I've thought about besides football. I didn't have the time or the desire to be with anyone else."

His confession was my undoing. "Really?"

He brushed my hair aside and cupped my face. "Swear on my life."

"We don't need to use anything. I believe you."

If there was one thing I was sure of, it was that JP would never do anything to risk my safety.

I sank my teeth into my bottom lip when he lined up at my entrance. I was convinced I couldn't take much more a few seconds ago. Oh, how wrong I was. The feeling of him finally sliding into me sent cries of relief through the room.

Rolling his hips forward, I felt him slowly stretch me until I was completely filled.

JP was big everywhere, and you wouldn't hear one complaint from me.

He thrust forward, and my nails went to his shoulders. Wrapping a leg around his middle, he pulled out and slammed forward, drawing pleasure from my body in places I didn't know were possible. Tears leaked from my eyes as he kept a rhythm that moved exactly in sync with mine. His hips swirled and ground, and I became an embarrassing mess of sighs and pants. With him being an athlete, he knew how to use his body; I just had no idea it could feel this incredible.

His kisses were patient, and his body's slow movement over mine drove me to the brink of insanity. I couldn't figure out if he was teasing or torturing me. I was mindless and helpless and completely at his mercy. That bundle of nerves I tried to hold back didn't stand a chance.

My back arched underneath him, begging and pleading with him to finish this. Instead of giving me what my body craved, he shifted his hips, creating a new friction, and I couldn't decide if I wanted a release or to revel in this feeling forever.

My fingers trailed down his spine, letting him take what he needed from me. I could feel the muscles in his back as he thrust harder. He pulled out and drove his hips forward, hitting the spot where I needed him most.

I hugged his body to mine and urged him to end this because I couldn't take much more. I never felt anything like this. He was deep inside me but still didn't feel close enough. JP was deliberate and controlled with his movements; he was fast and slow, and I couldn't keep up.

Circling his finger against my swollen clit, I understood why I'd avoided him all these years. The feeling was too much. I should have mentally prepared better because now I wasn't sure if I'd be able to come back from this.

"I can't take much more," I warned as that familiar sensation pushed through me.

"Yes, you can." He wrapped my hair in his fist and pumped harder. "You. Me. This," he said as that ache building inside me started to crest to the surface, "was meant to happen." His thrusts turned rough; his thighs began to shake, and that little thread of control I held on to disintegrated. "But make no mistake, we will not be done because I want more than this. This is not the end, it's just the fucking beginning." He cursed under his breath and released himself inside me.

CHAPTER 10

JP

PROPPING MY FACE IN MY HAND, I GRINNED AT THE SIGHT before me. Last night was incredible and completely unexpected. I couldn't even begin to comprehend what I was feeling.

It's been ages since I slept in the same bed with a woman. It was too intimate and often led to mixed signals and the person drawing the wrong conclusions about my intentions. With Rylee, I wanted to take my time and savor every second. For the first time in my adult life, I was considering something more. Maybe because I'd gone so long without human touch, I had forgotten how good that connection felt.

There were no awkward kisses or moments of hesitation. We just clicked.

My fingers skimmed along her back, feeling like the luckiest guy on earth. How I got her in my bed was a damn miracle. It felt like she saw past the JP (Just Playin') Watson or whatever the media was calling me this week. This type of contentment should have scared me, but all I could think about was how I could convince her to stay.

"Morning." She lifted her head and squinted her eyes.

I dropped a kiss on her hair. "Morning, Sunshine."

She was quiet for a second while my hands silently roamed her body. "Why do you call me Sunshine?"

I pulled the covers up over her shoulder. "Because you're always glaring at me."

She swatted my shoulder and narrowed her eyes. "I do not glare."

I brought the pads of my thumbs against her skin to help smooth out the tightness around her eyes. "What do you call this?"

"Bullshit."

My chest rumbled with laughter when she pushed my hands away so she could cover her face. "How did you sleep?"

"Horrible?"

I arched an eyebrow. "Horrible?" I repeated back.

"Yes, because you snore." She yawned, and I couldn't help but smile down at her. "*Loud*," she emphasized.

"I do not." I totally did, like a congested bulldog.

"You might want to check with your doctor about that. My dad has a CPAP machine, he could probably give you a referral."

Yanking the covers down, I started tickling her sides. "You think you're just little miss peace and quiet? I got news for you sweetheart, you snore too."

She squirmed and tried to swat my hands away. "I only snore when I drink alcohol."

"You didn't drink that much." I stopped and stared at her breast. My heart sped up, and I slicked my tongue over my teeth. Shit! She wasn't going to be happy with me when she saw the love bites I left behind.

"What's the matter?" Her laughter stopped when she noticed my face.

My fingers traced the bruises I left along her skin. "It looks like I got a little carried away last night. I hope you're not mad."

Her hand reached up and cupped my face. "Does it look like I'm mad to you?"

Her eyes were soft, and her lips were tilted in a lazy smile. "No, but I won't fight you if you want to pay me back," I teased while waggling my eyebrows.

She tried to nudge me off. "Nice try, but I need to get going. My neighbor took care of my dog last night, but he's got a grooming appointment that I need to take him to this afternoon."

I swallowed and hated the thought of her leaving so soon. "Can I at least cook you breakfast before you go?"

Her lips pressed together, and my heart thumped erratically while it seemed like she took forever to answer me. "You don't have to do that."

"I want to."

She tried to hide her smile, but I still caught it. "Okay."

I kissed her lips briefly, trying to ignore the way my fingers itched to touch her all over again. "You can use my bathroom to get dressed. I'll shower in the guest bath to save time, unless you want to conserve water and take a shower together."

She rolled her eyes and pushed away. "We both know that won't save either of us any time."

After a quick shower, I walked into the kitchen to see what I had in my fridge. I pushed the containers of fruits and veggies aside, finding a couple of eggs, coffee creamer, and a bottle of syrup. I bent at the legs and remembered a loaf of frozen sourdough bread in the freezer.

I opened a few empty cabinets, wondering if I had anything else to cook; I pushed past the tubs of protein powder, boxes of oatmeal, and packages of protein bars and came up short. I walked back to the fridge, grabbed a container of berries, and set it on the counter. I made a mental note to buy a few things for next time. The thought hit me when I was in the middle of defrosting the bread in the microwave. Pulling on the back of my neck, I waited and waited for the panic to hit me, but it never came. This connection didn't feel fleeting or temporary; oddly, I was okay with that.

I turned to the sound of soft footsteps descending the stairs. My grin was automatic at the sight in front of me. Her hair was wet from the shower, her smile was sheepish, and I loved knowing it was because of me. But it was the sight of her naked silhouette under one of my white dress shirts that made me want to throw her over my shoulder like a caveman and drag her back to my bedroom.

Her eyes traveled down my chest to the towel hanging along my hips. She was definitely checking me out, which was fine and dandy with me. "Do you always cook breakfast in nothing but a towel for your guests?"

My smile widened. "Do you always steal men's dress shirts?"

"It was either this or walk through your house naked to get my clothes." She pointed to the haphazard pile on the floor.

"Sorry. I should have brought those up to you."

"You don't look sorry." She stepped forward, her eyes sweeping over me from head to toe. Those big brown eyes filled with heat, so I raised my hand and stepped back.

"Don't go getting any ideas, little lady. I'm trying to be a gentleman here, so don't you even think about seducing me. You're the one who said you had to go, remember?"

She groaned. "That was before I saw you freshly showered, wearing nothing but a towel."

"Would you like me to drop it?"

Her soft laugh floated through my kitchen. "Maybe after breakfast."

I turned my back and faced the stove to hide my hard-on. I was a strong man, but I only had so much restraint. My cock was throbbing, and I was half-tempted to throw her over my kitchen countertop—again.

"You shouldn't tease a man like that," I said, keeping my eyes on the griddle. "Especially since he's one second away from dragging you back into bed."

"It's cute that you think you're in charge."

Setting the spatula down, I stalked toward her. "It sounds like somebody needs a reminder."

She dragged her finger along my exposed shoulder. "Maybe I do."

"Woman." I leaned back and pointed the spatula at her. "Sit down and stop tempting me."

"Fine." She huffed in annoyance. She was so stinkin' cute. "But only because it smells so good in here, and I'm hungry."

She poured herself a cup of coffee and sat down at the table. I could feel her eyes on my back, so I might have used a little more muscle than I needed to when flipping the French toast in the pan. I've never been more thankful for all the extra work I put in at the gym.

Rylee stared down at her coffee cup. "Do you want to talk about the elephant in the room, or just keep avoiding the conversation?"

I made a show of glancing around the kitchen. "I don't see an elephant."

"JP," she sighed, "we need to talk about this."

"Says who?" I slid her plate in front of her and crossed my arms.

"Sit down and be serious for a second."

"Rylee." I walked to her side of the table and sat

beside her. "Let's not define this or overthink things, okay. We both wanted what happened last night, and I really hope it will happen again. We don't need to complicate things." I leaned forward to brush my thumb along the bottom of her chin. "I told you last night that I've wanted you for a while now but convinced myself I could never have you."

She pursed her lips. "Because of Maverick?"

"Partly yes." I held out my hand, and she took it. "There are things I'm not comfortable talking about, but I want to be as truthful as I can with you. I carry a lot of baggage, Rylee, and I'm not even close to being ready to unpack it."

"JP, we all carry baggage."

I shook my head. "Mine takes up too much space in my mind. That's why I avoid relationships. It's not fair to my friends, my family, the people that are close to me."

Her eyes softened, and I saw a hint of pity there, and I hated it. "Look, I'm not a psychologist okay, but even I know that storing any type of emotional baggage away doesn't make *it* go away. At some point, you have to deal with it."

"That's just it, Rylee." I turned her hand over and linked our fingers together. My palms were starting to sweat. "I haven't dealt with it. I've gone out of my way to avoid it. I've spent my entire adult life putting a certain image out there that I wanted people to see. I smile when I'm supposed to and laugh when it's expected. Pretend to be happy even when all the energy is sucked out of me. I 'fake it till I make it', but with you, things seem real, and I don't want to pretend anymore."

She slid her free hand over my lower back. "You will never have to pretend with me and just so we are clear, you better not ever fake anything with me either. Regardless of whether or not anything comes out of this, you can always trust me to be real with you too."

"What exactly is *this*, Rylee?"

She blew out a long breath and looked away. "I don't know yet."

"Me either, but how about this," I tilted her face to meet mine, "why don't we figure it out together? One day at a time. No labels, no expectations. Just two people trying to figure their shit out."

I could see her overthinking and worried I'd said the wrong thing. This was uncharted territory for me, so I didn't know what the hell I was doing. The look she gave me did nothing to calm my nerves.

"I'm not sure how I'm supposed to respond to that. It's one thing if this is just sex, but I'm not sure I could handle walking into your house and seeing some bimbo sitting on your lap. I'm just not made that way. And let's be real here, you're not known to be an exclusive type of guy."

"Says who?" I drew back, offended. "You're basing this assumption off of an image that I put out for the media and the public. I just told you that's not the real me. My feelings for you are authentic. There is nothing fake about our interactions. I've been candid with you, and I can assure you that there won't be any other women."

"So, you're saying that we're exclusive?"

"Sure." I shrugged. I thought I had already covered this, so either I wasn't convincing, or she didn't believe me.

"You're serious?"

I looked into those brown eyes that had owned me since I first noticed them. "As long as I have you in my bed, I don't have the need or desire for anyone else. But this isn't just about what happens in the bedroom, it's about you and me. I've waited forever for you to give me a chance, and I don't want to do anything to fuck this up."

She set her cup down and crawled into my lap. Her hands folded along my neck while mine went to her ass. "You really are sweet."

"I can be." I picked up the fork, sliced off a piece of French toast, and brought it to her mouth. "Open."

She opened her mouth and moaned. "You probably shouldn't do that while sitting on my lap," I said, adjusting myself underneath the flimsy white towel.

She giggled. "Why are you still wearing that thing?"

"I didn't want the French toast to burn, and then you walked into the kitchen and distracted me before I had a chance to put sweats on."

"I'm not sorry one bit for distracting you." She picked up a strawberry and brought it to my mouth. "My turn."

I opened up and sucked the strawberry from her fingers. When the juice ran down my chin, she pulled it away and licked it off my skin. Fuck! She was hot, and I was one lucky son of a bitch. I gripped her hips painfully as my erection rubbed against her bare pussy. "How sore are you, because I want you again?" My hands ran along her smooth thighs.

"I'm a little sore but I can take it," she said, undoing a few buttons of my shirt, exposing her chest to me. I swiped another strawberry off the plate, bit off the tip, and squeezed the rest of the juice along her hard nipple. I closed my mouth along the peak and sucked hard.

"So sweet," I said, moving over to her other breast. She moaned and spread her legs. I knew she would go again, but there were other ways I could make her feel good.

I trailed my hand down her chest, past her stomach, and pressed my thumb against her clit. Her hips shot forward, her head flew back, and her mouth opened. I slammed my lips down onto hers, feeling myself grow harder and thicker. I grabbed an ice cube from the glass and ran it along her slit.

"Oh, God," she cried out as I pressed the ice cube along her clit. My mouth watered at the sight of her. I inserted the ice cube inside while keeping a firm grip so it wouldn't slip from my finger. She squeezed my thigh and dry-humped me with only a flimsy towel between us. Rylee moved up and down; I could feel her getting close to the edge. I took the ice cube out and replaced it with my fingers. I knew the exact spot that would set her off, and with her groans growing louder and the way she pulsed and trembled, I wrapped my free hand around her hair and pulled her mouth back to mine. I kissed her, swallowing all her sounds until I felt her come all over my hand.

Her eyes were closed, and her hair was a mild mess. It was an image I never wanted to forget.

After a few breaths, I held her face in my hands and asked, "Aren't you glad you stayed for breakfast now?"

"That was so good, I might have to stay for lunch." She sighed into my touch.

I chuckled against her mouth and gave her a few minutes to get her breathing under control.

When I set her down on her feet, our eyes locked, and I wondered if she felt the same things I was. Happy. Content. Sated.

She pressed her lips to mine, and I could taste the strawberry on her tongue. It was crazy how much I wanted and needed her again.

She untied the knot holding my towel together, letting it fall to the floor. "Rylee, what are you doing?" I asked as she closed her hand over my erection.

"Thanking you. For breakfast, of course." She winked and dropped to her knees on my kitchen floor.

"Is that so?" I groaned as her hand gripped my cock and pulled it forward. I dreamed of this moment so many times in my head, but nothing compared to the sight in front of me.

"Yes." She wet her lips and stared up at me. "I also want to know what you taste like?"

Jesus, Fuck!

I hissed in a breath when she sucked me into her mouth. My hands dipped into her hair as her tongue slid over my shaft. I guided myself in and out, trying to stay in control, but I lost all common sense when she drew me into the back of her throat. I couldn't think with her warm mouth wrapped around my cock. My head fell back as I let the sensation take over. It felt incredible, and fuck me. I'd never be able to be in this kitchen again and not think about this moment. I could feel myself growing thicker; my balls were growing painfully tight. My hips had a mind of their own when they started pumping with reckless abandon. I tightened my hold on her hair, urging her to take me farther. When she scraped her nails down my thighs, I finally let the release I was chasing break free. I tried to pull out, but she just sucked me harder. My legs shook as I pumped faster. She held on tight, and when I came, I thought I was going to collapse to the floor.

I pulled out, dragged her to my chest, and captured her mouth with mine. I poured all my desperation and need into our kiss.

I held her tight, loving the way she melted into me. I could feel my walls cracking and shaking. I had no doubt she would find a way through eventually; I just needed to make sure I was ready.

CHAPTER 11

JP

"I screwed up, Mike," I said to my brother as I walked to the window and peeked outside.

"So, what else is new?" I could tell from the traffic noises in the background that he was on his way to my niece's soccer game. Mike was three years older than me, married to a great girl, and had an adorable kid. I was envious of my older brother for many things, but mainly that he had his shit together.

I felt my jaw tic. "You could be a little more empathetic, bro."

"Why don't you just tell me what you did."

I gave my hair a nervous tug. I was going to regret this; I just knew it. "I slept with Maverick's sister."

"You did what?" It sounded like he was choking on his coffee. "What the hell were you thinking?"

I knew calling him was a bad idea, but it wasn't like I had any other options.

"Trust me, you don't want to know." I turned away from the window and walked back over to the bed to lie down. I might have felt guilty for what happened last night, but I sure as hell didn't regret it. "Things just kind of happened," I tried to explain. In reality, it felt like a long time coming. The plan was to have a nice dinner and get to know each other better, but when things heated up and she gave me an opening, I jumped right in. There was no way I could have slowed down; I had no control when it came to that woman.

"Come on, JP. I know you've had a few concussions, but your brain isn't that bad yet. You had to know this was a bad idea."

I adjusted a few pillows behind my back so I could sit up straighter. "It didn't feel like a bad idea."

"Are you going to tell him?"

My stomach muscles clenched at the thought of my friend finding out. I felt guilty, dirty, and downright fucking awful. Would he hate me? Kick my ass? Cut me off? Any of those were a possibility.

"I should, I just don't know what to say to him," I said, running a hand through my hair. I felt myself getting defensive. I wasn't usually one to shy away from anything, but Maverick was important to me, and the last thing I wanted to do was ruin our friendship over this.

"Let's back up for a second." He lowered his voice while I shifted to the side. "Is there more going on here? Do you have feelings for her?"

My mind went back to last night, with how we worked through our physical feelings, and then this morning when we did it again. When she left, I was feeling disappointed. I wanted more. More of her time, her laugh, her kisses. I wasn't that guy, but if I was being honest with myself, my feelings for Rylee ran much deeper than I cared to admit.

I swallowed hard. "I care for her, but what if things don't work out?" There were a million reasons why we shouldn't be together, and there was a really big chance I'd screw up somehow. Then what?

"I need to say something, and I don't want you to take this the wrong way."

My hands tightened around the phone while I braced myself.

"Being monogamous isn't your thing. It hasn't been for a while, and Rylee isn't some random woman you test things out with. This is your best friend's sister, so you better make damn sure you know what you want. Shouldn't all your energy be on football, considering you only have a couple more years left in the league?"

There was a lot to unpack from what he just said. He had some valid points, but I was trusting my instincts. There was nothing about Rylee that felt wrong. In fact, I couldn't remember the last time something felt so right.

"Am I supposed to let bad timing stop me from being with someone I want to be with?"

"I'm not saying that at all, but if you want to be with her, then you have to tell him."

I flopped my head back on my pillow and stared at the ceiling. "I know, and I will. I just need to find the right time and figure out what to say."

"The sooner the better." He sighed into the phone. "Listen, I hate to cut things off here, but we just pulled into the parking lot. Brenna's game is about to start."

I glanced at the clock and hopped off the bed. "You better get a move on it. Tell her I said good luck."

"I'll call you later tonight so we can revisit this conversation."

"I can't wait," I said, walking into my closet to grab a pair of sneakers. I needed to get a good run in before it got too hot.

Mike laughed. "You better answer when I call, because we are not done, brother."

"Don't you do enough interrogating during your day job? Are you not pulling enough people over for broken taillights, Deputy Watson?"

"If I were you, I'd worry more about a broken friendship than broken taillights."

I rolled my eyes. "You couldn't help yourself, could you?"

'That's what you get for making fun of my profession."

"Whatever." I hung up, laced my sneakers, and grabbed my earbuds off the nightstand. Maybe the fresh air would clear my head.

———

I was grabbing lunchmeat and veggies from the fridge when my mom's name flashed across the screen. After running six miles, I was starving and just wanted to eat my lunch in peace.

When the phone buzzed again, I swiped the answer button. It wasn't like I could ignore her.

"Hey, Mom," I said, carrying everything to the table and kicking my feet up on the opposite chair. "How's it going?"

"I don't know. Why don't you tell me?"

"What are you talking about?" I asked and took a sip of my water.

"I heard you have a girlfriend."

Water went spraying from my nose. Never again was I calling my brother for advice.

"I don't have a girlfriend," I gritted out and threw my head back.

"But do you want this girl to be your girlfriend?"

"Mom, slow down."

She sighed heavily into the phone. "I don't know why you insist on this funny business. You haven't had a relationship since Caroline. I worry about you."

Caroline was a sensitive subject for me, so I quickly changed it. "How's everything going in The Sunshine State?"

My mom lived in a gated community just north of West Palm Beach. After my parents divorced, she wanted a fresh start, and Florida was where she felt most at peace. After convincing my brother to put his pride aside, my mother finally allowed me to provide a house and some income so she could take care of herself. I knew I could never give her back the son she lost, so I might have been overcompensating with the house, but she deserved it.

"The weather has been beautiful. I joined a women's golf league and we play every Wednesday afternoon. I've also been volunteering at the children's hospital a few days a week, so I'm keeping busy."

"That's great, Mom." I smiled at the phone. I was happy to hear that she was making friends and doing things that interested her.

"Now that the season is over, are you going to come visit me?"

I slapped a piece of cheese and turkey together and rolled it up. "I'll look at flights today," I said between bites. "Are you planning on attending the charity dinner next month?"

The Justin Watson Foundation was a charity I started in my brother's name. It provided housing for families who had to travel for medical treatments. It also offered tutoring, homecooked meals, and daycare to keep families close together so they could get the care they needed. It was a cause very near and dear to my heart and one I didn't mind supporting.

"As long as you promise to seat me and your father at separate tables."

I swallowed quickly and reached for my water. Having my parents in the same room would be uncomfortable enough; keeping them apart would be damn near impossible.

I chuckled, feeling a little uneasy. "I'm not sure how much control I have over the seating arrangement, but I will do my best."

This conversation was a reminder of how broken my family was. After my brother passed away, my family was never the same. My mother was drowning in grief, and my father made little effort to keep his family intact. I never forgave him for giving up on us or throwing his marriage away when things got tough. Our relationship was strained at best, but I would have to be on my best behavior. He had as much of a right to be there as I did. There wasn't anything I wouldn't do for this foundation. If I had to laugh at dumb jokes and rub a few elbows to raise funds for a good cause, then so be it.

"I'm sorry, that was insensitive. I don't mean to put you in the middle. I don't hate your father, it's just hard seeing him with someone else."

"It's okay." I felt the same way but didn't need to add to her frustration by admitting that. She had her own issues to deal with.

"No, it's not. They are presenting you with an award, in memory of your brother. I can put my differences aside for one night. Justin would be proud of you, son, as am I. If I have to sit next to your father and that floozy he married while you get recognized for all the good you've done, then that's what I will do."

My throat got tight. "Thanks, Mom."

"So, back to this girl. Tell me more."

Talking about this with my mother was weird, and I reminded myself to be careful with how much I shared with her. I didn't want her to get her hopes up.

I dragged a hand over my face and blew out a long breath. "I like her a lot, Mom, but it's a little complicated because she's Maverick's sister."

"Oh." She paused. I could envision her eyebrows pulling together. "I wasn't expecting that."

"Maverick doesn't know yet," I said, playing with the grapes on my plate.

"Can I give you a piece of advice?"

It wasn't like I could tell her no; she was my mother, after all. "Go for it."

"I know starting a new relationship isn't easy for you, and if this girl makes you happy, then don't let anything stand in your way. I hate the thought of you being alone and miserable."

"I'm not miserable," I said, trying to reassure her. "I have football, my friends, I keep myself busy."

"But you don't have a partner to share your life with. Maybe this girl is the one."

I ran a hand along the top of my head. "I'm easing myself into this. I don't want to rush into anything. I want to do this right."

I was starting to develop real feelings for Rylee, but I needed to be careful and not lead her down a path that wouldn't go anywhere.

"Does she make you happy?"

I looked off to the side, feeling my chest grow tight. "She does, but I feel like I don't deserve her. She deserves someone so much better than me. Someone that can give her one hundred percent."

"Now you listen to me right now." Her tone held that no-nonsense air. "The idea that you've planted in your head that you're not enough is ridiculous. And I'm not just saying that because I gave birth to you. You are a wonderful, kind, compassionate man. But sometimes, son, you can be a total blockhead. What happened with Caroline was an accident. What is it going to take for you to realize that?"

"I don't want to talk about Caroline."

"What else is new?" I knew she had good intentions, but talking about my ex-girlfriend would never be easy for me, and I'll never forgive myself for what happened to her.

"I'm sorry." Her voice grew soft. "I know it's a tough topic for you, but if you ever want to move forward, you're going to have to let her go."

I swallowed hard. "I have let her go, but that doesn't mean I can just shed the guilt completely."

"You're right. Baby steps. So, tell me about this woman who has caught your attention."

"I'm pretty sure you've met her before, at least in passing."

"Well, I would like to properly meet her. Maybe you could bring her to the charity dinner next month."

"Maybe." My eyes darted around the room. "Like I said, things are new, but I'll give it some thought."

She squealed into the phone, and I couldn't help but laugh. "She must be someone special, because, JP, this is huge progress for you."

My mom has been harping on me for years to find someone to settle down with. The last thing I needed was for her to get ideas in her head and start playing matchmaker.

"Mom, please slow down."

"I'll try." She sighed into the phone. "I just think it's wonderful. I haven't heard you this happy in a long time."

There was no denying that Rylee was breathing life back into me. There was also this feeling of dread deep in my bones that I couldn't ignore. That somehow, someway, I would end up letting her down.

CHAPTER 12
RYLEE

Leaning forward, I glanced at the screen, ensuring everything looked good. "I'm sending over the document now," I told Miles, our VP of Finance. We'd been on a conference call for the past hour, fine-tuning some attendance projections with his team.

"Great!" he said into the speakerphone. "I'll look it over one last time tonight to make sure we didn't miss anything."

"Sounds good." I unglued my eyes from my computer screen and sipped my water. "I hope you guys have a safe flight. I'll see you all back in the office tomorrow."

"Can't wait," Miles grumbled. "Chicago is fucking freezing."

I laughed, hung up the phone, and typed out a quick response to our customer service team with an update.

We were hosting a good-sized medical conference next month in the main ballroom at our Tennessee location. The managing director who was in charge of events was out on maternity leave. I was asked to step in and make sure that every detail had been attended to and that our client would be happy with their experience.

Pulling this stuff off was never easy; you had to hustle, be flexible, and manage the vendors and their teams. If you messed things up, word got around, and you lost events. And losing too many events would eventually put you out of work. Fortunately for me, I was good at what I did. I loved the fast pace of the business and the idea of impressing my clients.

I glanced up when I heard a knock on my office door. "Come in."

My face broke out into a huge smile at the attractive man I had the pleasure of getting to know pretty damn well over the weekend, standing in my doorway.

"Hey, gorgeous."

"Wow! This is a surprise." I blinked rapidly as JP quickly shut the door behind him.

"A good one I hope." In his arm, he held a lovely bouquet of colorful flowers.

"Only the best." I couldn't stop smiling. "Those are beautiful. Are they for me?"

"Actually, I bought them for the receptionist out in the lobby."

"Funny." I fidgeted under his stare. After everything we did over the weekend, I couldn't believe I was acting so shy. I smoothed a hand down my blouse and did my best to get my nerves under control. My hair was pushed back in a ponytail, my heels were on the floor near my desk, and my shirt was slightly wrinkled. Not my best look, but there wasn't anything I could do about it.

Meanwhile, he was just a few steps away and looking pretty damn good in a simple pair of dark jeans and a white hoodie. I stared, not knowing what to do with myself.

Was I supposed to greet him with a kiss? A hug? A handshake? I had no clue.

When he brought his free hand up to his stubbled chin, I had to close my legs at the memory of how good it felt between my thighs. I took a minute to gather myself and wished I could have snuck in a quick coat of mascara or worn a different outfit to work today because JP looked hot without putting an ounce of work into his appearance. Impressing people wasn't his style, but apparently, making me lose self-control was.

"Are you just going to sit there and ogle me all day or come over and give me a proper greeting?"

Busted!

I pushed my rolling chair back and sauntered toward him. He closed the remaining steps between us with a smirk playing at the corner of his lips that I couldn't wait to kiss off. I slid my hands up his arms and gripped his face, forcing his mouth on mine. The kiss was greedy, impatient, and probably sloppy, but all I could focus on was how much I needed it. It was ridiculous how addicted I had become. I'd never felt like this before—ever.

"Damn." He brushed his lips against mine, soft and sweet. "Let me leave for a second and come back in because that was one helluva welcome."

My arms wrapped around his neck as his hands went to my ass. He trailed his lips to the shell of my ear and brought the lobe into his mouth with his teeth.

"Feel free to stop by anytime." I sighed, backing away slightly before I got too comfortable. I wasn't sure how I would be able to focus on work after this.

His hands dropped to the side, and he took a step back. If you had told me a week ago that I would be making out with my brother's best friend, let alone in my office in the middle of a work week, I would have thought you were crazy. It was mind-blowing how much had changed in the last seventy-two hours.

"What are you doing here?" I asked, taking my reading glasses off. I forgot I had them on.

"I came here to take you to lunch." He pointed to my glasses. "You look hot as fuck in those. Why did you take them off?"

"I only wear them when I'm working or reading." I set the glasses on my desk and straightened my blouse. "How come you didn't tell me about these lunch plans? Not that I'm complaining," I quickly added.

"It wouldn't be a surprise if I told you, would it?" He winked and placed the vase on the edge of my desk. "Plus, I wanted to check out your office." He glanced around the small room. It wasn't much, just a desk with two small chairs and a few filing cabinets. On the plus side, it had a bay window that overlooked the courtyard. It wouldn't be long before the cherry blossoms and dogwoods would be in full bloom.

"Knock. Knock," I heard a voice call out. "Hey, Ry, I wanted to…" Dominick's feet paused on the carpet when he realized I wasn't alone. "Sorry, am I interrupting?" His eyes narrowed, and I didn't like that one bit. Dominick was also my ex, whom I avoided as much as possible.

"Do you need something?" I asked, spinning around and walking over to my desk. I took a seat and wanted to roll my eyes when I spotted Dominick sizing JP up. My ex spent a fair amount of time at the gym, but he was a sorry comparison to the All-Star Wide Receiver standing off to the side.

Dominick spotted the flowers on my desk; his eyes seemed to be glued there. "I wanted to talk to you about an event we just added to the calendar."

He was always using an excuse to stop by my office.

Most of the time, it was at the end of the day, and he would suggest drinks or sometimes dinner. Sometimes, he would find me in passing and manufacture reasons why he needed to talk to me. He wasn't discreet about it, and it didn't matter how many times I blew him off, Dominick wouldn't take the hint.

"Can it wait?" I asked, reaching for my purse under my desk. "We were just on our way out to lunch."

"Sure." He simply nodded, held out his hand, and tried to force a smile that wasn't even close to genuine. "Dom Cavallaro. You're JP Watson, we've met briefly a few times when Rylee was my girlfriend."

He just had to go and make things freaking awkward.

JP tilted his lips into a smirk. "Sorry, can't say I remember meeting you, but then again, anyone standing next to Rylee is pretty forgettable."

I shoved as much as I could into my purse so I could get the hell out of there before the pissing match started.

"Are you two dating?" His gaze turned hard as stone, and it annoyed me how standoffish he was coming across. What in the ever-loving hell was his problem?

"It's new," I said before JP had a chance to answer.

Dominick rubbed his palm along his chin. My ex was an attractive man with his tan skin, thick black hair, and muscular build, but having the two men together in the same room, I couldn't help but notice how opposite they were.

Dominick was polished, whereas JP was rugged. He was also arrogant when JP was simply confident. From their physical appearance to their personalities, they were night and day. The biggest difference though, was that I felt absolutely nothing at all for my ex other than regret for all the time I wasted that I'd never get back.

"Okay, then." Dominick pulled on the sleeves of his

dress shirt. "Seeing that you already have plans for lunch, how about we meet for dinner?"

You've got to be freaking kidding me. He was testing me, trying to figure out how serious things were.

"Sorry." JP walked over and held the door open, giving him a not-so-subtle hint. "Rylee isn't available tonight or any other night in the foreseeable future. Your interruption has made us late for lunch, so please excuse us while we get on with our day."

Oh, wow. Normally, I wouldn't let something like this fly, but my ex was acting like an ass, and it looked like JP was one second away from losing his cool.

Dominick shoved his hands in his front pockets. "Seeing that you're so busy, I'll call you later."

As soon as he disappeared down the hall, I sighed with relief. "Are you ready?" I asked, throwing my purse over my shoulder.

"Come here." JP shut the door and held his hand out.

I walked into his arms. "I thought we were leaving?"

"We are." He grabbed my waist, pulling me closer. "I didn't know you worked with your ex?"

"The subject never came up." I looked up at him, catching a hint of insecurity on his handsome face.

"What does he do here?" He swallowed, seeming uncomfortable.

"He's our in-house legal counsel. We have five properties, so he travels between the facilities, but this is his home base."

Our weekend had been so intense, and I was still trying to wrap my head around all that transpired. And JP's reaction to my ex only added another layer of confusion.

"You know he wants you back, right?"

That was something I already knew, but I wasn't going to admit that to JP.

I brushed a strand of hair off his forehead. "Doesn't matter if he does. It won't be happening."

His arms tightened around me. "I don't like him. He's annoying."

"Join the club. He's not my favorite person at the moment either."

He searched my eyes. "Sorry if I overstepped my bounds."

I played with the strings of his hoodie. "No apology necessary. Clearly, he was provoking you."

A crease formed in the middle of his eyebrows. "I was expecting more pushback from you."

I laughed. "Sorry to disappoint you."

He brought his hands up to cup my cheeks. "I was jealous."

We didn't have a label, and no promises were made, but he had no reason to be jealous. There was no one else for me now; he was all I wanted.

His thumb brushed along my bottom lip. "You're quiet. What's going on in that pretty little head of yours?"

I stood on my tiptoes and wrapped my arms around his neck. "I like you a lot."

His eyes sparkled. "The feeling is mutual."

"You have no reason to be jealous. Not of him or anyone else."

A boyish smile broke out across his face. "Same goes for you, Sunshine."

———

"This place looks interesting," I said, eyeing the worn leather booths, high-back wood chairs, and mismatched tables.

When we pulled into the parking lot of the little hole-in-the-wall Mexican restaurant, I joked and told him that it looked as old as the Alamo.

JP laughed. "What's the matter, princess, afraid they're not going to have any organic chicken or fresh wild caught fish for your tacos?"

I flipped him off, and the hostess showed us to our table.

I unrolled my silverware while he did the same. A young, handsome waiter stopped by to pour water into our glasses. "Would you like to hear the specials?"

"Yes, please," I said, flipping open my menu while he went over the extra choices. We decided to share a plate of nachos and the chicken fajita entrée.

After he took our order, JP leaned back in the booth and studied me. "How was your weekend?"

I dipped my chip into the bowl of salsa. "You mean what was left of it?"

"Yeah, I guess I ate up most of it." His eyes went wide at the innuendo. I wanted to laugh because he sure did eat it up. "That came out wrong."

"I think it came out just fine."

He shoved a hand through his dark hair, messing it up. "You're enjoying this, aren't you? Watching me sweat it out."

I folded my hands under my chin and smiled. "Quite a bit, actually."

It was weird and downright concerning how much I was enjoying his discomfort. He didn't strike me as the type to get all twisted up over a girl. It was most likely the other way around for him.

He sipped his water. "You're evil, you know."

"I can't help it. You're cute when you're acting all bashful." He threw his head back in laughter. "Seriously, though. This was a nice surprise. I'm happy to see you."

He seemed nervous as he drew his finger along the plastic placemats. "I should have called you yesterday."

I reached for his hand. "This is better."

The waiter dropped off our plates. The portions were huge, but everything looked delicious.

"Now that the season is over, are you ready for some downtime?" I asked, laying the chicken and peppers into the tortilla.

He handed me an extra napkin and started fixing his plate. "I'm looking forward to being able to eat normal food like this for the next few months because once the season starts, I have to follow a strict diet."

I always admired the dedication and commitment that it took to compete at the level that he did. I was all too familiar with the sacrifices pro athletes had to make and how tough it got on their bodies, especially as they got older.

"Do you have any pregame rituals?" I carefully took a bite of my fajita, trying not to spill anything on my work clothes.

He smiled shyly. "I eat a glazed donut for breakfast every game day."

"A donut?" I asked, in between bites of my food. "I should have known."

"Yep, it was mine and Justin's thing when we were kids. My mom would pick up donuts from the local bakery in town every Saturday morning before my high school games."

"That's sweet." I patted the corner of my mouth with a napkin and was about to say more when his phone rang.

He dug it out of his pocket, rolled his eyes, and sent the call to voice mail.

"You can answer that?"

He leaned forward to scoop some nachos on his plate.

"Nah, just my dad."

"Do you not get along?" He looked like he would rather juggle hand grenades than answer that question.

"We have a complicated relationship."

It seemed like whenever the topic of his home life came up, he got uncomfortable.

"Your parents are divorced, right?"

He dropped his eyes to the table. "They split up after my brother died."

The death of his younger brother, Justin, was public knowledge, as well as his parents' divorce. I've seen his mom at a few games but never his dad.

I reached for his hand across the table. "I'm sorry that you lost your brother and your family had to go through that."

He sat up, lacing our fingers together. "I'm not sorry about my parents," he said, surprising me. "They were miserable together. Between the doctor visits, hospital stays, and dealing with Justin's illness for so long, it became too much for them. I was thankful that I had football to keep me busy because I didn't have to deal with all the shit going on at home."

"I've never been in your shoes, but I know dealing with a family member's terminal illness can cause a lot of stress on the caregivers."

"That's correct, but nothing can prepare you for what happens after they pass away. My mom and I have always been close, but there was a period of time where she became so crippled with her own grief, I thought I lost her too. And my dad, well, he just moved on with his life and I doubted whether he even gave a shit about us at all. He would reach out from time to time but not enough and it always felt like it was out of obligation."

Never, ever, had I appreciated my parents more than I

did at that moment. Maverick and I were lucky to have parents who loved and supported us. We had a great childhood and were both close to our mom and dad. It was hard for me to picture such a different set of circumstances. My chest split wide open for him.

"How often does he call now?" I pointed to his phone.

"Whenever he needs something." He shrugged. "Mostly money, but he wasn't always that way."

I was trying not to judge, but it was hard. "Does he work?"

He sipped his water. "He's the chief of police in the town I was raised in."

I tilted my head to the side and stared at him. I wanted to learn more but wasn't sure if I should keep going. "We don't have to talk about this if you don't want to," I said, leaning back in my chair and giving him an out.

"It's fine." He shrugged and stretched his long legs out. "It is what it is, but thankfully my mom is doing better, she's the one I worry about."

"Will they come to your games next season?"

"My mom yes, as for my dad, it will depend on whether or not he has someone he wants to impress or if he needs money."

I simply stared; my heart ached for him with every word he spoke. "I don't think I am going to be your father's biggest fan anytime soon."

"How about mine?"

"Definitely." I bit back a grin and reached for his hand again. "What about your older brother? Is their relationship complicated too?"

"Nope, but Mike is a sheriff's deputy, so he and my dad have more in common." His eyes flickered across the restaurant. I could practically feel his thoughts churning in his head. "Speaking of brothers, I want to tell yours."

"Tell him what, exactly?" I asked, trying to keep my tone even and giving my brain a minute to catch up.

He cleared his throat, looking slightly uncomfortable. "That we are seeing each other. He asked me to hang out yesterday and I blew him off. I don't want to keep avoiding him."

I frowned. "Do you really think that's a good idea? Shouldn't we wait?"

His eyes narrowed. "Wait for what? For him to find out from someone else?"

"We don't even know what we are doing yet?"

His glare turned lethal. "As much as I hate hiding our relationship from Maverick, I hate that you think that more. While I still have no clue what we are doing, I know whatever it is, I want to keep doing it—with you. I don't want to sneak around behind his back and worry about him catching us."

"Okay." I held my hand out. "I didn't mean to get you so worked up, but have you given this enough thought? This could turn into a big deal. Are you sure you're ready for that? There is a possibility that this type of news won't be very well received, and I'm not just talking about with my brother."

He raised an eyebrow. "I have no idea where you're going with this."

My face softened at how clueless he was. "People would know, your fans, your agent, your teammates. Are you really okay with everyone knowing about us?"

He ran a hand over the top of his head. "I don't feel as though I have to announce it to the world, but if people see us holding hands, or kissing in public, they can draw their own conclusions."

Now that thought scared me. He wasn't just an average guy who had a normal profession. JP was a well-known athlete. He had fans and lived a life that could be challenging at best. I learned a lot while watching my brother go through everything in the public eye.

"What will you tell them if they ask?" My palms felt clammy all of a sudden.

He held my gaze and studied me very carefully. "What are you fishing for, Rylee?"

"I just want to make sure you know what you're getting us into. You've been single for as long as I've known you. Now, all of a sudden, you want to date me? You don't think we're moving a little too fast?"

"I know what I want, Rylee, and that's you—exclusively. This isn't just sex for me, and what I feel for you is the furthest thing from casual. I want you all for myself and for you to know that I am all yours."

He was making it sound way too easy. I've been hurt in the past, and while I think we would be great together, I was still concerned about how it would all work out.

"You just signed a two-year deal. Your career will make it hard. Sure, we'll have the next few months, but once the season starts, we will barely see each other. Your focus will be on your team. I know the type of time and dedication it takes to play at your level. Do you really think this is the right time to start a relationship?"

"Will it be hard? Yes. Is it the right time? Hell, if I know. I wasn't looking for you. I wasn't planning on you, yet here we are." He squeezed my hand. "I've got two years left, Rylee. I'm starting to think about a future beyond football. I look at my friends, your brother, and I see what they have. And I want that," he said, surprising me. "If you sign up for this ride with me, it won't be just during the off-season. I will give you all I am capable of giving you. I want you by my side. The rest will sort itself out."

CHAPTER 13
RYLEE

"I can't believe I'm actually doing this," JP said into my neck as we stood hand in hand outside my brother's front door. "Tell me again how everything is going to be fine."

"He has it coming," I joked, trying to figure out a way to calm him down. This might have been his idea, but he was freaking out, like ready to lose his shit. They had been friends for years. Hell, he probably knew my brother better than I did. But if I was sure of anything, I knew Maverick would be okay with this. "Relax, he's going to be more worried about you than me."

JP laughed, kissed my cheek, and rang the doorbell. "I wish I could be as calm as you are right now."

"The sooner we get this over with, the better it will be."

JP wanted to talk to Maverick privately, but I insisted on being here, claiming it was payback for him showing up at my parents' front door with my best friend. I wasn't sure what Maverick's reaction would be, but I wanted to participate in this conversation. Not that I thought my brother would give JP a hard time, but I wanted to play it safe.

The door swung open, and Maverick's eyes immediately fell to our joined hands. His eyes bounced back and forth between us. "What's going on? What are you guys doing here?"

We had an entire speech planned out in our heads and practiced all day yesterday, but suddenly neither of us could remember a word of it.

Kinley peeked her head over his shoulder and smirked. "Well, it looks like our night just got a lot more interesting."

I haven't told her what's been happening, but I could tell by her smiling eyes that she didn't have a single issue with us being together.

"Hey, man. Sorry for just showing up like this. We hope it's not a bad time, but we brought beer." JP lifted up a twelve-pack to show my brother.

"And cupcakes." I held out the big pink box.

I wanted to laugh at the thought of softening my brother up with beer and cupcakes.

"I asked you both a question." Maverick kept his sight on his best friend. "I would really like to know what my best friend is doing here with my little sister?"

"And I would really like you to change your tone," I said, hating that things were starting out like this.

I should have called him and explained that we would be stopping by, but that would have led to questions I didn't want to answer over the phone. If anyone should understand, it should be him. It wasn't long before Maverick and Kinley showed up at my parents' house to announce that Kinley was pregnant with his baby.

"Are you guys sleeping together?" His face went pale like the thought made him physically ill.

I smiled like a smartass. "Not at this exact moment." JP cursed under his breath next to me, but I just shrugged. "We are technically standing outside your front door, waiting for you to invite us in."

Maverick didn't say anything; he just rubbed his jaw. "This is fucking weird."

"It doesn't have to be, but it will be really awkward if you make us stand out here in the hall all night."

He blinked a few times. I wasn't sure if he was upset or just surprised. "Let's go to the kitchen because I need a fucking drink."

Kinley eyed the box of cupcakes. "I'm going to check on Zander. Will you make sure your brother doesn't eat all those?"

I patted her shoulder. "If he doesn't change his attitude, you're going to get the entire box."

Following my brother and JP, I set the box in the center of the kitchen table. Maverick went to the fridge and pulled out a bottle of wine Kinley had opened. "Is white, okay?"

"That's fine," I said, reaching for a glass out of the cabinet while he popped open two beers from the twelve-pack.

After the three of us had a cold drink in our hands, we all settled around the table and waited for Kinley to come back into the room. I took the cupcakes from the box and plated them on dessert plates.

"Cupcakes?" Maverick crossed his arms.

"They are red velvet, your favorite, but if you don't want them…" I reached for his plate, but he grabbed it before I could touch it.

"I didn't say I didn't want them, so hands off." He peeled the wrapper off and took a huge bite.

"You could show a little more gratitude, you know."

"I'm just a little shocked. I wasn't expecting this." He set the rest of his dessert down and scrubbed a hand over his face. "How long has this been going on?"

"Not long." JP sat up straighter in his chair. "If you're going to punch me, you've got one shot, okay?"

"I'm not going to punch you." Maverick eyed him from across the table. "But I am going to give you one hell of a lecture."

Kinley returned to the room and slid into the seat next to my brother. "Are you serious?"

"Yes," Maverick said with no hesitation.

Kinley folded her arms across her chest. "Just remember how easy your sister went on us."

God, I loved her. There was a reason why she was my best friend.

Maverick turned to his wife. "Can you cut me some slack and give me a minute to adjust here?"

JP leaned forward, resting his arms on the table. "I know this is a surprise, but we wouldn't be here right now if I didn't care about her. I've had feelings for Rylee for a while now, but I never acted on them out of respect for our friendship. The last thing I want is for things to be awkward between us. I know this is a lot to take in, and if you need time to adjust, I understand. But I wanted you to find out from me, not anyone else."

"I always suspected that you liked her. You weren't exactly subtle when she was around."

"Really?" JP sipped his drink and rested his hand on my chair. "I'm surprised you never called me out."

"It wasn't just you." Maverick scratched the back of his neck. "You both would look at each other a certain way, but neither of you said anything, so I brushed it off."

JP smirked while giving me the side-eye. "I always knew you had a thing for me."

I rolled my eyes. "Yet it only took you eight years to ask me out."

His fingers toyed with the ends of my hair. "I was waiting for the right time to make my move."

"The continents of Pangea moved faster than you did," I teased.

Kinley folded her hands under her chin, beaming at us like a proud parent. "This makes me so happy."

"I'm not opposed to this," my brother said. "As long as you treat her differently than all the other women you've…" he paused, searching for the right words, "been with over the years."

"Trust me, Rylee is different. You don't have to worry about that."

"Good." My brother studied us closely. "I know you're both adults and you can't control how you feel, and I also know you wouldn't be here if things weren't serious."

"Whoa." I put my hands up. "Back the bus up. We are not even close to serious."

Maverick whipped his head to JP. "Excuse me?"

"What she's trying to say is that things are new and the reason why we are here is that I didn't want this weighing me down. I didn't want to feel like we were sneaking around behind your back. I respect our friendship too much."

I've never seen JP so out of sorts before, and it made me want to reach over and give him a big old hug.

"I appreciate that." Maverick stopped and let out a huge sigh. "But please don't take this the wrong way." He leaned forward, resting his arms on the table. The tension in the room kicked up around ten degrees. "You have a reputation and as Rylee's brother that has me concerned."

"Oh, my God. You did not just say that," I said, coming to JP's defense.

Kinley's eyes were bouncing back and forth between the three of us. She rested her hand over my brother's. "I think what my husband is trying to say is, despite your reputation as being a ladies' man"—she fired my brother with a look—"he's giving you the benefit of the doubt. He knows what happens between you two is none of his business and it's for both of you to figure out. Isn't that right, dear?"

God, I wanted to reach across the kitchen and kiss my best friend. If anyone could knock sense into my brother's big fat head and put him in his place, it was Kinley.

"Come on," Maverick whined. "Don't make me out to be the bad guy here."

Kinley sipped her wine and fully turned to face my brother. "You're not a bad guy, but you need to show her the same courtesy she showed us."

Maverick shoved a hand through his hair. "JP, you've been my friend for years. I know you would never do anything to intentionally hurt Rylee, but you need to understand something, I might not insert myself in your relationship, but when you fuck up and things go south, there might be no going back for us."

A muscle in JP's jaw ticked. "Thanks for the vote of confidence, *friend*. Can I ask why you're so sure I'm going to fuck up?"

Maverick took a long pull from his beer. "We're men; it's what we're famous for."

They shared a laugh, but I didn't.

"Mav, I'm not going to sit here and listen to this, and might I remind you that you went and got my friend pregnant and didn't even know who the hell she was at the time? So, you're in no place to be judging anyone."

He blanched. "Was that necessary?"

"Yes, it was necessary. JP has been torn up and worried

about your reaction. I don't think you understand how much having your approval would mean to him. And you don't need to worry about me. I'm no wallflower. I can take care of myself just fine."

My brother sighed and turned to his friend. "She's right, and I know from firsthand experience that coming here wasn't easy to do. I appreciate you manning up and having this conversation with me face-to-face."

JP nodded. "I don't want things to be weird between us."

"I don't either. But she's my sister and you're my best friend. I want the best for both of you. And most importantly, I want you both happy, so who am I to stand in your way."

I smiled at my brother. "Thanks, Mav."

He might have annoyed me at times, but I was lucky to have him looking out for me.

"Yeah." He cleared his throat. "And, JP, just a heads-up, my sister can be a pain in the ass, so I hope you know what you're signing yourself up for."

Or maybe not.

CHAPTER 14

JP

"What is all this?" Rylee paused mid-step when she saw all the ingredients on my kitchen counter.

My bare feet padded across the kitchen. "What does it look like?" I slid her overnight bag off her shoulder and unhooked Oakley's leash from his collar.

He ran across the room where I had a dog dish and toys set up by the sliding glass door.

"I assumed we were going to order takeout?" Her eyes surveyed all the ingredients, trying to figure out what we were making.

"Nope." I gave her a quick peck on the lips and directed her over to the counter, where I had all the food prepped. "We are making my favorite meal."

"Which is?" she asked, playing with the buttons of her black and white flannel.

"Chicken Riggies."

Her nose scrunched up. "What on earth is that?"

Chuckling, I poured a glass of wine and slid it over to her. "It's a popular dish in Upstate New York."

"Sounds interesting." Her eyebrows drew together when I handed her an apron. "Um…I don't cook."

"At all?" I stared at her in disbelief.

"Does a grilled cheese count?"

My mouth hung open. "How is that possible? I've been to your parents' house, your mom is an amazing cook. She had to have taught you a few things over the years."

She shrugged. "She tried, but I was never good at it."

I tied the strings to the apron along her back. "Do you bake?"

Her snort said it all.

"My mind is blown," I said, guiding her over to the chopped vegetables. "Looks like you are going to get your first official cooking class."

"You can't expect me to help you." Her eyes looked scared. "I didn't sign up for this."

"It's not hard."

She sighed. "Okay, but don't say I didn't warn you."

"First, we are going to sauté the chicken." I placed my hands on her shoulders and guided her over to the stove. I added the olive oil to the pan and waited until it sizzled before adding the chicken.

"Where did you learn to cook?" she asked, moving the chicken around with the wooden spoon.

I dropped the plate in the sink to rinse it off. "I waited tables when I was in high school. My buddy Adam was the chef, so I would hang out in the kitchen with him when we weren't busy."

"I bet you were pretty popular with the ladies."

"They were all old and married, but they tipped pretty good." I smirked.

"I bet they did." She nudged me in the side. "How about your mom, did she cook?"

"Yep." I sipped my wine. "But with three boys, she

didn't want us hanging out in the kitchen. It was her space. The only time we were allowed in was when dishes needed to be washed or the trash needed to be taken out."

She laughed. "The only way Maverick would find his way in the kitchen was if there was a plate of cookies that needed to be eaten."

"Now, that's not true. He can grill, I know that for a fact." I raised a brow and grabbed a wet cloth to wipe down the counter. "So, stop lying."

She huffed, not liking being called out. "I'm not lying; I just don't want you thinking he's more domesticated than me. Grilling a steak doesn't make him a chef."

A laugh bubbled out of me. "Competitive much?"

"I'm just jealous that you are better than me at this. I assumed you had a personal chef who did all your cooking."

"I believe what you're trying to say is you're impressed." I pressed my body against her back and put my hand on her hip to look over her shoulder. I allowed my breath to tickle her ear. "You're doing a good job."

She turned in my arms and poked me in the side. "It's early yet, give me time."

We worked around each other comfortably in my kitchen. Every few minutes, I would brush my hands along her side or purposely breathe into her neck while giving her directions. I liked having her in my space more than I expected.

My phone buzzed in my pocket, breaking through my thoughts. I pulled it out and rolled my eyes.

"Rhett, what's up?"

"Are you open to hanging out tonight?" I could hear a loud nineties rap song playing in the background. "I can gather up the crew and pick up the booze."

I glanced at Rylee, who was paying extra attention to the chicken. "Not tonight, buddy."

"Why, whatcha doin'?"

"I've got company." I winked, giving Rylee's hip a squeeze.

"You invited people over and didn't tell me?"

"I have a guest, not people."

Rylee bit down on her bottom lip and smiled.

"Wait." He turned down the music. "What kind of guest?"

I could hear the confusion in his voice, and knowing Rhett, it would take me hours to explain this recent development to him. "Would you like to say hi and find out for yourself?" Rylee giggled while turning the burner down on the stove.

"Is that Rylee? Did you finally make your move?" he whispered into the phone.

"Yes, we're dating."

Silence.

"Did you hear what I said?"

"Yeah, I just can't believe it. Does Mav know?"

"Yes."

"Did he punch you?"

"No."

"Did she put out yet?"

Click.

I put my phone on silent when it started ringing again.

The tears streaming down Rylee's cheeks indicated she heard the entire conversation. I, however, was not amused.

I leaned my hip against the counter and instructed her to turn the burner off. "He's not that funny."

"Oh, come on." She wiped her face and moved toward me. I widened my stance so she could stand in between my legs. "Cut him some slack. He can't help himself."

One palm went to the back of her neck. "Why are you defending the little shithead? Not to mention he gossips like a third grader. Everyone is going to be talking about us."

"Is that a bad thing?" She licked her lips in invitation, and I wasn't going to deny her.

"Nope, especially since I can do this whenever I want now." I yanked her to my chest and captured her mouth with mine. It started soft but quickly deepened. I've kissed my fair share of women, but there was something about the feel of her in my arms that felt like the most perfect thing in my life.

Before we had another repeat in my kitchen, like last weekend, I grabbed her arms and pulled back. We were both breathing pretty heavily, neither one of us was ready for the kiss to be over.

She tilted her head to the side. "Why did you stop?"

My chest rose and fell as I took a step back. "Because I put a lot of effort into cooking this meal. It's my way of impressing you."

"You don't need to impress me with your culinary skills." She angled her head over to the stove. "Although, maybe someday you'll let me return the favor."

I arched an eyebrow. "What kind of favor?"

She swatted my shoulder. "Not that kind, you pervert. The cooking kind. I want to try to cook you dinner next time."

"Not in my kitchen, you're not."

She looked genuinely offended. "You don't trust me?"

"If you want to cook, you can experiment in your own kitchen."

She put her hands on her hips. "If you are so worried about your precious little Williams and Sonoma cookware, I could always experiment in someone else's kitchen."

She squealed when I picked her up and threw her over my shoulder. I placed her in the chair and pointed. "Stay right there and stop being a pain in my ass."

She picked up her phone and started scrolling through social media. "Looks like my plan to get out of cooking worked." She smirked.

"That was amazing." Rylee patted her stomach while I snuck a piece of chicken behind my back for Oakley. She had a stupid rule about not giving him any table food, but I had a feeling the dog got scraps when she wasn't looking. He was way too good about mooching for a dog who was supposed to be on a special diet.

"See." I smiled and stretched my legs out. "And it was easy, right?"

"Easier than scrubbing the baking sheet." She sighed. "I owe you a new pan."

I don't think I laughed as much as I did while trying to teach Rylee how to cook. She wasn't lying when she said she was terrible at it. She burnt the garlic bread because instead of setting the oven to bake, she accidentally set it to broil. Poor Oakley probably lost an eardrum when the smoke detector went off. It took us almost an hour to get him out from underneath the table. His first time sleeping over, and he was traumatized.

"It's fine, but if you would have kept the apron on like I told you to, you wouldn't have stains all over your shirt." I pointed to her chest.

"I was not wearing an apron that said, *'I'm going to rub your butt and pull on your pork.'*" She rolled her eyes. "Besides, it wasn't my fault that the sauce was bubbling over."

We both laughed and went back to our meal. Over

dinner, we didn't talk about anything too serious; we just lightly bantered back and forth. It was hard not to smile around her. She was fun, caring, always seemed to be in a good mood, and sexy as hell. I could easily see myself falling for her. Hell, I've been falling for her little by little over the past eight years.

"I like having you guys here," I said, giving Oakley's ear a good scratch.

"You and Oakley seemed to be getting attached."

His head popped up at his name. "We are. I think he likes having the space to run around too. I always wanted a dog, but with my crazy travel schedule, it never made sense to get one."

"Don't go getting any ideas because you can't have mine."

"Well, I have you both for now, right? And you and Oakley are a packaged deal. Come on." I took her by the hand and led her to my outdoor sectional. She squealed when I pulled her on top of me and positioned her on my lap. Oakley ran in circles around my yard, sniffing every patch of grass he could find until he found the perfect spot to do his business.

She kissed the side of my neck. "If you wanted me to sit on your lap, all you had to do was ask."

Oh, I had something to ask her, all right. I'd been gearing myself up all night. My brother had texted me earlier asking if I was bringing Rylee to the foundation dinner next month. I've never brought a woman back home and never wanted to until now. The last relationship I had was when I was eighteen. Having her meet my family was a big deal, especially since my relationship with my dad was so strained. I entwined our fingers. "Actually, I do need to ask you something."

"Okay." Her eyebrows drew together.

"You know how I run a foundation in my brother's name, right?"

"Do you need my help with the planning?"

My eyes softened. I had a feeling she would do anything I asked. "I don't need your help with the planning, but I was wondering if you'd like to be my date? I'm being honored with an award."

"JP!" Her eyes lit up in surprise. "Of course, I'll be your date. That's wonderful."

I leaned in, kissing the top of her nose. "Thank you. It's in Upstate New York, and I would need you for a whole weekend. You can check your work schedule and let me know for sure."

She looked into my eyes and held my gaze. I thought she was going to kiss me, but she kept her mouth at a distance. "I don't need to check my calendar, because nothing is more important than being there for you. If you want me there, then I will be there."

My shoulders relaxed, and I exhaled a long breath. My need to have her there was overriding my fear of bringing her there.

"Thank you." I settled a blanket around her shoulders. "I hate going home, but having you there will make it more bearable. You settle me in ways that I can't explain."

"Hey." She cupped my cheek, sensing my unease. "Is everything okay?"

"Yeah." I pressed a kiss to her nose.

"Are you sure? Because it seems like something is weighing on you."

I shifted her on my lap. "Inviting someone into that part of my life isn't easy for me because I don't trust a lot of people."

She trailed her fingers along my shoulder. "But you trust me, right?"

"Not only do I trust you, but I can be myself with you. I feel comfortable when we're together, even though you make me want for things I shouldn't."

She frowned like she wasn't happy with that answer. "Have you ever considered that maybe the things you shouldn't want are exactly what you need?"

Fuck! She had no idea how close to the truth those words were. "What if I need you right now?"

She dipped her nails underneath my shirt. "Then take me. I'm all yours."

And I did. We made love soft and slow. My body filled her in the only ways I knew how. Just the feeling of her around me made me lose focus, forget, and wish for things I knew could never be possible.

CHAPTER 15

RYLEE

"I'M SORRY, I'M LATE," KINLEY SAID, SLIDING INTO THE chair across from me.

I waved her off. "It's fine."

I called her yesterday and asked if she wanted to meet for dinner. Since she's been with my brother, we don't get a lot of one-on-one time anymore. I sent JP out on a guys' night, needing a little break from the intensity of our relationship. I needed to clear my head, and Kinley needed a break after spending all day taking care of my sick nephew.

"Zander kept trying to peel his pajamas off and was giving your brother a hard time." She took a sip of the martini I ordered for her. "He's been running a low-grade fever for the past two days and has been absolutely miserable."

"Did you call your pediatrician?"

She flopped back, looking worn out and exhausted. "They think it's a viral infection, but I'm ninety-nine percent sure it has something to do with his teething."

"Poor guy."

She nodded her head and placed her napkin on her lap. "Enough about my chaotic life. How are things going with JP?"

A blush crept up my neck, remembering our early morning shower. "Things are going great."

She clasped her hands under her chin. "I love you two together."

"I think you are enjoying this way too much." I laughed.

"He's a great guy and you are my best friend, so of course, I'm happy."

I smiled as our server placed a breadbasket down. I was starving after a long day of work. "Do you need a minute to look over the menu, or do you ladies know what you want?"

"You go first," I said. "I'll be able to pick something."

After placing our order, Kinley leaned forward. "Can I tell you how much I love you for choosing an Italian restaurant. I've been on a strict diet and trying to get back to my normal weight before I had Zander and it isn't easy. I haven't had real food in what feels like forever and today happens to be my cheat day."

I rolled my eyes. "You look great. You don't need to lose weight."

Since Kinley has been with my brother, she's been obsessed with her appearance. The fans and media could be pretty harsh, and after being thrown in the spotlight last year, she's been very self-conscience about her looks.

She chuckled. "Tell that to my stomach."

"Knock it off, you look great."

She waved me off. "Sorry, moving on." She held up a piece of bread and dipped it in oil. "Now, circling back to JP, how are things going? I feel like I never see you anymore."

"I know." I sighed. "JP and I were just saying that we need to get together."

Her lips quirked to the side. "Your brother has been moping around the house, saying you stole his friend from him."

I laughed. "We just want to give him some time before we shove our relationship in his face."

She nodded. "I understand, but I can say with one hundred percent certainty that it's okay. Maverick is fine with the two of you together, as long as JP doesn't do anything stupid."

My heart began to pound, and it was probably nothing, but our conversation from the other night wasn't sitting right with me. Whenever we would talk about his past, he would get tense. I didn't want to pressure him or make him feel guilty, but I couldn't shake the feeling that he was hiding something.

Kinley studied me for a few seconds. "Rylee, what's the matter?"

"I don't know." I chewed on my bottom lip nervously, not sure how to explain this.

She gave me a pointed look.

"Okay." I sat up straighter, not knowing how much I should share with her. "I feel like he's keeping something from me."

Her jaw dropped. "Like another woman? That kind of something?"

"I don't think that's it. It's just a feeling and he said some things in passing that didn't make sense."

"Like what?"

"He said, '*I have you for now.*' And '*You make me want for things I shouldn't.*'"

She frowned. "Why didn't you ask him what he meant?"

"I was caught off guard and didn't want to bring too much attention to it."

"Hmm."

"Do you think he sees this as just temporary? Does it sound like he was trying to tell me something?"

She shook her head. "No, I've gotten to know JP pretty well, and I've never known him to date anyone until you, but it doesn't matter what I think. What's important is how *you* feel."

"I feel like he's going to break my heart." I let the confession slip without a second thought.

"Rylee, are you in love with him?"

"Not yet, but I can see it happening." Somewhere between all the dates and sleepovers, things changed. When I was with him, I felt happy and content. He felt like everything I'd wanted and wished for but never knew I needed. The smiles, the laughs, the bantering, the lovemaking, was more than I ever thought possible. No one else has ever or could ever compete with that.

"Then I think you should give him the benefit of the doubt. I don't think he would risk his friendship with Maverick if this was just temporary for him."

I took a huge sip of my drink. "Did you miss the part where I said he would probably break my heart?"

She raised an eyebrow at me. "If anyone is going to get their heart broken, it's most likely him."

"Yeah, okay," I said, letting her know that I didn't believe her.

"Rylee, that man has gone and caught feelings for you. Whatever it is that you think is happening is not one-sided. Now, tell me why you are so convinced that he is going to break your heart?"

I knew she meant well, but there was a twist in my stomach that wouldn't go away. "Kinley, he has gorgeous women throwing themselves at him all the time. How long before he gets bored or realizes that he doesn't want to be tied down?"

She let out a laugh, and I looked at her like she had lost her mind. "Girl, you must be blind. That man only has eyes for you. He doesn't even notice anyone in the room when you're around. You have nothing to worry about in that regard." She sat up straighter in her chair. "As for him getting bored, if anyone can keep that man on his toes, it's you. I really think things will work out for you guys."

God! I hoped she was right.

CHAPTER 16

JP

"Gotta say, your girl is cool as hell. I don't know many women that would tell their man to go hang with the boys," Rhett smirked, "unless you pissed her off and she wanted you out of her hair for the night."

I rolled my eyes. "Just because we're dating, it doesn't mean we have to spend every second together."

I was trying to play it off like it was my idea when it was Rylee who insisted we do things with our friends tonight. We've been spending every second together for the last two weeks, watching reruns of *Friends*, eating takeout and doing simple things like playing cards and board games. Spending the evenings with her and Oakley curled up at my side had become my favorite part of the day, but she felt bad that I'd been blowing off my boys and insisted we needed to balance our friends and our relationship.

"You look happy, man. I don't think I've ever seen you look so relaxed." Morris took a bite of a chicken wing and smiled at me.

"I am happy." I took a sip of my beer. "Rylee is

different. She's down to earth, cool as fuck, and makes me laugh. I don't want to jinx what I have going on, but things are going pretty well."

Beckett's eyebrows arched. "Sounds serious to me."

"You plan on putting a ring on it?" Rhett asked while giving the cards a good shuffle.

"The only ring in my future is the Super Bowl ring," I said, picking up my cards as he dealt them across the table. "Right now, all I'm planning on is kicking your ass at poker tonight."

"Unless my memory is off, you suck at poker." Morris smirked and tossed ten dollars' worth of chips into the center of the table.

He wasn't wrong. Playing cards was like playing golf; even if you sucked at it, you still played. For the past three years, we got together one Wednesday night a month for poker during our off-season. Over time, marriage, kids, and life, in general, have whittled our original group of eight down to four.

"These cards suck," Beckett grumbled, tossing two cards into the pile.

Rhett dealt him two more. Everyone pulled new cards, and the bid moved around the table.

"So, Mav is cool with you dating his sister, huh?" Morris asked and glared at Beckett, who raised the bid five dollars.

"Yeah, and thank fuck for that. Makes my life a hell of a lot easier." I sighed, folding on a shitty pair of threes. As the guys said, I sucked.

Morris laid down three tens, figuring the pot was all his. Beckett flipped over a hand full of garbage, and Rhett dramatically laid down a full house—aces over kings. The guy was so damn lucky at cards; it was ridiculous.

"I'm calling dibs on best man." Rhett grinned while soaking up his winnings.

"If anyone is best man, it's going to be Mav," Morris said and popped a chip in his mouth.

"Nope." Rhett shook his head. "Best man throws the bachelor party. And unlike Beckett's pathetic little snooze fest. JP here deserves the best. I'm talking Vegas, strippers, casinos. The whole shebang."

"Jesus, will you guys knock it off. I'm not getting married." I was, however, going to need to get wasted if they kept this up.

"Ever?" Rhett looked offended by my answer. "Because you really like Rylee, right?"

I more than liked Rylee. She was the first girl in a long time that I'd been with that I had actual feelings for. I was comfortable with her. I liked falling asleep with her in my arms and waking up with her in the mornings. There were so many things about her that were different; it was as if she had turned on a switch inside of me.

"Just because I have feelings for her, that doesn't mean I'm going to marry her. This is pretty new territory for me, boys." I scratched the back of my neck. "Besides, I'm not sure if marriage is an option for me."

There was no doubt I wanted a wife and kids someday, but as long as I was anchored to my past, there was a good chance that marriage would never be in the cards for me.

"Why the hell not?" Beckett asked. "Do you have some deep, dark secret that you're hiding from us, or are you just against marriage altogether?"

He was hitting too close to home. I loved my friends and trusted them, just not enough to confide in them about my past and the real reason why I might never get married. I wasn't ready to share that with anyone. They didn't know about Caroline. I protected her and our past, mainly to avoid dragging her and her family into the NFL media circus. That was the least I could do, considering all I took away from them.

"I really don't want to answer that, so let's change the subject."

They all stared at me in silence; even Rhett was quiet. Of course, I looked like an asshole.

"Does Rylee know that?" Morris asked.

"Know what?" I leaned back and crossed my arms. Since when did poker night turn into a therapy session?

"That there are no wedding bells in her future?" He looked me in the eye, and I didn't like being painted as the bad guy. Just because I didn't have the desire to rush out and put a ring on her finger, that didn't make me a horrible human.

"We've only been dating for a few weeks, so it's not like the topic has come up." I pulled on my hair in frustration. Their interest in my personal life was starting to tick me off.

"But if you never plan on making that type of commitment, shouldn't you tell her?" Morris arched an eyebrow that said, *"You are a fucking idiot."*

"Guys, this is stupid." They were getting in my head, and the last thing I needed was for them to drag this shit out of me.

"No, it's really not." Beckett eyed me suspiciously. "You need to have those conversations up front to make sure you're on the same page. Otherwise, you're just wasting her time."

I never thought of it like that. There was no doubt I wanted more with Rylee, but was she expecting more than I could give her? Was I going to allow her to get in too deep with me, knowing I'd never be able to give myself to her fully?

"I agree." Rhett sipped his beer, and we all stared at him. He was the last person you would expect to hand out relationship advice. "Rylee is a cool chick. If you go and hurt her, things will get fucking messy."

Anger pricked at my nerves because there was enough truth to that statement than I cared to admit. "Why does everyone have so little faith in me? Is it wrong of me to want to just enjoy the moment and not want to think about what comes next?"

"All we are trying to say is, have you thought this through?" Morris asked. "We know you care about her, but you better figure out your shit and come up with a plan."

I sat up in my seat and rubbed my jaw. "My plan is not to mess things up, how's that?"

"It's a start," Beckett stated the obvious. "But you finally got your chance with her, so don't blow it."

"Are you ladies done with all this Dr. Phil bullshit? I came here tonight to play poker and donate some of my cash to you poor suckers, not trade relationship advice and recipes."

"Speaking of trades, I heard a rumor," Beckett said, shuffling the cards. "My agent also represents Donaldson. Word is that he's getting traded to Denver."

"No shit." I sat back and studied my cards. Kevin Donaldson has been playing like crap all season, so I shouldn't have been surprised, but we still needed him on the team. We already had two defensive tackles out on injury with no guarantee they would be back next year. "Any idea who we are getting to replace him?"

"Nope." Beckett tossed a chip in the pile. "From what I gathered, he wanted out of his contract for personal reasons."

I scratched the side of my jaw. "Do you think it has anything to do with him not getting along with anyone on the team?" It was no secret that the front office had a love/hate relationship with him. Kevin was moody, never smiled, and didn't play nice with his teammates, but he was damn good at stopping running backs and tipping passes at the line of scrimmage.

"Possibly," Beckett said. "But I think it's more than that. His kids are young, and he's originally from Colorado."

"Let's not forget his hot model wife." Rhett winked. "Although, it seems like we have too many guys, dropping like flies once they get the white picket fence and two point five kids."

"What about you, Rhett? When are you going to settle down and make Daddy happy?" I asked, turning the tables on him.

Rhett shivered at the thought. Rhett came from old money. His dad was a senator, and his mom was a federal judge. They weren't very supportive of his decision to join the NFL, and it was no secret that they had a serious job and a list of vetted prospects waiting for him when he was done playing the field, both figurately and literally. We all assumed that was why he messed around so much because he was afraid of life outside of the NFL.

"The thought of that much responsibility gives me nightmares, man," he said, pouring himself a glass of whiskey.

"You don't know what you're missing." Morris smirked.

"Nah, I like my freedom too much," Rhett said, throwing his drink back.

I wished my reasons were as simple as his. If I weren't so concerned about the skeletons in my closet being exposed and insecure about my past, I'd be in a much better position to commit. My biggest fear was that once I shared that part of myself with Rylee, it was possible she wouldn't want me anymore. And that thought terrified me because now that I had her, I didn't want to let her go.

CHAPTER 17
RYLEE

"SURPRISE!" MY FAMILY YELLED THE SECOND WE STEPPED inside my mom's kitchen.

My feet halted in place at all the balloons and decorations filling the room.

"What is all this?" I asked, glancing around and smiling as my dad came forward to hug me.

"Did you honestly think your mother wouldn't acknowledge your birthday?" I squeezed him back, picking up on the faint familiar smell of Marlboro Lights. He tried to disguise it with cologne, but I could still smell it on his shirt collar.

An elbow nudged me in the side. "You can thank that hunk of a man over there for the surprise," Kinley said, beaming at me.

My head turned to JP. "You planned this?"

His mouth tipped up in a grin. "Happy birthday, Sunshine."

My mom placed a glass of wine in my hand and kissed my cheek. "He called me and asked if we were planning on doing anything special for your birthday. I told him we usually just do a quiet family dinner at home with your favorite meal. He insisted on the decorations and the cake."

My eyes filled with unshed tears. This man could have done something over the top and extravagant. Instead, he called my freakin' mom and planned a dinner with my family. Who does that after only a few weeks of dating? A keeper, that's who.

He was standing only a few feet away with his hands shoved into the front pockets of his jeans. My eyes locked onto his; they were swimming with heat and intimacy. The tip of his tongue darted over his bottom lip, and I felt my entire body grow warm. He was so getting laid tonight.

My brother cleared his throat and whispered in my ear, "Stop eye-fucking my friend. It's weird."

"I'm trying to control myself but it's hard," I whispered loud enough to where everyone could hear me.

JP's dimple popped out, causing Maverick to shake his head. "I think I'm going to check on dinner."

My eyes followed my brother to the stove, where my mom pulled the eggplant parmesan out of the oven. A crockpot was filled with homemade sauce and meatballs. There was a basket of fresh Italian bread sitting next to it.

We all piled into the dining room while Zander was sleeping peacefully in the den.

"Mrs. Cross," JP said from across the table. "How is it possible that you are such an amazing cook, yet your daughter can't cook anything fit for a dog?"

I put my knife and fork down on my plate and kicked him under the table. "I'd be careful if I were you," I quipped back.

"I'm sorry, JP, but I think my culinary skills got passed down to my son. Cooking has never been Rylee's thing."

I grimaced. "Thanks, Mom."

"You're welcome, honey."

The entire table shared a laugh until Zander started wailing from his spot in the living room.

My brother jumped up, putting his hand on Kinley's shoulder. "I'll get him."

He kissed her temple, making us all swoon. "He's really good with him." My mom smiled.

"Better than me." Kinley watched my brother walk out of the room. They were so madly in love that it was ridiculous. It was hard to believe that he was once a strong, intense, intimidating athlete who could stare down men twice his size, but one look at his wife and he turned to mush.

Maverick came back in a minute later, cradling Zander's head. The poor kid let out a high-pitched cry. Maverick rocked him back and forth, whispering soothing words into his ear, but nothing was calming him down.

"He's got a set of pipes on him, huh?" JP laughed while my brother continued to rub Zander's back, but it was no use.

"Do you think he's hungry?" my mom asked.

Maverick eyed his wife like he wasn't sure what to do. "Nah, he ate before his nap, and his diaper is clean. We think he's cutting his first tooth."

"I used to put a little whiskey on your gums when you and your sister were teething. It calmed you right down. Want me to give it a try?" my dad asked.

Maverick and Kinley both shouted, "No!" at the same time.

Dad threw his hands up in surrender. "All right, it was just a suggestion."

JP was still laughing when he stood up. "Why don't you let me give it a shot?"

My head snapped to his in surprise. Zander's wails

grew louder, so Maverick rolled his eyes and handed his son over to JP. "As much as it pains me to do this, he doesn't seem to be calming down."

I wasn't sure why I was so surprised when JP rested Zander on his chest and laid his head on his shoulder. He kissed his temple softly and bounced him up and down. My ovaries were hyper-aware of my hot boyfriend being the only one who seemed to get my nephew to relax.

Don't go getting any ideas, I told myself.

JP shot me a wink as Zander's cries turned into soft sighs.

"You're a natural, JP." My mom beamed at him from across the table. "Have you ever thought of having kids of your own someday?"

JP stiffened, and I wasn't the only one who noticed it. Kinley's eyes cut to mine, and I shrugged my shoulders. JP and I haven't been dating long enough to discuss kids or marriage. I had no idea where he stood, but judging by the sleeping baby on his chest, he would make a wonderful father someday. However, he looked terrified by the thought.

My mind started to wander. What would I do if we wanted different things? Could I handle a relationship if we weren't on the same page? Could I sacrifice a future of the things I desired most just to have one with him? The fear of it all gripped me so tightly that it felt like I was losing it.

I was freaking myself out for no reason and allowing my insecurities to get in my head.

"Mom." I stood and started clearing the dishes. "Why don't we get the cake ready?"

Kinley and I brought the food to the kitchen while Zander was conked out on JP's chest. I started scrubbing a pan a little harder than I needed to.

"Hey, are you okay?" Kinley asked, setting a few plates off to the side.

"I'm trying not to overthink things right now," I said, putting the salad dressing back in the fridge and sitting on one of the kitchen stools.

"Overthink about what?" She leaned over to start the coffee maker.

I dropped my voice to a whisper. "About how JP froze up like a statue when Mom asked if he wanted kids someday." I gripped the counter, unsure why his reaction bugged me so much. Maybe because I always thought he was too perfect, and reality was starting to settle in.

"I wouldn't read too much into it."

"Do you think I'm wasting my time with him?" When I looked at him, I saw a future I wanted more than my next breath. But my gut feeling was telling me we wanted different things.

"I don't know, you tell me?"

"You saw his reaction, right? I wasn't imagining it, was I?"

She poured herself a glass of water. "He seemed a little uncomfortable, but I feel like JP needs baby steps. The relationship is new, and from the looks of it, he is crazy about you. I wouldn't get too ahead of yourself. Even if he isn't open to the idea now, he could change his mind." She squeezed my hand. "One step at a time."

———

We were in the middle of enjoying dessert when my mom insisted it was time to open presents. She loved fussing over us on birthdays and sometimes forgot that my brother and I were adults.

I set the cake fork down and was mid-chew when JP placed two boxes in my hand.

"You look pretty excited to give these to me." My lips lifted in a smile.

He shrugged his shoulders. "I hope you like them."

Without waiting another second, I opened the bigger box first. It was wrapped in football-themed wrapping paper, and when I finally opened the lid, I understood why. I pulled out the Atlanta Arrows jersey with the name "WATSON" on the back and stitched with his player number 23.

He smiled sheepishly. "I figured you would want a new jersey now that your brother's retired."

"My jersey still sells out online, thank you very fucking much," my brother boasted from the other end of the table.

"Maverick's is a little old and worn." I held up JP's jersey so everyone could see it. "I guess it was time for a new one."

"Where is your loyalty?" Maverick threw his napkin across the table, hitting me square in the cheek.

I was just about to send a Solo cup right at his forehead when my mom put her hands out. "Enough you two."

JP's chest shook with laughter as he pushed the small box into my lap. I set the jersey aside and slowly undid the tape. When I saw what was inside, I half-smiled and half-laughed. I pulled it out to reveal a beautiful gold chain with a sunshine pendant. "This is perfect." I held it out so everyone could see. "Will you put this on me?"

He nodded and leaned forward. I pushed my hair to the side so he could clasp the chain around my neck.

My eyes wandered over to the man who seemed to fit right in with my family. He and Maverick have been talking nonstop about the upcoming season. My mom and

Kinley were fussing over my nephew, and my dad was probably sneaking a cigarette out in the garage. This was hands down one of the best birthdays I ever had.

I picked up a few dishes and brought them to the kitchen. There was a piece of broken glass sitting on top of the garbage I had forgotten about, so when I went to pick it up, I cut my finger. *Son of a bitch.*

"Mom, is the first aid kit still in the bathroom closet?"

She came rushing into the kitchen. "What happened?"

I held my finger out, which was starting to bleed. "Just a little cut. It's fine."

She shook her head. "Yes, let me get it."

I waved her off. "I've had paper cuts worse than this."

Once I found the right size Band-Aid from the kit, I wrapped it tightly around my pointer finger. It wasn't bad, and it felt much better once it was all bandaged up.

I had just finished putting the kit away when the bathroom door swung open. In two quick strides, JP had me pinned against the vanity. "Let me see the cut."

I held up my finger. "As good as new, but if you want to kiss it and make it better, I'm not opposed to that."

An amused glint lit his eyes, and my senses went on high alert. "I plan on kissing every inch of you when I get you home later."

"Good, because that's what I wished for when I blew out my candles."

He chuckled against my neck. "Did you have a good birthday?"

"Minus the cut, it was the best," I murmured as he scraped his stubble along my cheek.

He tipped my chin up with his thumb and lowered his mouth to mine. His fingers dug into my hips, pulling me closer. The kiss was slow and tender; he was doing everything he could to keep it light. I tried to deepen the kiss, but he was holding himself back, not wanting to get too excited in my parents' bathroom. The feeling of his length growing thicker through his jeans wasn't helping matters.

JP lifted me up and moved me to a sitting position on the vanity to trail his mouth along my neck. My chest rose and fell, and I didn't need to turn around and look in the mirror to know my cheeks were completely flushed. It didn't take much with him to get me worked up.

The door creaked open, and my brother's groan was hard to ignore.

"Oh, for fuck's sake." Maverick threw his hands over his eyes. "I don't need to see this shit."

I giggled into JP's shoulder. "Buddy, this is G-rated compared to what we normally do. And after hooking up with my friend, I'd say you deserve it."

"I married her," he said, trying to defend himself. He peeked through his fingers and lifted his head slowly, making sure there wasn't much to see.

"I don't care. I've had to endure watching you two love-sick fools for the past year and a half. This is just a warmup, so buckle up buttercup."

JP's smile was so big it caused his dimples to pop out.

Maverick threw his hands up and walked away. "I'm moving, preferably, to another continent where I don't have to be tortured like this."

He could act disgusted all he wanted, but he's often told me how much of a difference he's noticed with his best friend since we got together.

JP eased back, his large hands framing my face. "Are you ever going to take it easy on him?"

I patted his cheek. "Eventually, but not anytime soon."

CHAPTER 18

JP

THERE WAS A QUIET KNOCK, LIKE THE PERSON ON THE other side was afraid to make too much noise.

"Come in," I yelled as best as I could.

Rylee slowly opened the door and sighed. She took her shoes off and tiptoed over to the couch. I sat up and pushed my mussed-up hair back.

"I brought soup and medicine."

"You're an angel." My voice was hoarse and raspy from coughing.

She set the bag down on the coffee table. "Please tell me you sound worse than you feel."

I attempted a grin. "Why don't you come a little closer and get a better look?"

"How about you take these and eat a little bit first?" She held out a few pills and a bottle of water.

"Are you my nurse now?" I asked and grabbed the pills from her palm. I've been lying flat on my back all day, so even the slightest movement was uncomfortable. It felt like I'd been run over by a bus.

It turned out that Zander had a nasty bug. Everyone at Rylee's birthday dinner caught it but her and her mom.

"I am, but there will be no role playing, so don't get any ideas?" she said, arranging a few pillows so I could prop my body up a little bit more.

"You could have at least worn one of those short, white nurse outfits so I could cop an easy feel?"

She pointed to the pills in my palm. "Why don't you swallow those first, and then we'll talk about a sponge bath, Mr. Watson."

"Now you're speaking my language."

She rolled her eyes and placed her hand against my forehead. "You definitely have a fever. Let's give the medicine a few minutes to kick in and drink this Gatorade." She pulled out the purple bottle, and I smiled because that was my favorite flavor. "Then I'll help you in the shower."

"Is that a nice way of saying I stink?"

"Honey, your entire house stinks. Do you have any scented candles that I can light?"

"I can't say that I do, but there is a can of Lysol under the kitchen sink."

She walked to the kitchen, and I watched her shuffle through cabinets. After spending a few minutes looking over my bare shelves, she placed her hands on her hips and spun around.

"I forgot to get crackers for the soup. You have no food. I'll have to run to the store."

"You don't have to run anywhere. I have some protein bars in the garage."

"You can't live off protein bars. That's just sad." She grabbed a bowl and utensils and placed them on the coffee table. She flipped the lid off the soup and fed me a spoonful. My taste buds weren't a hundred percent, but the warm chicken broth felt good going down.

I couldn't remember the last time someone took care of me. Sure, I had a woman who came in once a week and cleaned, but only because I paid her to. A neighbor down the street owned a landscaping company and looked after my yard. And in return, I gave him seats to every home game. So, he didn't count either. The guys on the team would stop by and check in, but they wouldn't think to show up at my door with soup and medicine when I was sick.

The only person who would do that was someone who genuinely cared about me.

"Thank you for all this," I said in between bites. "I'm sure there are a million other things you could be doing."

Her smile was automatic. "Taking care of you and making sure you get better is my number one priority."

I reached for her hand. "I'm grateful that you're here."

She squeezed my fingers. "Ready for that shower now, stinky?"

I laughed as she tried to help me up and led me to the shower. I was capable of doing more than she knew, but I didn't see the harm in milking my situation for a little extra TLC.

There was nothing sexual about how she helped me wash myself, which was a damn shame if you asked me. My dick apparently agreed with me because he was getting ideas of his own.

After a good scrub down, I wrapped Rylee up in my arms. "Can you stay here tonight, or do you need to get home to Oakley?"

"I was thinking of staying, but would you mind if I went home and got him?"

"Of course not. You're always welcome to bring him."

"Thank you." She kissed the corner of my mouth. "Let's get you situated on the couch before I leave. I can always pick up dinner on my way back if you're feeling up to it."

"Sounds good." I pulled her in for a deeper kiss. "Just nothing too heavy for me."

"Got it." She raced across the room to slip her shoes on. "Why don't you pick out a movie and text me if you think of anything else. I'll be back soon."

———

A few hours later, we were cuddled on the couch with Oakley, passed out at our feet. The food, shower, and change of clothes had me feeling a lot better, but my eyelids still felt heavy. All I wanted to do was lie with her and sleep.

Rylee's head was resting on my chest, her leg was wrapped over mine, and I'd never felt so content in my life.

Her phone buzzed on the coffee table. I grabbed it, flipped the screen over, and frowned. "Why is Dominick calling you?"

She lifted off my chest and silenced her phone. "Probably something work-related."

"Probably?" I scooted back on the couch to put a little space between us so I could look at her. "Work related?" I looked at the time. "At ten thirty at night?"

Her eyes snapped to mine. "Is it a crime to call someone after a certain time?"

"So, if one of my ex-hookups called right now, you would be okay with that?"

"That's different."

"The fuck it is." I raised my voice.

Oakley's head popped up from the end of the couch.

"Our relationship is strictly professional now. You have nothing to worry about."

I pointed to her phone. "What on earth could he need at ten thirty at night?"

"He probably wants to talk about the conference coming up in Nashville."

My eyes bugged out of my head. "You're going away with him? To a conference?"

"He needs to meet with our team in Tennessee to go over some legal documents."

"Rylee, that sounds fishy as fuck. Why would they need to send their in-house lawyer to a conference?"

"I don't know. Why don't you ask the owner of the company. He is the one that requested that we both attend."

"Maybe I will."

"Woah!" Her hand shot out to my chest. "I'm going to stop you right there because I'm not liking your tone there, buddy."

"Well, I don't like the fact that you were planning on going away with your ex-boyfriend without telling me."

She hopped off the couch. "First off, I'm not going away with Dom. We have a work convention. There will be thousands of other people there in attendance. Second, Dom isn't a threat to you in any way, shape, or form. Third, the reason why it hasn't come up in conversation is because Dom never crosses my mind. I don't even think of him outside of work. That's how insignificant he is. And last, I would never cheat on you or anyone, ever."

I sighed. "I'm sorry for snapping at you. I know you're not a cheater. I was caught off guard, that's all."

"And I apologize for not telling you sooner." She walked back over to sit on my lap. "You have to trust me like I trust you. If anyone should be jealous, it's me. You could dump me today and find someone prettier, smarter, younger, or whatever the hell you wanted."

I squeezed her side. "I don't want anyone else but you."

She looked into my eyes. "Neither do I."

"I'm sorry if I'm coming across as a jerk. It's been a long time since I've been in a relationship."

Rylee brushed her fingers along my forehead. "I didn't realize you were ever in a relationship. I assumed you've always been single."

I cleared my throat and trained my gaze across the room. "It was a long time ago."

"Was it serious?"

"Yeah, it was." A burning sensation started to grow in my chest. I wasn't prepared to talk about this. It was uncomfortable, and whenever the topic of my ex came up, my skin got itchy.

"What happened?"

I threaded my fingers through hers. "Remember, I told you that I had a lot of baggage?"

"Yes." She swallowed. "I'm assuming this has something to do with it."

"It has everything to do with it. I want to tell you, because you deserve to know, I'm just so tired right now, but I promise we will talk about it, okay?" I squeezed her hand.

She seemed like she wanted to say something but changed her mind. "Okay, I just have to ask you one question, and I'll leave you alone."

"What's the question?"

"Do I have anything to worry about? Do you still have feelings for this person?"

I cupped her cheek to stare into her eyes and give her a portion of the truth. "You have nothing to worry about, Rylee. I swear, it's just you I want."

She kept her face neutral. If she realized how I avoided the second part of her question, she wasn't calling me out on it. Eventually, I would have to tell her. But with coming clean came the risk of losing her, and I wasn't quite ready to let her go yet.

Once I got through the benefit next week, I would tell her everything.

CHAPTER 19
RYLEE

"This is a cute little town," I said as we approached a sign that said, "Welcome to Skaneateles."

The main drag was lined with boutique-style shops, restaurants, an old bank, and a bed-and-breakfast. It was quaint and beautiful. People were strolling around in their winter jackets, walking their dogs, and browsing the shops.

"You should see it in the summertime, it's busting at the seams with seasonal residents," JP said, as we passed by a long pier that flowed out into the frozen lake with a little park on the right. "Lots of money in this small town."

"You never had the desire to buy a place here?"

It wasn't like he couldn't afford it, and from what he told me, a few celebrities owned vacation homes here.

"Nah, spring training starts at the end of July, and the weather doesn't warm up until the end of May. It wouldn't be worth it to me because I would barely use it," he said, taking a left at the firehouse.

JP's mind seemed a million miles away from the moment we boarded the flight in Atlanta. I couldn't tell if he was bothered about seeing his dad or nervous about the banquet. This was the most he's said during our thirty-minute drive from the airport.

"Maybe we could come back during the summer and visit some of the wineries."

Just as I said that, I noticed the big Victorian mansions that were splayed along the hill overlooking the lake.

"You might want to get through this weekend first before you go making plans to come back."

He glanced in his mirror and pulled down a long gravel driveway where a white, modest lake house came into view.

"You could do a better job at putting my mind at ease," I joked, sensing how anxious he was. JP has been dreading this visit, and my gut told me it was much more than just his complicated relationship with his dad.

"Sorry." He killed the engine and ran a hand through his hair. "I just need to get through these next two nights, and then I'll be back to normal."

"Hey." I grabbed his hand. "Are you going to be okay?"

"Yeah." He sighed. "Sorry, if I'm freaking you out. I'll be fine. Being around my dad makes me agitated."

I stared down at our joined hands. "If it gets to be too much, just say the word and we are out of here."

He lowered his head; his nose brushed against mine. "Thank you for coming. It means a lot to me that you're here."

"I would do anything for you."

We grabbed our bags and ushered them into the house. There was an older version of JP standing in the doorway. He looked exactly as I pictured him in my head. Dark brown hair, the same green eyes, only Greg Watson had a weathered face, and it looked a little too tan for this time of year.

"Dad."

"Hello, son, it's been so long, I almost didn't recognize you," he said, coolly. "I see you brought your friend."

JP's hand stiffened on my back. "I told you her name when we spoke, but then again, I was interrupting your happy hour, so it makes sense that you wouldn't remember."

Jesus! We were off to a great start. I pulled my carry-on to the side and slipped my boots off.

"I'm Rylee. It's a pleasure to meet you, Mr. Watson." I thrust my hand forward, trying to cut through the tension.

"Welcome, Rylee." He shook my hand and looked over my shoulder. "Do you need any help bringing in your things?"

"We're good," JP said as we followed his dad into the living room.

The house was an open-concept that looked like it had been recently renovated. JP told me on the drive here that his parents sold his childhood home after the divorce. While this house wasn't huge, I could tell by the upgraded kitchen and top-of-the-line appliances that this was considered prime real estate. And way out of the salary range for a small-town police chief.

"How was your flight?" Greg asked, walking over to a built-in cabinet with fully stocked liquor.

"It was a direct flight, so not bad." JP sat down on the long white sectional and stretched his legs out.

"Good." Greg pulled a bottle of Kettle One from the shelf. "What can I get you guys to drink?"

"I'll have a glass of wine, white if you have some, please."

JP squeezed my leg. "I'll have a vodka tonic, light on the tonic."

After making us both a drink, Greg sat directly across

from us. My gaze moved across the room, looking for family photos or mementos, but my eyes were coming up short. Unlike my parents' house, where I was sure my mom still had artwork from my brothers and my elementary school days, these white walls were empty and depressing. If it weren't for the pile of shoes by the front door, you wouldn't even know anyone lived here.

"You have a lovely home," I said, trying to come up with a nice conversation starter.

"Thank you." He swirled the liquid around in his tumbler. "It's been a long time since my son has brought a girlfriend home. Never thought I'd see it happen again."

Maybe I'd get some answers about the mystery girlfriend after all. Ever since our conversation the night he was sick, I've been holding back questions and felt like a fool for letting him off so easily. He promised we would talk about it, and my spirit sank with each passing day that we didn't.

"Sorry, I'm late." A dainty woman with long auburn hair stood in the entryway. She was younger than I expected, probably no more than a few years older than me.

"Vicky." Greg stood and helped her take off her coat.

"Hello, JP, welcome."

"Vicky," he said with a nod. There was no hug, no kiss on the cheek, not even a handshake.

The woman shifted on her feet, unsure what to do. After another beat of awkward silence, I stood up, held out my hand, and introduced myself. This was my first time meeting his family, regardless of their issues, I wanted to make a good first impression. JP, however, didn't move; he just sat in his seat and sipped his drink.

We exchanged small talk and walked into the small dining area off to the side. The table was set with fine china and crystal glasses. You could tell Vicky put a lot of effort into tonight.

Greg walked back into the room, holding a casserole dish. He placed it in the middle of the table and kissed Vicky's head before getting the salad on the counter.

"Do you have your speech all memorized?" Vicky asked JP. She's been looking for things to talk to him about, but he wasn't giving her much to work with.

"I hope so." He piled food on his plate.

Greg cleared his throat. "That playoff game against San Diego was brutal."

"You watched?"

Greg's spoon paused as he scooped chicken out of the casserole dish. "I met a few friends at the Lakehouse Pub so we could watch it. You looked good out there despite the loss."

"You could have actually seen it in person if you really wanted to." His tone had a bite to it that had all heads swirling in his direction.

"Some of us have to work a *real* job. I can't just jump on a plane whenever I want."

JP's fork dropped on his plate. "Don't start with this bullshit."

Greg met his son's stare. "What bullshit? You know I don't get much time off. It's pretty much a one-man show around here. I have no one to cover for me."

His jaw was clenched, and a muscle twitched in his cheek. "But you managed to find the time to take your wife to Hawaii for two weeks."

"We needed the time away. Am I not allowed to take a vacation?"

"I find it ironic that you went on that little trip right after I paid to have the roof replaced on the house."

"You offered to pay the bill."

"Because you were complaining about not having any money."

"Is this about your hurt feelings? Because if it means that much to you, I'll come to one of your games. But you'll have to help me out with the cost of the ticket. The airlines keep jacking up their prices, it's almost impossible to find a good deal these days."

"Unbelievable." When I glanced at JP, he looked like he was fighting like hell to keep it together.

"What is your problem? I said I would go, didn't I?"

"What about calling me, Dad? Have you ever thought about just calling me to check and see how I'm doing?"

I put my hand over his, partly to get him to calm down, the other to show support.

"The phone works both ways, son."

I bristled at how fast this dinner went downhill. JP brought me thinking maybe, just maybe, we could at the very least enjoy a simple dinner. The night was turning into a shitshow and now I understood why he was so agitated about coming here.

"I'm going to get the dessert." Vicky stood abruptly and rushed back into the kitchen.

The food was barely touched; I don't think anyone cared about dessert.

Once she was out of earshot, Greg glared at his son from across the table. "Why are you being so rude?"

An aggravated sigh left him. "You really want to go there, Dad?"

"Yes, I want to know why you are always so pissed at me?"

"Maybe because you only call me if you want something, and the only way you'll come to my games is if I pay you to. You don't think that's fucked up?"

He rubbed his forehead. "I don't have the kind of cash

lying around that you do. I don't think I ask for very much."

"Really, Dad?" JP's eyebrow rose. "Then why did I get an email from the mayor, asking if I could meet with the two of you when I was in town to discuss the Amphitheater project? I had no fucking clue what she was talking about, but she was under the assumption that I was going to attach my name and help fund your latest little venture."

Greg held his hand out. "Before you go shooting it down, hear me out. We've already secured a few investors, but we're still short on cash. I was going to talk to you about it but things kind of went sideways before I could broach the topic with you."

JP's stare was murderous. "I'm not giving this project a single cent."

Greg's head reared back. "I already told the mayor we could count on your support."

JP stood from his seat. "I'm fucking leaving."

"Where are you going to go?"

He pulled out his phone and handed it to me. "Can you look online and find us a room nearby? I'm going to grab our things."

"Sure." I unlocked his phone and started searching for a place to stay. A little distance would do the two men some good.

"You're really going to leave like this?" Greg said to JP's back as he started walking away. "What am I supposed to tell the mayor?"

JP paused to face his father. "Tell her I said hello, and good luck."

CHAPTER 20

JP

I lifted the lid on the hot tub and dipped my hand inside to check the water temperature. After adjusting a few controls on the panel, I turned the jets on high and stripped down. I sank into the warm, bubbling water and leaned against the back.

A fresh layer of snow was on the ground, the sky was dark, and the stars were out. I closed my eyes and inhaled the crisp, pure air, and watched the steam rise over the water. It was pure bliss.

After that disastrous dinner, Rylee and I weren't having any luck finding a hotel nearby—one of the inconveniences of living in a small town. I called my buddy Adam, who owned a place on the lake. He was away on business but had his housekeeper meet us with the key. I couldn't take another second of listening to my dad's bullshit, so staying here worked out much better.

I turned my head when I heard the sliding glass door open.

"Jesus." I swallowed, allowing my hungry eyes to rake over her from top to bottom. "When I told you to pack a swimsuit, I meant something other than a scrap of material."

She spun around, giving me a view of the back. "Sorry, buddy, but all I own are bikinis. I don't like one-pieces because they are really inconvenient when you have to go to the bathroom."

Her black bikini top looked like it would come undone with one tiny tug of my fingers. And don't even get me started on the bottoms. Her ass was on full display, leaving nothing to the imagination.

I draped an arm along the hot tub and quirked a brow. "You coming?"

"I don't know, am I?"

"Have you ever not with me?" I replied smoothly.

A smile twisted her lips. "Is that why you invited me out here?" she asked, not giving me the satisfaction of answering my question. We both knew the truth, but my ego was big enough that I didn't need confirmation.

"Why don't you step inside the water and find out." I noticed her face turned red, and it had nothing to do with the cool temperature outside.

She tiptoed over, while I sat and admired all the toned, smooth skin she was flashing me.

Rylee slid her legs over the edge of the hot tub and into the steaming water. "Now that you got me here, what do you plan on doing with me?"

I smiled, watching her slip her body completely underneath, causing a little splash. "First," I grabbed her by the hips and pulled her onto my lap, "you're going to lose this top." I untied the knot in the back, causing it to land in the water. "Next," I slid the wet fabric down her legs, "we're going to ditch these bottoms." I threw them over the edge, enjoying the amused expression on her face.

"And now?" She wrapped her arms around my neck, staring into my eyes.

"And now I'm really going to get you wet."

I slid my palm up her thigh and leaned in, taking her lips with mine. She relaxed into my kiss while my hands continued their own journey. Her soft sigh spurred me on, and for a moment, I allowed all my troubled thoughts to drift away.

The steam from the hot tub floated around us as I slowly slid her up and down along my shaft, showing her the effect she had on me. She gasped and started twisting in my lap, searching for the right friction that would bring her a release. I was already hard but wanted to ensure she had her orgasm before me. I pressed my lips to her neck and thrust my fingers inside her. She ground against me and squeezed her legs along my thighs.

My hands reached up to cup her breasts before pulling one in my mouth. The louder she moaned, the harder I sucked.

"God, I'm so close." She dragged her nails down my shoulders and raked her fingers down my chest. "I want you inside me."

"I want you to take whatever you need," I told her.

She molded herself closer and rubbed against my aching cock. I wanted to lose myself in her touch, her body, and her strength. Everything about her was light and warm, and little by little she was healing the parts of me that I thought were broken.

I pushed my swollen head at her opening, and in one fluid motion, I shoved inside her. We moved together, slow and deep. Rylee was panting and moaning, and a feeling of possessiveness took over me. I pushed her hair to the side as she proceeded to grind down on me. Her deep brown eyes fluttered closed, and the passion I brought out of her was written all over her face.

"I swear, it gets better and better every time with you," I said, stretching her to the limit, while she took every inch.

This physical connection I had with her was the most intense feeling I'd ever had. I felt it in her touch, with how she kissed me and gave herself to me so freely. She was mine in every way that mattered. She understood me. She saw me. She was the kind of special I knew I'd never find again. That thought hit me hard because I knew I had to give her all of me. She deserved it all.

Rylee urged me to go deeper, so I rocked my hips into her and filled her up. My lips moved across her skin; she had me so fucking needy that every move I made had my vision going fuzzy. I settled my hands on her hips and started thrusting in and out. There was no space between us, only shared air and frantic heartbeats.

"Nothing has ever compared to this." She closed her eyes, getting lost in the moment, and then a second later, she fell forward, calling out my name.

The feeling of her spasming around me had my own release dripping out of me. I groaned and fell silent, allowing my body a minute to soak up the moment.

I pressed a firm kiss to her lips. These past few weeks we've spent together nonstop have been the best of my life. Typically, my world revolved around football and partying. But getting to know all the little things about Rylee that I've learned had me questioning everything.

And they were little things like how she loved macaroni salad but hated mayonnaise, and how she would get annoyed when I tried to look at my phone during dinner. She would complain that I talked too much during a movie but loved to have a conversation while watching sports highlights. The girl loved going for walks but despised exercising, something I would never understand.

Even things that I would typically find annoying, I thought were cute, like her need to sleep with four pillows every night and the way she hogged all the covers. From her favorite foods to her biggest pet peeves, I'd learned them all. But at the end of the day, did all that really matter if I wasn't being completely honest with her? Was it fair that we knew all these little things about each other while avoiding all the big stuff?

Like, where did we go from here? She deserved every part of me, not just the pieces I allowed her to have. In reality, I was grateful to have her in my life, but I still struggled every goddamned day with trying to be enough for her. Grateful for the time we had yet waiting for the moment to come when she decided she wanted more.

She brushed her cheek along my stubbled jaw. "Why are you so quiet all of a sudden?"

I positioned her so she was sitting on my lap. "Just thinking about what happened earlier, I wouldn't blame you if you wanted to cut this weekend short and leave early."

Her hands went around my neck. "I'm not going to get scared away from one shitty dinner with your father."

"It's not just that." I swallowed hard as she studied my face. "There is a reason why I avoid this town and only come back if I absolutely have to."

"I've got news for you, buddy, I'm not going anywhere. Wherever you go, I go. I got your back."

A relaxed smile lifted my lips. "I was nervous about bringing you here, but after today, I'm glad I did. Thanks for sticking it out with me."

"JP." She hesitated for a moment. "I know something is bothering you, something bigger than the mess with your dad. Whatever it is, you can talk to me. I know you don't trust easily, but whatever you share stays between us. I just want you to know that."

"I do trust you, Rylee. I promise, once we put this weekend behind us, I will tell you everything."

She pursed her lips. "Fair enough. Just so you know, we all have things from our past that make us vulnerable and question things."

"Are you talking from experience?" I kneaded my fingers into her hip.

"Do you really want to know?"

"Only if you feel comfortable talking about it." I more than wanted to know, but she deserved the same courtesy she showed me.

"You're the first guy I've dated where I haven't had to worry about being used to get to my brother."

"Your ex, Dickhead Dom, used you to get to Mav?"

Her fingers played with the ends of my hair. "I don't think that was his intention, but I don't think he minded the perks that went along with dating me. I was referring to guys in college and shortly after, when Maverick became famous. It was hard having a football god as your brother because I never knew if the guy at the time really wanted me for me, or if I was just a means to an end. There were a couple of losers that I knew for sure were using me, and one I really liked, that one stung."

Hatred and jealousy filled my bones for every man who came before me and was too stupid to appreciate what they had. For making her think she was anything less than what she was. To me, she was slowly becoming my everything.

"Please tell me Mav kicked their ass."

"He doesn't know about them."

I shook my head. "I want names and addresses."

Her eyes crinkled in the corners. "You going to defend my honor, big guy?"

"I will gladly kick any guy in the nuts who treated you wrong."

She threw her head back in laughter. It was such a beautiful sound. "Look at you, getting all protective of me."

I pulled her flush against my chest; I couldn't get her close enough. "Rylee, you're way too good for a man like me, and those assholes didn't deserve a second of your time. If they couldn't see the beautiful, smart woman you are, then it's their fucking loss and my gain."

"Thank you." Her hands ran along my shoulders. "For what it's worth, I'm glad things didn't work out with them either, because I wouldn't be here with you if they did."

I pushed a wet strand of hair behind her ear. "I don't ever want to lose you."

"Why do you think you'll lose me?"

I looked into her eyes and swallowed hard. Every fear, every doubt came rushing to the forefront of my brain.

"Because I'm afraid once I tell you about my past, you'll realize I'm not worth the trouble."

"You're really scared to tell me, aren't you?"

"I'm terrified."

"Well, unless it's illegal or involves cheating, then there is nothing you can tell me that will scare me away."

Fuck, I hoped she was right.

CHAPTER 21
RYLEE

I GAVE MYSELF A LITTLE TWIRL, ADMIRING THE FLOOR-length blue gown. My heart pounded with nerves because I wanted to look beautiful for him. This was our first public appearance, and I wanted him to be proud to have me on his arm.

A swift, heavy knock sounded on the bedroom door. "Rylee, we have to go."

"I'm coming," I called out, running a hand along my hips. The dress was strapless and hugged every curve I had. There was a slit that ran along the side and stopped mid-thigh. The material felt tight, but not too tight where I couldn't breathe.

Another knock. "Rylee, please hurry up. I can't be late."

I blew out a deep breath and slowly opened the door.

JP was adjusting his tie when he looked up. "Holy shit!" He froze, and I did the same.

Just the sight of him in a simple, tailored, black suit, with a pale blue tie that perfectly matched my dress, made my knees go weak.

"Do I look okay?"

His eyes were dark as they took me in. "You look stunning." The rough tone of his voice sent a shiver down my spine. "Every woman in the room is going to be jealous."

I walked over and brushed a kiss on his cheek. "It will be because I'll be the one on your arm."

"Ready?" He held out his hand.

I placed my palm in his. "I guess so, considering you won't give me five more minutes."

"You don't need five more minutes. You look perfect." He brought his mouth to my ear. "I'm not sure how I'm going to keep my hands off you. All I keep thinking of is how badly I want to fuck you in that dress."

"Don't forget the heels." I stretched my leg out to show off my sparkly Jimmy Choo's.

He groaned. "Trust me, there is no way we are forgetting those later."

He helped me into my coat and out to the car. Both of us were going to have a hard time keeping our hands off each other tonight.

When we stepped inside the venue, my eyes wandered, taking in the tiny details, and getting caught up in the ambiance of the room. A live band played music, and servers carried trays with bite-sized hors d'oeuvres. The ballroom was dark, with flickering candles. It was also dripping in money. I was happy to see so many supporting this cause.

A waiter passed by, and JP grabbed two flutes of champagne. "Want to check out the silent auction?"

"I'd love to."

Unfortunately, we didn't make it very far before he was stopped by someone trying to lock him down in a conversation. His eyes were full of apology, but I brushed him off and told him to do what he had to do. He was here to raise money for his charity and get recognized for his hard work. That was the whole point of this dinner. JP couldn't help it that he was the center of attention, and everyone wanted their one-on-one time with him.

I strolled over to the first auction table and put a bid in for a weekend stay at a local winery. There was a little bit of everything, from restaurant gift cards, spa packages, memorabilia, and tickets donated by the NFL.

A familiar hand rested on my back. "I'm sorry."

I turned around, giving him a reassuring smile. "No need to apologize."

"Yes, I do," he said into my ear. "Here comes my family."

My eyes widened when I spotted his mother, brother, and sister-in-law walking toward us. Mike, who I'd met briefly before, greeted me first. "Rylee, it's good to see you."

"It's good to see you as well." I pinned a bright smile on my face, even though I was freaking out.

His mom rushed over and was clinging to him in seconds. I was surprised at how tall she was. "It's good to see you, son." She pulled back and clutched his cheeks. It was apparent that JP inherited her eyes, but the rest of his features were all his dad's.

"How's my favorite lady doing?" His smile was warm and affectionate. It was endearing watching the two of them together.

"Better, now that I have both of my boys in the same room." She adjusted his tie and ran a hand down her purple gown.

He chucked softly and placed a hand on my back. "Mom, this is Rylee, my girlfriend."

She stepped forward with open arms. "Hi, I'm

Jennie, it's so nice to finally meet you. I've heard so much about you. I can't tell you how happy I am that you are here."

"It's a pleasure to meet you." Her grip on me was tight and warm; it was impossible not to like her.

"Has he been showing you around town?"

"He has. I absolutely love it here."

Mike leaned in. "You might feel a differently if you stick around for a few more days. We are supposed to get two feet of snow toward the end of next week."

I laughed. "I remember going to one of my brother's playoff games in Buffalo. They had to pay the fans to shovel out the seats before they could start the game."

"I remember that game well." Mike smirked, taking a slow sip of his drink. "I bet Maverick is happy to be retired."

"He is, although I feel bad for my sister-in-law, who has to deal with him all day long."

"You two are so cute together." Rachel, Mike's wife, smiled. "Can I get a picture?"

JP pulled me to his side while Rachel handed her drink to Mike.

"I think this will be our first official photo as a couple," I said, resting my hand on his chest.

JP looped his arm along my waist, practically branding me to his side. "Well, then, I guess it's time the world knows I'm taken."

I found myself faltering and unable to stop the grin from spreading across my face. When I glanced at his mom, she had tears welling in her eyes.

"Jennie, are you okay?" I asked her once Rachel was done taking our picture.

She waved me off. "I'm fine. I'm just so happy."

JP pulled his mom into a hug and kissed the top of her

head. She lightly pushed him away. "You're going to make me cry harder if you go getting all mushy on me."

"We can't have that now." He chuckled and reached for my hand. "I hope you guys don't mind, but I promised this pretty lady a dance," he said, handing my flute glass to the passing waiter. "And I'd like to take her for a spin on the dance floor before things get hectic."

Mike patted his shoulder. "Go have some fun. We'll save you both a seat at the table."

He guided me through the crowd, trying to find a section that wasn't occupied. A few people stopped to introduce themselves, but he kept his hand in mine the entire time.

"You're an excellent dancer." I smiled, happy to have him all to myself for a moment.

"You can thank the trainers, they are the ones who made us take the dance classes." He spun me around before bringing me back to his chest.

"I think I remember my brother mentioning that." I wrapped my hands around the back of his neck. "Did you enjoy the lessons?"

I allowed him to take the lead and fell into line with his steps. "They weren't my favorite, but the dance instructors were cute, making the lessons more bearable." I swatted his chest playfully. "What?" He laughed. "You asked, remember?"

I pressed my cheek against his chest. He was so big that I felt small in his arms. "Your mom is adorable."

"I think she likes you." He jerked his head over to where his mom sat, talking to a few people. His dad and stepmom were on the other side of the room. I wondered if that was on purpose.

"I hope so. I still have yet to win her over."

He spun me around before pulling me back in. "If anyone can do it, it's you."

"I think it's great that your family is here tonight to show their support."

He tipped my chin up to meet his eyes. "The only one I care about being here tonight is you."

My heart hammered in my chest. I was so in love with him, and I wanted to tell him so badly, but instead, I closed my eyes and relaxed into him. His arms were enough. These feelings were enough.

When the song ended, we pulled apart and joined his family at the table. After an hour of talking and laughing, it was time for JP to give his speech. The room was silent as he spoke about the Justin Watson Foundation's importance to him. There wasn't a dry eye in the house when he told stories about his younger brother. If he was nervous, he didn't show it. He was composed and knew how to command a room. By the time he was finished, I was so damned proud of him.

I stood from my seat as he returned to the table. "You were incredible." I smoothed a hand over his chest and stole a quick kiss before he got pulled away in another conversation.

He chuckled. "Thanks."

His smile slipped from his face, and I followed his gaze to an older couple approaching our table. "JP. It's good to see you."

"Charles, Michelle." He adjusted his tie, and I noticed his hands were shaking. "How are you? I didn't know you both would be here tonight."

"We are doing well." The woman looked back and forth between us, her gaze filled with questions. "We thought about reaching out to let you know we were coming, but we didn't want to bother you."

"You could never bother me."

"We just wanted to support you. It's a wonderful cause, and you have done so much for our family." She sniffed, and he rubbed her back in a soothing gesture. "I'm sorry. I didn't mean to cry, and I always seem to do that with you."

"Would you like a tissue?" I pulled one out of my clutch and leaned forward to hand it to her.

"Oh. Thank you." She smiled as another tear rolled down her cheek before wiping it away.

"Of course."

Her lips pursed. "Are you a friend of JP's?"

My eyes connected with his. They were weary, scared, and filled with nervousness.

He cleared his throat and held his hand out for me. "She's actually my girlfriend. Rylee, this is Charles and Michelle Kerr."

Surprise lingered in their eyes for a beat, while his family sat at the table, all of them looking uneasy.

What on earth was going on?

"It's nice to meet you both." I smiled tightly, feeling the need to do something other than just stand there.

"You as well," the gentleman finally spoke. "We are glad to see that you are finally moving on and starting to live your life. Caroline would want that for you."

My head swirled in his direction, but he avoided my gaze. He dropped my hand and clenched his fist at the side.

Who was Caroline?

"Thank you. That means a lot to me."

Unease crawled up the back of my neck. I felt like I was trying to put puzzle pieces together that wouldn't fit.

The woman reached out and squeezed his elbow. "It was time, JP."

I waited until they walked away before I turned to him. "Who was that couple, and who is Caroline?"

"Not here."

He grabbed my hand and led me through the ballroom. We walked back through the front entrance until we reached a little sitting area off to the side. There were three wooden benches curved around a giant outdoor stone fireplace.

"Let's sit," he said softly, removing his suit jacket to wrap it around my shoulders.

"JP, you're scaring me."

"This isn't how I wanted you to find out about this, but I guess there was never going to be a perfect time," he said, gripping his hair and tugging at the ends in frustration.

"Take a deep breath." I rubbed his back, while trying to get my heart rate to calm down.

"Caroline Kerr was my high school girlfriend and Michelle and Charles are her parents." His shoulders bunched underneath his dress shirt. He dropped his eyes to the ground, and I hated that this conversation made him so uncomfortable.

"During our senior year, Caroline and I were invited to spend the weekend at our friend Shane's cabin. His parents were away, so he thought it would be a good idea to throw a little party for our friend group."

I moved closer because he was shaking so badly, I was afraid he would bolt at any second. "We don't have to do this now if it's too much."

His eyes met mine. "I need to get this off my chest."

He was finally talking about this, and even though I wanted to know, the pain in his voice was almost too much for my heart.

"Okay," I said, feeling my pulse race because I had a feeling how this story was going to end.

"I worked at the restaurant that day, so I showed up late. By the time I got there, everyone was trashed. Shane wanted to take the boat out on the lake, but he was too stoned to drive, so I offered to take everyone out for a ride. I thought it would be fun to mess around with them a little bit." He looked haunted, like it was taking all his energy to talk about this. "I started driving fast and randomly steering the boat a little too hard. A bigger boat had just passed us. Normally, I would slow down, but I was so distracted and ended up hitting the wake pretty hard. I hadn't realized it at the time, but Caroline had moved to the rear of the boat to get a drink out of the cooler. Suddenly, everyone was screaming at me to stop. Her body lurched backward, she hit her head, and fell into the water."

I watched as the events of that day flashed across his face. The agony in his voice cracked my heart wide open. My lips parted, but I was unable to speak. Instead, I gripped his hand and wrapped my fingers around his.

He wet his lips. "The second I realized what happened, I slowed down and turned back to where she fell. By the time I got to her, she was unconscious, and barely breathing. We called nine-one-one, and they airlifted her to the hospital. The doctors said the blunt force caused traumatic swelling in her brain. Because of my recklessness, she has been in a vegetative state ever since."

I gasped. "Oh, JP. I am so sorry."

He shook his head. "She's been confined to a wheelchair, unable to speak and communicate since that day. It's my fault, Rylee, so please don't try to make me feel better?"

I could hear the faint chatter of the guests in the ballroom, but all I could focus on was him. "What happened was a terrible accident."

"It doesn't change the fact that I was the one driving the boat. It doesn't make the guilt go away."

I tilted my head to the side and stared at him. "You tried to save her. You did all you could."

"Rylee, you don't understand. I can't untangle myself from this. It's a part of who I am. That day changed me."

A part of me understood where his guilt was coming from, and I wouldn't hold that against him. But I would do my damnedest to make him understand that day didn't have to define who he was.

"Of course it did. It's completely normal to feel that way, but you've been dealing with survivor's guilt all these years. She might not have died, but you still lost her."

"And now I'm afraid that I'm going to lose you too."

The defeat in his voice was almost too much to bear.

"What has you so convinced that you will lose me?"

He gritted his teeth. "Because what I have to offer you will never be enough."

"What are you talking about?"

He blew out a frustrated breath. "I might not love her the way I used to, but a huge piece of me is in that hospital room with her. How is that fair to you? You deserve all of me."

"So, you're just going to push me away? Do my feelings not matter?" I shook my head. "I'm sorry for all that you had to endure. Your pain, your past, and your anger, it's all a part of you. None of that scares me and nothing could make me love you any less."

His head whipped to mine. "You love me?"

I did not mean to blurt that out. That wasn't how I planned on telling him.

I moved in a little closer, refusing to acknowledge the panic in his expression. "You're very easy to love and you may think I am wasting my time with you, but you are wrong. You deserve to be happy and you deserve to be loved."

His throat bobbed, and I worried I was pushing him too fast.

"You shouldn't have to deal with the consequences of my actions. I'm the one who carries this burden, and I don't want you to have to give up anything to be with me."

"What would I be giving up, JP? Help me understand this."

He shook his head. "I don't know if we will ever be more than what we are right now. I know I was young, but I was planning on spending the rest of my life with her. Why should I get to move on when she can't? I don't know if I will ever be ready to give you the future that you deserve, and you shouldn't have to settle for less."

I jerked back, feeling hurt and offended. "Why are you trying to push me away?"

"Push you?" He scoffed. "You should already be running in another direction by now."

Not a chance. My love for him didn't come with a set of conditions. He was everything I wanted and nothing like what I was looking for. And now that I had him, he was crazy if he thought I would give him up without a fight.

"I'm not going anywhere." My palm rested against his cheek. I was determined to get through to the stubborn man. "My feelings for you are what they are. I know what I can handle and what I can't. People change, life changes. Maybe there is a future for us or maybe there isn't. But I know that we won't know if we don't try."

"You really want to stay with me, after everything I just told you? Don't you want time to process all this?"

Tears ran down my cheeks. "You're worth taking a chance on. I don't need time to come up with reasons on why we can't be together, because I choose you. You are the only man I want, so stop trying to convince me that my love is wasted on you."

He pressed his forehead against mine. "I don't know how I got so lucky, but I swear to God, I will never take a moment with you for granted." He paused. "Please don't give up on me."

I gripped his chin, bringing his gaze to mine. "I can do better than that. I promise to fight for every moment we have."

He shook his head. "It's not going to be easy."

I brought my lips to his, needing him to hear the truth in my words. "If it isn't hard, then it's not worth it."

CHAPTER 22

JP

"Yes!" I stood from my seat and shouted as number eight's three-point shot swooshed through the net. Syracuse was now ahead by eleven points, and Maryland's lead scorer was still on the bench, holding his injured right hand. From the fall he took at the end of the first quarter, there was a good chance his shooting hand was broken.

"Lucky break with Maryland's point guard, no pun intended." My brother took a sip of his beer and stretched his legs out.

"It's called home court advantage."

"Give us time, we can still screw this up."

Mike and I were enjoying a college basketball game in one of the box suites at the Carrier Dome. We were huge Syracuse Orange basketball fans growing up. As we got older, we made it a tradition to attend at least one game a year together.

"I talked to Dad. He mentioned things got a little tense at dinner," he said, tossing a handful of popcorn in his mouth. "I gotta be honest, I'm glad I missed that one."

"It was the same old bullshit."

"I figured, for what it's worth, I'm sorry."

I stared down at the foam on the top of my beer. "He is who he is. I don't see him changing anytime soon."

He nodded his head. "Rylee was probably wondering what she got herself into."

"She was a champ. Way more understanding than she needed to be, about everything."

He side-eyed me. "Things seem to be going good between you two."

"Better than I expected." I sipped my beer and kept my eyes on the game.

"I could tell from the way you looked at her."

I rolled my shoulders, feeling tension come on. "How did I look at her?"

"Like she was the only woman in the room." He smiled smugly.

"That's what happens when you spend time with someone you really like." I shot him a look and turned my attention back to the game.

"Like, huh? It looked as though you more than 'like' to me."

He wasn't wrong. My confession didn't send her running for the hills like I thought it would. If anything, it made us stronger. It made me realize how lucky I was to have her in my life. And it made me wonder if maybe, just maybe, we could do this.

"We've been seeing each other and having a good time."

He leaned forward. "She's the first woman you've been serious with since Caroline."

He was hitting a nerve and trying to trick me into admitting how I really felt. "She is, and before you start getting any crazy ideas, we are still trying to figure out the next steps."

"Want my two cents?"

"No."

"Great, here it is." He held his hand up when I started to protest. "I'm not going to tell you what to do because you're going to do whatever the hell you want, but you need to let Caroline go, brother. It's been twelve years, and all the blame and guilt you put yourself through doesn't change what happened. You were eighteen. We all did stupid shit back then, it could have been any one of us behind the wheel. Yet, you were the only person on that boat who jumped in the water to try to save her. What happened was a freak accident. The only person that blames you is you. You've finally found something good; it's time to let yourself off the hook."

I guess we were going there. "How do you know that no one blames me? And why are we talking about this now?"

"I saw Chuck and Michelle at the banquet. I heard what they said. They don't have an ounce of animosity toward you. If anything, they are grateful and appreciate everything you've done for Caroline. Taking care of her financially wasn't your responsibility, but you did, and you still do. That's the type of guy you are. You take care of the people you care about."

Seeing Chuck and Michelle was unexpected, but even I had to admit, it wasn't as bad as I imagined. I didn't keep in touch with them, but they still reached out to me every year to thank me for helping with Caroline's medical bills. It was the least I could do, seeing it was my fault. I made more money than I could ever spend in one lifetime, so the financial contribution was the easy part for me. I would still trade places with her in a heartbeat or hand over every cent I owned if it would make her whole again.

I scratched the side of my jaw. "What's your point, Mike?"

He turned in his seat and studied me. "I know what Caroline meant to you, but it's well past time you start focusing on your future. Rylee is a great girl. She's smart, beautiful, funny, and for some reason she cares about you, so don't screw it up. This may be your only chance at happiness."

My brother was one of the few people who didn't kiss my ass and gave it to me straight. Something I appreciated and hated.

"I don't know how to do that and still live with myself. It fucks with my head just thinking about it. And Rylee, who's to say I won't end up hurting her?"

"Are you sure it's not your own heart you're trying to protect?"

"I'd rather rip my own heart out than do anything to hurt Rylee."

"That may be true, but by playing it safe, you risk losing her. You'll never move forward if you don't make some changes. What if she's the one?"

My feelings for her have evolved significantly since we've been together. She has become someone important to me. I see things more clearly since I've been with her. She has accepted me for who I am, not what I am. And I don't question her loyalty or her feelings.

There was no doubt in my mind that she was the one for me, but was I the one for her?

"When did you and Rachel figure out that you two belonged together?" I asked, draining the rest of my drink.

"I realized it right after she broke up with me." His eyes got a distant look as if he were reliving the memory.

"I don't remember you guys breaking up."

"Because I didn't tell anybody. We'd been together for

a little over a year, but I was spending too much time focused on other things, and I didn't notice her drifting away from me. It wasn't until she left me that I realized I couldn't live without her. I'm a better man because of her. She centers me, calms me." He shrugged. "She's my person. I feel it in my bones and I've never felt that way about another living soul."

Everything he said was exactly how I felt about Rylee.

There was no doubt in my mind that my younger self had loved Caroline, but real-life responsibilities hadn't hit us yet. With Rylee, my feelings have grown at a slower pace. She knew versions of me that no one else did. She was comfortable and safe and everything I needed at this point in my life. Being with her was easy, but having a future with her would be impossible if I didn't let go of my past and learn to forgive myself.

The last part of my brother's sentence really hit home, though.

I've never felt that way about another living soul.

Rylee told me she loved me, but before I said those words to her, I needed to mend my heart back together so I could give her the whole thing. Not just bits and pieces of it.

———

It felt like I was traveling through a time machine as I took my time driving along the back roads to the Saratoga Rehabilitation Center. Some buildings looked the same, while others had been replaced. This trip was a final goodbye and the longer I drove, the more I could feel the anxiety building in my body.

I tapped my fingers on the steering wheel as I pulled my rented SUV into the visitor's lot. The light rain was tapering off, so I gave myself a few minutes, waiting for the sky to dry up and get my thoughts in order.

The outside of the building was well maintained, with beautiful ivy crawling up the century old brick facade. This facility was the best in the state. They tried to make it as close to home as possible for the residents, but as you got further into the building, the bright lights and antiseptic smell were a stark reminder of where you were. I wasn't sure what I would say or where I would even start, but this moment was long overdue.

Walking into her room, I thought I was prepared.

Oh, how wrong I was.

My throat tightened at seeing my teenage girlfriend trapped in her hospital bed. Her wheelchair sat next to a table overlooking a small lake; not that she could appreciate it, though. I stood over her bed, watching her sleep and memorizing every inch of her face. Her long, blond hair splayed along the pillow. Her face looked thin and pale; otherwise, she looked okay. Still, grief and regret cut through my heart, knowing I was responsible for her being here.

I grabbed the empty chair and pulled it close to her bed. "Hey, Caroline," I whispered softly, and leaned in to kiss her cheek. My eyes swept over her, looking for any sign that she was awake and could hear me. She didn't react to touch or voice; all she could do was blink her eyes, which we were told didn't mean anything.

"I saw your folks the other day," I sighed. "It's always hard for me to see them and not feel overcome with guilt. That pain in their eyes is still there, and even though they should hate me, they don't. You definitely inherited their grace and understanding and every time I look at your mom, I see you. I remember the girl you used to be." I hung my head.

Caroline was popular, and probably one of the sweetest girls you'd ever meet, everyone loved her, including me. I ran my fingers through her blond hair, which was a little darker now. Her skin might have aged, but she still looked the same. Every promise I made, every prayer, every dream came rushing to the surface of my brain. My heart squeezed with so many memories. The feeling of loss over a life she would never get to live crushed my spirit every time I saw her.

"Come on, JP," Shane said, throwing the key at my chest. "Just take us out for a quick spin before it gets dark out."

I looked down at my clothes. I still had my work uniform on, but all my friends were counting on me to take them out before it got dark. I didn't want to go out on the boat; I just wanted to relax and enjoy a cold beer, but I couldn't say no because I was the only sober person standing.

I spun in a circle, pointing at each and every one of them. "No waterskiing and no tubing. Just a quick ride along the lake."

"Yes, Captain." Shane clapped me on the shoulder, and everyone hopped in the boat.

We were just about to pull away from the dock before Donnie called out, "Wait, we need to grab the cooler."

Caroline came up and sat on my lap while a couple of the guys went back for the drinks. "Thanks, baby."

I nipped at her bottom lip. "You can thank me properly later."

She rested her hands on my shoulders. "I can't believe we get to spend the whole night together. It doesn't happen very often, so I want to take full advantage later."

She wasn't lying. Between our parents and our curfew, it almost never happened.

I squeezed her side. "A few more months, and we will be off to college. We'll be able to visit each other and spend weekends and breaks together."

She looked sad at the thought. "I hate the idea of being away from you."

"I do too, but I'll be thinking of you every second."

Her hands tightened around my shoulders. "I know we're young and we have our whole life ahead of us, but you're it for me, JP. You're my forever."

"And you're mine, Caroline." I kissed her lips while a few of our friends hooted and hollered about us "getting it on."

"Promise me you'll never love anyone but me."

I stared into her bright blue eyes. "I promise."

I sighed. So many dreams were ripped away from us, all because I was young and stupid.

I rubbed at my stinging nose. "I was just thinking about our last time together. I should have insisted you stay on my lap. I should have just said no when Shane asked me to drive. There are so many things I should have done differently." I looked down at her, waiting for a response I knew would never come.

I rubbed the inside of her wrist, and her eyes blinked open. I swallowed down the guilt that threatened to suffocate me. "This is harder than I thought, Caroline. I hope you don't hate me, and I pray to God that you understand. I know I promised you that you would always be the one, but things have changed."

I blew out a breath and wondered if I should have just stopped talking. My chest felt like it was breaking in half. "I would have done anything for you, and I would give anything to hear your laugh or see your gentle smile one more time. I know the doctors say that you'll never get any better than you are today, but I'm still praying for a miracle that somehow, you'll recover. If anyone deserves a second chance at life, it's you. But as I stare at you, I can see how your mind and your body have both settled into this place where no one can reach you."

I ran a thumb over the back of her hand, feeling a lone tear slide down my cheek. "I wish you could communicate with me, give me a sign, something that would ease my conscience."

I glanced over at the small wallet-size picture of us on her nightstand. It was taken at homecoming. I was suited up for the game, and she wore her cheerleading outfit. We were both so young and never got to go through anything hard in life. Our relationship was never tested. There was no guarantee we would have even made it. Just thinking about that made me feel guilty as hell, but it was the truth.

"This isn't easy for me, but I've found love again when I thought I never would. She is the exact opposite of you. She doesn't have your sweet personality, and you two look nothing alike. She's sassy, and drives me crazy." I emitted a small laugh. "She's good for me though. She's filled in the parts that you left behind. She makes me happy, and I'd like to think you'd want that for me. Maybe that makes me selfish, but I'm going to be honest with you. I'm scared. I'm scared I'm going to let her down; I'm scared of getting hurt again. You left a big hole in my heart, and I never ever want to go through that again. But I need to figure out how to make things work with her. And it feels like I'm letting you down, but she's reminded me that I still have enough pieces of my heart left to share with her. So, Caroline, in order to do that, I have to let you go. You will always be my first love and I will always cherish our time together."

I pushed to my feet and leaned over her bed. I pressed

a kiss to her forehead, feeling the finality of the situation wash over me. "Goodbye, Caroline."

I wiped my cheeks and walked out of her room. There was a sense of calm as I pushed through the lobby doors for the last time. I was walking to my car when I spotted the rainbow in the sky. Inhaling a deep breath, I started in the direction of my rented SUV.

It was time to go home to Rylee, where I belonged.

CHAPTER 23
RYLEE

"So, let's talk about that picture that's floating around on Instagram," Stephanie said over the salted rim of her strawberry margarita.

I flopped back in my chair and stared at my two coworkers. I should have seen this coming. "I'm not one to kiss and tell."

But I was pretty sure that the deep crimson red on my cheeks told them all they needed to know.

"Really?" she mocked. "Did you seriously think you could snag the hottest player in the NFL and us not grill you for information?"

I glanced at Lucy for help, who was the more serious of the two. "If it's any consolation, he looked really into you," she said, pushing the basket of chips my way.

"Please." Stephanie rolled her eyes. "He looked like he wanted to devour her on the spot."

"She has hearts in her eyes." Lucy smiled with glee. "I love this for you."

"Jesus." I choked on my frozen drink and looked around the half-full hotel bar to ensure no one was paying attention. We were seated in a booth by the window at the Garden Terrace. It was one of the three restaurants at our resort. I didn't need everyone I worked with listening to this conversation. "Do you think we could put this discussion off until we are somewhere more private?" I gave them a chiding look and took a bite of my salty pretzel.

She lifted her glass and took a huge swig. "No one is paying attention, unless you're worried about Dom catching wind of this."

"Not even a little. Dom doesn't have a say in anything that goes on in my personal life."

Lucy arched a dark eyebrow. "You're right, he doesn't, but he's been snooping around and asking about that sexy hot guy you've been dating."

"He really needs to get a life. We've been broken up for almost a year. I don't know why he's been acting so weird lately."

She clutched her glass tightly. "He's always been weird, you just chose to ignore it."

Stephanie snorted. "I heard the weird ones are freaks in bed."

I cringed. "I can tell you with one hundred percent certainty that Dom was nothing special."

They both broke out in a fit of giggles while I rubbed my temples.

Lucy leaned forward and whispered once she got her laughter under control. "I heard Dom got his ass chewed out last week for messing up a big deal."

I pressed my lips, trying to hold back my retort.

"Ohh, I heard about that," Stephanie said. "Gary was pissed."

"Do you know what happened, Rylee?" Lucy asked, while running her finger along the rim of her glass.

I cleared my throat and sat up in my seat. "I try to steer clear of Dom and all his drama, so that's the first I heard of it."

Although, that didn't surprise me one bit. He was such a screw-up. How upper management hasn't figured out that the man was nothing more than a functioning alcoholic, I would never understand. I was just glad that I was no longer associated with him because one day, things were going to catch up to him.

"Okay, switching gears," Stephanie's brows dipped in interest. "Tell us about this hunk of man who announced your relationship status on social media. Like how big is he and please tell me he's packing some good equipment down below because I will be very disappointed if he's not."

She seemed overexcited, and I hated to be the one to pop her balloon, but I wasn't sharing details with her or anyone about my personal life. JP was too well-known, and I wanted to respect his privacy.

"And here I thought having a couple drinks with my friends after work sounded relaxing. I had no idea our happy hour would turn into a Q and A session." I glared at my two friends, letting them know I wasn't going to give them an ounce of gossip to work with.

"I bet you he's a freak in the bedroom." Stephanie grinned, and I wanted to bang my head on the table.

I turned to her. "Are you saying he's weird?"

She flipped her hair over her shoulder. "I wouldn't know because I never met him. But based on how aggressive he is while running with a football, I would bet money he's aggressive in other areas." She wiggled her eyebrows.

I shifted in my seat. "Please stop objectifying my boyfriend."

She widened her eyes. "Do you think I'm the only woman in America who notices that body?"

Heat crept up the back of my neck. I was well aware and didn't need the reminder. I've seen the female fans drool over him and the comments online. I tried not to let them get to me, but it was hard.

I glared at her. "He's a person, not an object."

"Relax." Stephanie glared right back. "I'm married with kids. I don't get action that much anymore; I need to live vicariously through you."

"Wait, back up." Lucy squinted from across the table; her gaze was slightly unfocused from the shot she had just downed moments ago. "What do you mean you don't get action anymore? You're married, I'm pretty sure that comes with benefits."

Stephanie looked away, and I sensed we struck a nerve. "I'm convinced he's getting it somewhere else."

"Why would you think that?" I asked, scanning her face and hoping she was just overreacting.

"Because he's always tired, or stressed," she said, poking her straw around in her drink. "Either that or he doesn't find me attractive anymore."

"That's not possible," I said, scrunching up my nose at the thought. "I don't see Theo as the cheating type."

Her eyes started to fill with moisture. "Maybe he's just bored with me."

Just then, a text came through on my phone.

JP
How's happy hour?

I typed back.

I'm on my second margarita.

JP
You're not driving, right?

He's been out of town, and our messages have been short. The only silver lining was he was coming home tonight, and I planned on surprising him.

Aw, are you worried about me?

JP
I'm always worried about you and thinking about you...

There was a goofy smile on my face that would not go away.

"Why are your cheeks so red?" Stephanie leaned in close to peek at my screen.

I stuffed my phone away. "My cheeks aren't red."

"That was him, I know it." She pointed her finger. "You're smiling and you never smile."

I laughed. She sounded just like JP.

Lucy shook her head. "So, Rylee, how does it feel to be official? Are you worried at all about being in the public eye?"

I shrugged my shoulders. "Kind of late to start second-guessing myself now that I'm in love with the guy. I'm already all in."

Lucy opened her mouth and closed it.

"What?" I asked as they both stared at me.

Stephanie cleared her throat. "You just said you're in love with him."

"Oh, my God." Lucy's hand went to her mouth. "This is amazing. He must be the one."

I did a slow blink and wished my head wasn't so fuzzy so I had better control over what came out of my mouth. I had a good buzz going and wanted to keep it that way. "Let's not read too much into that statement."

It's only been a few days since the fundraiser, and I still felt a little protective of him. As much as I'd like to believe I could trust these two, I needed to be careful about what I said.

Lucy clapped her hands as the server placed a tray of drinks on our table. "Okay, you're obviously keeping some details close to the vest, but there has to be something you can share."

"Yeah." Stephanie sat back in her seat and crossed one leg over the other. "Throw us a bone here."

I arched an eyebrow at my friend. "Why is my relationship the only one in the spotlight?"

"Because her husband is an architect, and my boyfriend sells cars at the local Kia dealership," Lucy said in a bored tone. "Not all of us are lucky enough to snag Atlanta's most eligible bachelor."

I groaned like I needed a reminder of how much competition I had.

Stephanie leaned her arms along the table. "Does he have a six-pack or an eight-pack? I can't tell under that padded uniform."

I scrubbed a hand over my face. "I don't have enough alcohol flowing through my system to handle this conversation."

"You know what," Stephanie stood from her chair, "I think you're right. We need to order some shots."

I groaned and stared up at the ceiling. "This is last call for me. After this, you ladies are on your own."

An hour later, the table was covered with empty glasses and half-eaten plates of food. I took my credit card out of the binder and checked the airline app to confirm that JP's flight was on time. The margaritas I consumed had definitely hit my system; I was feeling good but not too drunk to where I couldn't follow through with my plan tonight.

———

The sound of the wheels of JP's luggage rolling against the floor had me jumping off the bed. I took a deep breath when he pushed his bedroom door open.

He lifted his eyes to mine. "Rylee. What are you doing here?"

Not the reaction I was hoping for.

He remained quiet as I stepped toward him in my black lace corset that I had spent a fortune on. He didn't move or seem affected, and I wasn't sure what to make of it.

"I thought I would surprise you." I tilted my head to the side. "Is everything okay?"

His hair was messy, his clothes were rumpled, and he seemed stressed.

"Rylee, I…" He looked like there was something on the tip of his tongue that he wanted to say. Instead, he scrubbed a hand down his face and shook his head. "It's been a long day and I'm exhausted. I was looking forward to coming home and crashing."

I tilted my head, trying to comprehend what was happening. He was on edge and looking everywhere but at me. But I'd been drinking, so those margaritas and shots might have made me imagine things.

"Let me help you relax before you crash." I trailed my mouth along his jaw and moved my hands to his zipper. His hand flew out and grabbed my wrist. I looked up; there was no smile on his lips, no warmth in his touch. He was completely turned off, and my heart fell into my stomach.

He let out a deep sigh and dropped my arm. "Rylee, I can't do this right now with you. I'm sorry."

He'd been on an airplane for the past few hours, so maybe he was a little tired, but JP was always in the mood. He moved around me, went to the bathroom, and started unpacking his toiletry bag. Was he honestly going to just get ready for bed?

"Did something happen?" I asked, crossing my arms across my chest. He was right across the room, yet he felt so far away. "Did I do something wrong?"

"Of course not." He leaned against the sink and pressed a hand to his forehead. "I went and saw Caroline today and it was an emotional visit."

That was not what I was expecting.

"I didn't know," I said, unsure of what I was supposed to say. Was I supposed to comfort him? Give him space? I had no idea what was going on in his head. "I thought you were going to a basketball game with your brother."

"I did, but then I drove to Saratoga and saw her this morning."

He went to see her and didn't tell me. Was he having second thoughts about us? Regrets? Because it felt like he didn't want me here, or maybe it was me that felt like I didn't belong.

"Okay." I swallowed, gripping the doorframe for support. "Do you want to talk about it?"

"Can we talk about this tomorrow?" he said between brushing his teeth. "I'm drained and just want to go to bed."

"Are you okay?"

"No, I'm not okay." He walked back into the bedroom, keeping his gaze on mine. "I'm devastated right now, and the last thing I want is to take my pain out on you."

"Please don't shut me out. Not after all the progress we made."

"I'm not shutting you out. I just need a minute. Can you give me a little breathing room here? Is that too much to ask?"

He was pulling away from me, and I was doing everything I could to pull him closer. I was scared that I was losing him, but that didn't give him the right to treat me like this.

"So, we're back to this again? You asking me for space and understanding. I thought we agreed to try. How is this trying?"

"Please don't pressure me right now. Just show some respect, let me get some sleep, and we'll talk in the morning."

I stepped back and stared at him, feeling the mortification and sadness wash over me. I came here tonight because I missed him and was excited to see him; instead of making love like I planned, I was left wondering where we stood. Tears welled up in my eyes and my chin quivered with humiliation.

I backed up into the bedroom and searched for my clothes. I needed a shield or an armor, some type of protection. It felt like he took a baseball bat to my damn heart.

Knowing that I might always come in second place wasn't a great feeling. Every insecurity I had about our relationship just came and punched me right in the gut.

He gripped the ends of his hair and blew out a frustrated breath. "I'm not trying to be an asshole; please tell me you understand."

I was tempted to say something about how wrong this was, but I wasn't that girl.

"Do you want me to go?" I asked, shifting on my feet. "I don't have my car, but I can call an Uber."

He shook his head. "No, I want you to stay."

I tiptoed to the dresser and pulled out one of his white T-shirts. JP took his jeans off and slipped under the covers. He looked tormented and broken, and there were so many questions on the tip of my tongue, but I didn't even know where to start.

I settled in next to him, and instead of reaching for me like he did every night, he stayed on his side of the bed. He stared up at the ceiling and didn't even look at me. Instead of kissing me good night or wrapping his arms around me, he turned off the lights and pulled the comforter over us. Once we were in the dark, I let the first tear fall. And once I could hear his soft snores and knew he was asleep, I flipped the covers off my body, quietly got dressed, walked downstairs, and called an Uber.

CHAPTER 24

JP

I stood outside Rylee's office door, trying to summon the courage to face her. I've spent the last three hours panicking about all the different thoughts there were probably running through her head. I'd thought about calling and apologizing a million times, but I was afraid anything I said would only make matters worse.

The last thing I expected when I got home was to see Rylee waiting for me in my bedroom. She looked downright beautiful last night, and part of me wanted to weep at the sight of her. But making love to her didn't feel right. I knew that's what she wanted and expected, but I couldn't touch her with the emotions of the day hanging over my head. I didn't realize how heavy of a load I was carrying until I said my final goodbye.

There wasn't a doubt in my mind that she was drawing the wrong conclusion, so it was time to fix the mess I made.

I knocked three times and pushed the door open.

The second I stepped inside her office, my heart slammed to a standstill. I was such a fuckup.

Her face was puffy; her eyes were red; she looked

utterly broken. All I wanted to do was pull her into my arms and make us whole again.

"Can we talk?" I asked, pushing through the ball of regret lodged in the back of my throat.

She wiped at her cheeks. "I'm getting ready to leave for the Nashville conference. Can we talk when I get back?"

Damn it! I forgot about that.

"I can't let you leave like this." She was slipping away; I could feel it. There was no way I was letting her leave for three days, thinking that I didn't want her. I needed her to understand what happened in Saratoga.

She stood from her chair and started packing up for her meetings. "I don't have time for this conversation right now."

I took a step closer, and when she didn't flinch, I took another. "I messed up. I'm sorry."

"Thank you for apologizing." She zipped up her computer bag and set it on the floor beside her luggage.

"You deserved one, but I'd like to take it a step further if you'd let me. I'd like for us to talk," I said quickly, not wanting to waste another second. "The things I said, the way I hurt you, was all wrong. I took my pain out on you and you didn't deserve that."

Her eyes flashed to mine. "You turned me away last night, JP, and not just physically. I was embarrassed, hurt, and angry. It felt like you didn't want me at all. I understand that you were dealing with something you weren't ready to talk about, but you could have still given me some type of reassurance that we were okay. You were cold and distant. Do you have any idea what that did to me? How it made me feel? I was confused, wondering if I did something wrong and second-guessing my place in your life."

"Rylee, you are the most important thing in my life. It's

my fault that you don't realize it. Hell, I didn't even realize it myself until recently."

She crossed her arms over her chest. "What are you saying?"

"I am hopelessly and desperately in love with you. I don't want to lose you."

She sucked in a breath of disbelief. "You love me?"

"I do, and I should have told you last night."

She wiped at her cheeks and took a few deep breaths. "Then why did you shut me out?"

"Because I was an emotional mess. Every time I see Caroline trapped in that fucking room, with a brain and a body that doesn't work anymore, I can't help but blame myself."

"JP, you were eighteen years old, it's time to stop punishing yourself. It was a freak accident."

"I was the one driving the boat."

"You were also the only one who jumped in after she fell into the water. You did everything you could. You saved her life."

"She has no quality of life because of me. She might be alive, but she sure as hell isn't living."

She crossed her arms again. "Just because you feel guilty doesn't mean you are. What about the other people that were on that boat that day? Do you think they shoulder some of the blame? Do you think they wonder if there was something they could have done to prevent it?"

"I don't know, but she wasn't their girlfriend, she was mine." I blew out a frustrated breath. "Look, I didn't come here to rehash my visit with her. I came here to explain what was going on in my head last night." I pulled on the back of my neck, pissed off that the words weren't coming out right. "You looked beautiful, and I know I messed up. I planned on waking up and explaining everything that happened yesterday, but when I noticed you were gone, I wanted to throw up. I don't ever want you to feel unwanted and I'm sorry I made you feel that way. I could have handled it better when I found you waiting for me, and if I could go back and do it all over again, I never would have shut you out."

She went to say something, but a knock sounded on her door.

"Hey, sorry to interrupt." Dominick poked his head inside. The sight of him had me clenching my fists in anger. "Just wanted to let you know that our car is waiting downstairs."

Her eyes filled with an apology. "I have to go."

I looked over at the overnight bag by her desk. "Rylee," I pleaded, "I need another minute."

I just laid myself bare at her feet, and she was leaving with *him.*

She turned to Dominick. "I'll be right down."

He nodded his head and closed the door.

"JP, I don't have time to talk. Let's finish this when I get back."

My shoulders deflated. "Please tell me we're okay."

She looked into my eyes, and I hated the hurt I saw. "Let's take this time apart and get our emotions in order so we can have a productive conversation when I return, okay?"

"I agree to everything but the time apart. I'm not all that thrilled with you leaving me under these circumstances, especially with your ex-boyfriend."

She glared at me. "Just when I thought we were making progress."

I scrubbed a hand through my hair. "I'm sorry. You're right. I'm edgy and frustrated because I want to make things right between us. I trust you. It's him I don't trust.

We both know he's not over you, and I don't want him to take advantage of how vulnerable you are right now."

Her body stiffened. "I think you need to stop talking before you dig a bigger hole for yourself."

I threw my hands up. "You're right. I'm sorry."

She walked over to her desk, grabbed her phone and keys, and stuffed them in her purse. "For the record, you have nothing to worry about."

She was wrong about that, but it wasn't her actions that had me concerned. Seeing that I was already skating on thin ice, I kept my mouth shut.

"Here, let me help you." I took her bag from her hand and threw it over my shoulder. I reached for her hand, thankful she didn't pull away, and walked her to the waiting car. I gave the bag to the driver and stepped up to her.

"Please, let me kiss you," I begged, leaning into her ear.

"Why?" She clenched her teeth. "So, you can make a point in front of Dominick or because you want to?"

"Please don't do this," I pleaded with her. "I need you."

She pressed her hand to my chest and met my eyes. "I know the feeling. That's how I felt last night."

There was so much at stake, and I hated everything about this. "Can I at least call you? There is a lot I need to explain."

"You've had lots of time to explain, and if I'm being honest, I'm exhausted. Just give me a little space, okay?" She wiped at her face, pushing away a tear that had fallen.

I was such a selfish asshole, and now I was paying for it dearly.

"I told you I was sorry for everything," I said, wishing I could wrap her in my arms and make all this disappear.

"I don't doubt that you're sorry, but I won't have a lot

of time to talk while I am away. We will sort things out when I get back. I'll see you in a few days."

And with those parting words, she slipped into the car and closed the door.

My gut churned when I watched the town car pull away from the curb. There was nothing left for me to do other than wait for her to come back to me.

CHAPTER 25
RYLEE

"I think I'm going to call it a night," Miles said, giving everyone a wave. "I'm ready to put all the 'crap' from today behind me and go back to my hotel. We all have an early morning flight, so don't get too crazy."

Our last meetings of the day were with the Physician Organization of Proctologists, or POOP, as they liked to refer to themselves. After spending the past eight hours listening to terrible butt jokes and puns, my coworkers and I were ready to unwind at a rooftop bar in downtown Nashville.

There was a live band playing countless country hits that were good enough to pull people out on the dance floor. Most of us were already three sheets to the wind. I was tipsy and sweaty, thanks to climbing six flights of stairs to enjoy the rooftop view. I took my phone out of my wristlet to take a picture of Broadway all lit up at night. The streets were packed with tourists moving from bar to bar. Nashville was a fun town, but I was ready to go home tomorrow. I sighed, noticing my battery was teetering on zero, so I quickly snapped a photo and put my phone away.

I walked over to the high-top table near the stage where our group was camped out. As soon as I sat down, a shot glass was placed in front of me. "Happy belated birthday," Dom said, pushing the tequila closer.

I glanced up, noticing his eyes were glassy. No surprise there. "Tequila?"

"Just remembering it was your favorite." He smiled sheepishly.

I didn't want to share a shot with him, but I didn't want to be rude, either. I managed to avoid him during the entire conference and was running out of excuses. "Thank you." I raised my drink in the air before throwing it back.

Diego and Noelle, our two coworkers, came over carrying a tray of drinks. I laughed when I spotted Diego's new cowboy hat and Noelle's sparkly new boots.

"You guys really went all out in the gift shop, huh?" I teased.

Noelle held out her leg. "Girl, these boots were made for dancing. Let's go," she said, disappearing into the crowd. Lucy and Stephanie were going to regret leaving the convention a day early. This was the most fun we'd had since we'd been here.

Diego tipped his hat forward and I had to bite back a laugh. "Dance with me, Rylee."

"I'm not drunk enough to dance with you." I shook my head and started backing away.

Diego was probably one of the most attractive men I had ever met besides JP. He was fun and cheerful, with curly dark hair and big brown eyes that reminded me of a golden retriever. And coming from Argentina, he took dancing way too seriously.

"You have to dance with me." He held up his phone to

show me his latest text exchange with his wife. "You are the only woman my Ana trusts me with."

"What about Noelle?" I pointed to where she was attempting to learn the two-step with a group of guys that looked half her age.

He waved his hands in the air. "She said to stay as far away from her as possible."

Noelle was known to be a shameless flirt, but she was completely harmless.

"One dance." I held up my finger and kicked my heels off.

I followed Diego out onto the packed dance floor. The man had moves, that was for sure. My efforts to keep up with his steps were embarrassing, but thankfully, I was too tipsy to care.

Dom stayed back but had the server replace our glasses every time they'd run empty. One song led to two, and after that, I lost count. I caught Dom watching me from the edge of the dance floor, never once making a move to come closer.

"Girl, that man still has it bad for you." I glanced over to where my ex stared at me with intensity over the rim of his whiskey.

I averted my gaze and focused on the strobe lights illuminating the dance floor. "Do me a favor and do not let him cut in."

He took my hand and twirled me around. "I got your back, *amiga*."

"Where the hell is Noelle, anyway?" I asked, taking another sip of my cosmo because I wasn't allowing it to go to waste at fourteen dollars a glass. Plus, it was hot and humid, so it was going down pretty easily.

His eyes were twinkling. "Probably getting laid."

"Go, Noelle." I raised my drink in the air. After the

week I had, I was glad someone was getting some action. I took a hefty sip from my glass, feeling the effects of the alcohol warm my veins. I thought going out with my coworkers would make my shitty mood go away, but I was still feeling down in the dumps.

As if Diego could read my mind, he lifted my chin. "Girl, you need to get out of this slump. Your problems will be waiting for you when you get home tomorrow. Try to have a little fun."

"I miss him." I swayed to the side a little as I said it.

Now that I had a little space and time to think, my heart was filling up with a bit of remorse for how I treated him. I don't know what possessed me to be so cold to him before I left, but I regretted it, and there wasn't a damn thing I could do about it until I landed back in Atlanta.

"We should go back," Diego said into my ear as a slow song started playing.

My gaze moved around the dance floor, taking in all the couples swaying to the music. God, I was a mess. I closed my eyes and tried to let the music settle my mind. Despite my best efforts, my thoughts drifted back to JP and how we left things.

"No, let's just dance," I said, resting my hand on his shoulder, wishing it belonged to someone else.

He stepped back, causing my hand to fall to the side. "Rylee, I would love to, but I gotta take a piss."

"Can't you hold it for five more minutes?"

He gave me a look. "Did you see all those beers I drank?"

"But I love this song. I want to dance to one more. Please, Diego."

A hand landed on Diego's shoulder. "I can take it from here."

My eyes flicked to Diego, and I pleaded with him not

to leave me alone with my ex. I didn't like the way Dom had been watching me tonight.

Diego leaned in and whispered, "I know you're using me as a buffer, but I really am close to pissing my pants."

I gave my friend the evil eye and turned to Dom. "That's okay, I'm ready for a break anyway."

His stare was unwavering. "You were just begging Diego for one more song. You really can't spare me one dance?"

He has been trying to give me space and hasn't done anything terrible. Maybe we could find some middle ground and manage to move forward.

Diego grabbed my arm and leaned in. "I'll be quick."

I hesitated before I finally gave in. "Okay."

"Come on, Rylee. I know how much you love to dance." Dom wrapped his hand around mine and I tried not to squirm uncomfortably in his grasp. Maybe I was overacting, but this felt like a really bad idea.

Dom slid his hands along my hips while I kept the drink in one hand and the other on his shoulder. That was as close as we were going to get. Our bodies moved in sync with the beat while I kept my gaze everywhere but on him. But oh, how I could feel his eyes rake down my body, doing a slow sweep. Whenever he tried to move in an inch, I would move back. Dom and I have danced many times, but his arms weren't the ones I wanted touching me. Everything about this felt wrong.

"Dom," I started backing away, "I can't, I'm sorry."

"Wait." He reached for my hand. "Tell me you didn't feel anything just now."

Was he insane?

"The only thing I felt was regret because I never should have danced with you in the first place."

He grabbed my chin. "I don't believe you."

I could smell the whiskey on his breath, and every hair on end stood at attention. "Get your hands off me."

"Not before I do this." He slammed his mouth down on mine, catching me completely off guard. It took my brain a minute to realize what was happening. When he tried to part my lips open, I shoved him back.

"What the hell do you think you're doing?" My hand went to my lips as I tried to wipe the taste of the kiss away. JP would kill him.

He held his hand up in surrender. "Whoa, calm down, it was just a kiss. Nothing we haven't done before."

My eyes burned with tears. I was not an emotional person, but I was in love with someone else, and the thought of another man's lips on mine made me sick to my stomach. "I have a boyfriend, and even if I didn't you don't kiss me without my permission."

"I'm sorry," he slurred and ran his hand through his sweaty hair. "I'm drunk and wasn't thinking. I got carried away."

"That's no excuse. Don't ever touch me again!" I stormed off the dance floor and ran smack into Diego and Noelle.

"Rylee." Noelle stumbled into me. "I'm sorry I left you."

"Everything okay?" Diego asked, his eyes bouncing back and forth between Dom and me.

Dom waved his hands in the air. "Everything is fine. It was just a simple misunderstanding."

I scoffed and crossed my arms. "It was more than that and you know it. I was trying to be nice and you took advantage of that."

"Rylee, come on, cut me some slack. Don't cause a scene. We've all been drinking."

"I'm ready to leave." I set my drink down on the ledge.

I couldn't believe how quickly this night went downhill. I didn't even want to think about the fallout if JP ever found out what had happened tonight. If the situation were reversed, I would be livid.

Dom stepped back, creating a little distance. "I'll order our Uber to take us back to the hotel."

I took a deep breath, attempting to calm myself down. I just wanted to go back to my hotel room, crawl under the covers, and forget this night ever happened.

The black SUV pulled up to the curb. We all jumped in. Noelle and I sat in the second row, and Diego and Dom sat in the third. I rested my head against the back of the seat, watching the neon-colored lights whizz by.

I was missing JP, so I slid my phone out to text him and let him know I was thinking of him, but my battery was dead. I threw it on the leather seat and felt my eyelids grow heavy from exhaustion.

Noelle tried to talk to me, but I was too tired to keep up a conversation. I had changed my plans to a six-a.m. flight and needed to get a few hours of sleep. The past week had been weighing me down, and the longer I sat, the more guilty I felt. Dom's kiss played in my mind like a bad dream on repeat.

Maybe tonight was the universe's way of telling me never to touch a drop of alcohol again.

CHAPTER 26
JP

Normally, I was calm and collected, even during the most extreme circumstances. It was rare for me to feel this out of control. I don't ever remember feeling so caught off guard in my life.

The last thing I ever expected to find while scrolling through Instagram were tags of my fucking girlfriend dancing with another man. I could almost look past that because there had to be a reasonable explanation, but what really sent fire through my veins was the second picture of her and Dom. His arms were wrapped around her waist, and her hand was on his chest. They looked pretty damn cozy, and there was no denying the way he looked at her. Like he was one second away from taking her right there on that dance floor.

What. The. Fuck!

I spent these past two nights missing the hell out of her and torn up about how I treated her. All I wanted to do was make things right and get her to understand how much she meant to me. Meanwhile, she was out getting hammered at a club, letting him put his hands all over her.

She was so damn busy that she couldn't spare me a five-minute phone call, but she had time to hang out with him. Yeah, she looked busy all right.

My fingers squeezed the phone case so hard I was afraid it would crack. I was going to kill the son of a bitch. Sure, my ego took a hit, but I couldn't let this one slide. He had to make a move on her when I was hundreds of miles away. Just like he had to have known there would be a price to pay.

I should have listened to my instincts and begged her… to what, not leave with him? That was absurd. I had no control over her work schedule, but I should have insisted on driving her to the airport at least, instead of just backing off. After looking at these pictures, giving her the space she asked of me was the wrong move.

A sharp burn stung my eyes. I was going to destroy the weaselly fucker with my bare hands. I snatched my keys off the counter and stormed out the door.

My knuckles were white from gripping the steering wheel so hard as I sped along the interstate. By the time I reached my destination, my jaw was locked with fury. I sat in my truck like a stalker, waiting for either of them to pull into the employee parking lot. Showing up when I was this upset probably wasn't my best plan, but I had to confront both of them—two birds with one stone and all that.

If Rylee would just pick up her phone or return her messages, I wouldn't be as pissed off as I was. Rationally, I knew there had to be a damn good reason for all this, but my mind wouldn't settle down until I talked to her.

My eyes were trained on the main entrance of the hotel. Guests and employees were making their way through the parking lot, and a row of rideshares were waiting in the circular driveway, ready to drop travelers off at the airport.

I had no idea what I would say, but when I spotted the fucker exit his white Tesla, I didn't hesitate. I didn't think twice. I threw my car door open and stalked toward him.

His head was down as he maneuvered around the parked cars. He must have sensed me because he turned just as my long strides caught up to him. The look on my face should have sent him running in the opposite direction. Instead, he pushed his sunglasses up to the top of his head and smirked.

"Can I help you?" His smile was sleazy as fuck.

"Don't act stupid," I spat.

"Oh, you must be looking for Rylee." He pulled a phone out of his briefcase. "I'm afraid she left this in my hotel room last night."

I didn't respond; I just drew my arm back and slammed my fist into his nose. Pain spread through my hand, but it was only a fraction of what he must have felt. It was stupid of me to lose control because my hand made me millions, and there was always someone standing nearby with a camera. But something about seeing blood trickle out of his nostrils was worth the risk.

"What the fuck, you psycho," he hissed, bringing both hands up to cover his nose.

"You ever think about touching my girlfriend again and I'll fuck up a lot more than your nose."

He crossed a line, and I was here to make sure he understood where that line was and who he was messing with.

"You don't deserve her, asshole," he panted out between heavy breaths. Satisfaction washed over me because I fucked up his nose pretty damn good.

"You're right, I don't, but she's still mine."

"She sure as fuck wasn't yours when I had my mouth and hands on her last night."

I landed another punch, this time to his gut. He stumbled forward and tripped, falling to his knees on the pavement. I was probably going to get sued up the ass for this, but it would be worth it. Did I believe she slept with him? No. It didn't matter how drunk she was; she wouldn't do that to me. She despised the piece of shit. But this jackass wanted me to think something happened.

"She wouldn't go near your tiny dick if it was the last one on the planet. Nice try."

He stood up and pulled out a pocket square from his suit coat. "You clearly don't know her as well as you think you do. She'll change her mind. Rylee and I have history. You of all people should respect that."

My eyebrows arched, not liking the confidence in his tone one bit. "I don't know what the hell you're implying, but you had your chance, and you blew it. She can't even stand being near you."

He squinted his beady little eyes at me. "You're right, I did blow it, and I'm going to get her back. And you're not going to stand in my way."

What on earth was he talking about? He was provoking me but making zero sense.

"Dude, are you drunk or high?" My eyes searched his face. He looked hungover but otherwise sober.

"No, I'm not drunk or high." He wiped at the blood running off his chin, staining the fabric of his white dress shirt in the process. "I'm just well-informed."

"Look, I'm out of patience, so whatever it is you're trying to say, just fucking say it."

"With pleasure." He puffed out his chest, seeming so damn sure of himself. "The beans have been spilled my friend. Your time is up. I know about Caroline and the boating accident. I know everything."

My body staggered backward as if I'd been hit square in the chest. "What did you just say?"

She wouldn't, I reminded myself. But how would he know?

"Did you really think you'd be able to keep your little secret forever?"

"What is it that you think you know?" I stared at him, not wanting to believe what I was hearing.

"I know about the accident you caused." He wiped at his nose. "I know that you made Rylee feel insignificant before she left for Nashville." He shrugged. "Don't worry though, I took care of that last night."

My breaths grew shallow, and my heart started to race. I felt lightheaded, blindsided, and ready to commit murder.

I hauled him up by his shirt collar, ready to strangle the little prick. "You do not want to mess with me."

"You don't scare me." His spittle landed on my cheek.

"Who told you about the accident?" I was seething and one second away from snapping his neck.

"I heard the whole thing from Rylee's lips."

I dropped him back on his feet. It felt like a cold, rusty knife was twisting in my stomach. I trusted no one, which was why I never talked about that day. I let my guard down just one time—something I never did. I know I messed up, but that didn't give her the right to share that information, especially with him, of all people. Never have I felt more betrayed in my entire life.

I spun in a circle, trying to slow my heart rate down. My vision was blurry as my eyes landed on the familiar pink phone case with Oakley's face covering the back.

I snatched it off the ground and shoved the phone into my pocket.

"If you even think about running that story to the press, I will make you regret the day you were born."

I was fiercely protective of Caroline and her privacy. Her family had been through enough. That's why I spent the last twelve years keeping the story buried in the past where it belonged. I wouldn't let this piece of shit use her to get what he wanted.

"Let Rylee go and I will. Otherwise, I'll sell that sob story to the highest bidder with zero fucks to give."

"You're delusional if you think you can blackmail me. I think you underestimate how powerful my name and popularity are in Atlanta, not to mention the entire damn country. You leak this to the press and you will become one of the most despised men on the planet. By the time my media team gets done, you'll be lucky to get a job sweeping up elephant shit at the zoo." I turned and strode to my truck. And because I was pretty damned peeved, I kicked a decent size rock toward his shiny white Tesla—smirking at the new dent right above the front right tire.

"You're going to pay for that, asshole."

"Good," I shouted back. "It was worth it."

Before I reached my truck, I spun around. "One more thing, I don't know what happened in Nashville, but I guarantee you, it will be the last time you ever lay a fucking hand on her." My knuckles were white, and I was itching to pound his smug face into the ground. "You're going to learn what happens when you touch things that don't belong to you."

And with that, I hopped in my truck, punched the start button, and flew out of the parking lot.

CHAPTER 27

RYLEE

THE POUNDING ON MY DOOR HAD ME SHOOTING STRAIGHT up in my bed. I blew the hair out of my face and looked at the time on my alarm clock. When my flight landed in Atlanta this morning, the first thing I did was open my laptop and log into my work email so I could let my boss know that I wouldn't be going into the office.

Dom sent me a notification, letting me know that he had my phone and would have it delivered today. I hadn't realized I left it in the Uber last night until I arrived at the airport this morning to check in for my flight.

I threw on a robe and trudged through my apartment with Oakley hot on my heels. I swung the door open, hoping it was a delivery person with my phone.

Only it wasn't a delivery person.

"JP?" I blinked, allowing my eyes to adjust to the sunlight behind his back.

"Surprised to see me?"

Normally, I was happy to see him, but after these past few days and with the way he was glaring at me, I wasn't sure how I was supposed to feel.

"Is everything okay?" I blinked as he leaned against the doorframe. His arms were folded over his chest, and his feet were crossed at the ankles.

"I've had an eventful morning."

Oakley trotted over, dropping a tennis ball at his feet. JP glanced down, his features softening slightly. He gave his furry friend a scratch behind the ear but made no attempt to pick up the ball and play with him. Sensing the tension, Oakley hung his head and moped his way over to the dog bed in the corner.

"Do you want a cup of coffee?" I asked, walking into the kitchen to turn my Keurig on.

"What I want is some answers," he said, slamming the door and stalking across the room.

I turned and arched an eyebrow. "Pardon me?"

"Rylee, I know I hurt you, and things were strained before you left for Nashville, but I never expected you to betray me so easily."

My eyebrows shot up to my hairline. "What are you talking about?"

He shoved his hands in his front pockets and stepped forward. "I really thought we could work this out, but after what you did, I don't even see that as an option on the table anymore."

"You want to tell me what the hell it is that you think I did?" I closed the cabinet, my coffee cup forgotten.

"I planned on talking to you. I wanted to fix things. And instead of talking to me, you went and ran your mouth to your ex, and God knows what else you did with him."

"I'm going to ask you this one more time," I said, trying my best to hold on to my composure. "What are you talking about?"

"Someone tagged you in an Instagram post. I showed

up at your office to find out why the fuck there were pictures of you dancing with your ex last night and some other guy. Instead, I ran into the douche himself."

I rubbed at my forehead, wishing I was less hungover and had gotten a little more sleep on the airplane. "I don't know what you saw on Instagram, but I can explain."

"Really?" he mocked. "While you're at it, can you explain to me what possessed you to tell Dominick about Caroline?"

My breath caught in my chest. "I did no such thing!"

"Then how does he know about the accident, Rylee?"

"I don't know." I started to panic, and my mind began sifting through our conversations. Dominick was the last person I would confide in. "You honestly think I would do that to you?"

He held his arms out. "I think it's pretty fucking obvious, don't you think? You've been with him for days. You were pissed, and instead of talking to me, you went and told him things that you knew I didn't want anyone to know about. I don't trust many people, Rylee, but I fucking trusted you."

I stared at him, mouth agape, feeling like I stepped into an alternate universe. "I wouldn't do that to you."

He threw something on my couch, and it took me a minute to realize it was my phone. My mind spun. So much confusion was rolling through me as pieces from last night started clicking into place.

"I know how you operate, Rylee. You were hurt and on the defensive. You needed your feelings validated, so you turned to the one man you knew wanted you. All to make yourself feel better."

I flew toward him so damn fast I was out of breath and ready to tear him a new one. He wanted to fight; I would give him a fight. "I don't know who you are right now, but this isn't you. I didn't say anything to Dominick. I have no idea how he got that information, but it wasn't me. You can either believe me or not."

"You were with him for the past two nights. How the hell else would he have found out?" His voice was getting louder with each passing second, causing Oakley's head to pop up from his dog bed. "I can count on one hand who knows what happened the night of Caroline's accident, Rylee."

"You really think I would go behind your back and betray you so easily?"

That made me angry, and a wave of hurt ripped through me.

"I'm starting to wonder how badly you did betray me. Did you cry on his shoulder? Did he give you the comfort and attention that I didn't give you? Were you so hurt that you fell into bed with your ex-boyfriend and allowed him to fuck the words right out of you?"

My hand connected with his cheek before he could say another word. His head whipped to the side, and I stumbled back. His face paled. My palm stung. What the hell was happening?

"You want the cold hard truth?" I shouted, getting angrier by the second, hating the tears forming in my eyes. "I have been faithful and loyal to you."

"Those pictures of you dancing at the club in Nashville say otherwise."

"I don't know what pictures you're talking about?"

"Maybe if you looked at your damn phone, it would jog your memory."

"JP, I haven't had my phone since last night. I left it in the Uber. Dom was having it sent…" I threw my hand over my mouth. "Oh, my God. What did he tell you happened?"

He looked at me with disgust. "Seeing you guys are so close again, why don't you ask him?"

"I swear to you, nothing happened. I don't care what you think you saw in a photo. I'm telling you, nothing happened. We were out at a club. We were all drinking. He asked me to dance. I didn't want to, but he made me feel bad, so I told him one dance. We all left in the same Uber and went back to our individual rooms."

He crossed his arms. "Anything else?"

Shit! The last thing I wanted was for him to find out about that kiss, but I wouldn't lie to him. I was damned if I do, damned if I don't.

"He kissed me, but I pushed him away."

His nostrils flared. "You let him fucking touch you!"

"No."

He stepped forward. "So, are you saying he forced himself on you?"

I swallowed, unsure how I was supposed to answer that. He was angry, and while I wasn't afraid of him, I knew whatever I said would only make things worse. "He didn't force himself on me, but he caught me off guard. The second I realized what was happening, I shoved him away."

He started pacing back and forth, tugging on his hair. "Rylee, I don't know if I can believe anything you say anymore. If I can't trust you, then I can't be with you."

He can't trust me? He can't be with me? He's going to believe whatever lies Dominick told him over me? What on earth was happening? How could he be so cold and cruel? How could he doubt me so easily?

Haven't I proven myself to him? Haven't I been supportive and understanding enough? What more could I possibly have done?

"So, you're done with me? Just like that without giving

me the benefit of the doubt? Why am I not surprised?" I shook my head, letting the tears fall down my face. "My love will never be enough for you, will it?"

"Don't turn this into something it isn't." His eyes filled with resolve. His decision had been made. As much as I didn't want to acknowledge it, trying to fight him on it was too much for me to handle. "This has nothing to do with how much I love you. It's about me not trusting you."

"Are you kidding me right now?"

He shook his head. "I don't know, Rylee. You looked pretty boozed-up in those pictures. Maybe you were too plastered to remember. But the truth of the matter is, whether you told him willingly or under the influence, he found out from you. I don't play games with my personal life. You of all people know that."

My heart felt like it was caving in. All the good, love, and laughter were falling apart right before my eyes. I had never seen him like this. I wanted to beg him to stop, plead with him, shake him, anything it took to get him to stop behaving like this.

"You realize you won't be able to take any of this bullshit back, right? When you realize how badly you messed up?"

His gaze dropped to the floor. His voice was distant and detached as he spoke. "The only thing I realize right now, is that we are hurting each other and that's the last thing I want. I think we should end things before any more damage can be done, and agree that it's for the best."

A strangled noise broke free. "If you're going to break my fucking heart, then at least have the decency to look me in the eye while you do it."

He wouldn't look at me. I was met with silence. This was pointless, and trying to reason with him while he was angry only made things worse. Deep down, I always knew he would break me in the end. If only I had listened to my head instead of my heart.

"Just go." I turned my back, not giving him the satisfaction of seeing me shed one more tear over him. "There is nothing left for us to say to each other."

I told myself that what we had was enough. I painted a pretty picture in my head and allowed myself to believe in things that weren't our reality. Now that I saw the truth and how badly he could hurt me, I realized how wrong I was. Not only did he break me, he destroyed me beyond repair.

"One more thing," he said so low I almost didn't hear him. "If you ever gave a damn about me at all, you won't breathe another word about the accident."

When the door slammed shut, I collapsed onto the floor and buried my head in my hands. How could so much change in a matter of minutes? I wanted to go back in time and never step foot on that airplane. I shouldn't have danced with Dominick. I should have made better decisions.

I sobbed in my hands because none of that mattered. I thought he trusted me. I thought we were moving forward, but apparently, I was wrong. After a simple misunderstanding and a conversation with a man who couldn't be trusted, everything was gone in the blink of an eye.

He lost faith in us. There was no healing, no recovering from this.

Oakley padded over; his eyes looked as heartbroken as mine as he rested his head in my lap. I threaded my fingers through his fur. "I know, buddy, it hurts, but we'll be okay."

Somehow, someway, we will be okay.

CHAPTER 28
RYLEE

I hadn't left my house for a couple of days. I only stepped outside to get the mail and let Oakley out to go to the bathroom. Even my dog was pissed at me because I hadn't had the energy to take him for a walk. He's been moping around the house almost as bad as me.

Getting over a famous NFL player whose face was everywhere wasn't easy. To make matters worse, my family loved him, so it wasn't like I could confide in them. Especially my brother, who was doing everything he could to stay out of our drama.

I sipped my water and pushed the Chinese food I ordered for dinner to the side. My stomach hurt too much to eat anything.

I missed the asshole. I loved him and had no idea what to do with my life now that he was no longer in it. I felt stuck. Stuck between wanting him back and wanting to move on and put him in my rearview mirror.

There was a knock at my front door, and before I could answer, it swung open.

When Maverick's eyes met mine, those damn tears came rushing out.

My brother's familiar arms wrapped around me. "I'm going to kick his ass, I promise."

I buried my face in his shirt and smiled, even though it was at odds with how I felt. "You didn't have to come rushing over here."

"Kinley told me to give you some time, but I had to see you."

I shook my head. "I'm fine, I swear."

His soothing hand rubbed circles along my back. "Rylee, I don't know what to say, I know I said I didn't want to get involved, but there is no way I can sit back and not do anything."

I rested my head on my brother's arm. "I've made a mess of things."

"No, you haven't. He should have believed you."

When I talked to Kinley, I realized that the only way Dom could have known about Caroline was from my conversation with JP in my office the day I left for Nashville. I was so concerned about making my flight and still messed up over the night before that I wasn't thinking straight. I should have locked my door. I shouldn't have made it so easy for him to overhear a private conversation. I should have done so many things differently. I might not have betrayed him like he thought, but I still felt partially responsible.

I played with the charm around my neck. "I don't know how to move on, Mav. I love him so much, in spite of everything. But I wasn't enough for him. He doesn't trust me. He wouldn't listen to me."

He pinched the bridge of his nose and took a deep breath. "Well, he sure as hell is going to listen to me. I'll send that fucker back, begging for forgiveness."

A small smile lifted on my lips. "Whatever you say won't make a difference."

"Rylee, say he does see the error of his ways. Would you take him back?"

"I honestly don't know. He still has this connection to Caroline that I can't compete with."

"I haven't spoken to him yet, but I don't believe that for one minute. The man is crazy about you, I don't care what he says. I saw it with my own eyes."

I wiped at my cheeks. "Did you know about her?"

He shook his head. "Not all of it. I knew he had a serious girlfriend in high school, but I didn't know the entire story until recently. I was a little hurt that he didn't trust me enough to tell me everything, but I understand why he wanted to keep it hidden."

I wiped under my eyes. "He doesn't trust very easily."

"No, he doesn't." His eyes grew soft. "He's a good guy, and I'm not making excuses for him, but I've known him for a long time. The way he acted was inexcusable, but there isn't a doubt in my mind that he loves you. I think this whole thing just fucked with his head. I truly believe when he takes a second to calm down, he will realize what a big mistake he made."

"You really haven't seen him?" I asked. I might have been hurt and angry, but I still cared about him.

He shook his head. "Not yet. I wanted to talk to you first. He might be my best friend, but you're my priority right now. I know you're hurting and it's my responsibility as your big brother to make sure you're okay."

I squeezed his hand. "Thank you. I'm fine, I promise."

"You don't have to be strong for me."

"I'm just a little heartbroken. I'll get over it. I just don't want you to get caught in the middle of this."

His eyes grew soft. "It's too late for that."

I leaned into his side. "Thanks for being such a good brother."

"No thanks necessary. But as your brother, I'm warning you now, if I ever see that sorry excuse of an ex of yours again, I will finish what JP started."

I sat up to face him fully. "What are you talking about? What did JP do?"

He leaned forward, resting his elbows on his knees. "Rhett might have mentioned that JP roughed Dom up a little bit before he showed up at your house the other day."

My hand flew to my mouth. "I had no idea."

Maverick's smile was wide. "Yep, and I can't say I'm sorry about that. I just wish I was there to land a punch myself."

I tapped my lip. "I haven't heard from Dominick since I've been back. Maybe it's time I pay him a visit."

Maverick looked nervous. "Rylee, what's going on in that head of yours?"

I patted his leg. "Trust me, you don't want to know."

———

I walked into the restaurant and spotted him immediately. Brushing past the hostess, I stormed over to the table where Dom and his little group of friends were having happy hour in the middle of a workday.

His head snapped up, and he looked scared when he saw my angry face. Good!

"Rylee." He smiled tightly and gave me a once-over. He knew I could be a loose cannon, so he should have expected this.

"I have some things I need to say to you. We can do this in front of your buddies here or in private, your choice."

I gave Cole and Gavin a little wave while Dom took a slow sip of his drink. He was lucky I was even giving him an option. Lord knew he didn't deserve one. I should have called him out and made sure everyone knew what a terrible person he was.

"I've been expecting you. Of course, I'd like to talk to you."

He was playing it off, trying to act like he was doing me a huge favor, sparing me a second of his time.

"How generous of you." Sarcasm rolled off the tip of my tongue.

"Uh…we've got to get back to work," Cole said right before they both jumped from their chairs, threw a few dollar bills on the table and scurried away, not even bothering to say goodbye. Smart move.

Dom held his hands up. "Before you lay into me, I want you to know that I have reasons for doing what I did."

I stared down at the little weasel, wondering what it was that I ever saw in him in the first place. Most people would find him attractive and charming, but they would be repulsed if they knew the real him.

"I don't care about your reasons," I hissed, feeling my cheeks heat. "JP broke up with me. Are you happy?"

"No, I'm not happy. Have you seen my face?"

I smiled, noticing the light bruising and swelling. "What did you expect? You lied and made him think things that weren't true."

He scoffed. "The guy is a psycho. He's unhinged and you should stay far away from him. If anything, you should be thanking me. I did you a favor."

"If you truly believe that, then the only one who is unhinged is you," I snapped back.

He rolled his eyes. "You're being dramatic."

The man was exasperating. How I managed to put up with him for two years, I would never understand.

"You ruined my life. JP doesn't want anything to do with me because of your lies."

He rattled the ice around in his tumbler without looking up. "They weren't really all lies though, were they? I heard everything, Rylee, and what little blanks were left to fill in were quickly found with a few internet searches."

"What have I ever done to you? Why would you do this?"

He lifted his gaze to mine, and I noticed his eyes were bloodshot. "It might not seem like it now, but I was simply looking out for you. You don't belong with him."

"Says, who?"

"Says the guy who is still in love with you," he said and went back to eating the hamburger on his plate. I opened my mouth and shut it at how casual he was being about this. I wanted to flip the table over and demand an apology for ruining my life, but one of us had to act like an adult.

"You love me, huh?" I leaned in, pushing his plate aside before he could take another bite. "That's a lie. The only person you love is yourself."

He shifted his eyes across the room, trying to see if anyone was paying attention.

"I knew you were going to be pissed, and I thought about all the different ways I could have explained this to you."

"The only thing I want from you is for you to admit what you did, to my face. There is no explanation needed other than you are an asshole."

Scowling, he pushed back in his seat and gritted his teeth. "I'm trying to protect you. Guys like him use and manipulate women like you."

"Women like me?" I crossed my arms. The guy was

digging himself a hole so deep he would need a ten-foot ladder to get out of it.

"You were vulnerable after our breakup. He thought he could just swoop in and try to take advantage of you."

"I was not vulnerable. I finally started thinking clearly." I leaned in so he would hear every word. "And he did not take advantage of me. I was over you before I even had my feet out the door. And if you're going to accuse anyone of manipulating, you might want to start with looking in the damn mirror."

"Rylee," he wiped at the corner of his mouth, "I'm working on myself. I cut back on my drinking. I want to be the man you deserve. Give me another chance to prove it to you."

"Dom." I sputtered out a laugh. "You're drinking right now." I pointed to the empty glass on the table.

He winced. "That was my only drink today. It was a business meeting."

I stared at him wide-eyed. Did he even realize how ridiculous he sounded? "I don't care if it was one or ten. It doesn't matter."

He ran a shaky hand through his hair. "Don't act like you don't care about me, because I know you do. Losing you was one of my biggest regrets. I saw a chance to get you back and I ran with it. I still love you, Rylee, and I couldn't go another day knowing you were with someone else."

He couldn't be serious. We have been broken up for almost a year. And during that year, he has slept his way through the city of Atlanta. This was all one big game to him because he couldn't accept the fact that I'd moved on to someone better. Dom's ego was too big. He couldn't handle the truth.

I pointed my finger at him, calling him out on his

bullshit. "You don't love me. You just want what you can't have. You use people and situations to get what you want, that's not love."

"You need to fucking relax." He scoffed. "I am being sincere. Don't tell me that I don't still love you, and I don't care what you say, I know you feel the same way about me."

I laughed bitterly. "You are kidding yourself, because here is the thing, Dom. I don't think I ever loved you and I can tell you with one hundred percent certainty, that what I feel for you is the exact opposite of that."

The corners of his eyes tightened. "Look, I get it. You're angry. Did I go about this all wrong? Yeah, but like I said, I was looking out for you. You don't belong with a guy like that."

"He is a good man. He has done nothing to you."

JP might have hurt me, but I wasn't innocent in all this. I should have made better decisions in Nashville. I never should have let Dom come near me, and now I was dealing with the consequences.

He glared. "Of course, you're going to defend him."

"You eavesdropped on a private conversation. What was said was none of your goddamned business. You knew I would find out. You knew I would be furious. You had no right to that information."

"I did it because I want you back."

"Well, I have news for you." I was simmering with rage, and my pot had finally boiled over. "After what you did to me, you will never have me back. Now that I know the man you really are, I hate you with every fiber of my being."

He tugged on the collar of his dress shirt. I could see his control slipping. "Once you realize what a mistake you're making, you'll be back and begging for forgiveness."

If I weren't so fired up, I'd laugh at the balls on this guy. For someone with a law degree from Duke University, he sure was thicker than a bowl of oatmeal. "I'm done." I leaned in, putting my face inches from his. "You are not worth a second more of my time. But I'm warning you, come near me again, or spread one dirty, nasty word about JP, and I'll let everyone in this company know what a drunk and disgrace you are. Don't forget I covered for your ass one too many times, and the only reason why I'm not singing like a bird right now is because I want the leverage to keep you quiet. One word to anyone about JP, and you are done. Do we understand each other?"

All it would take was one phone call to the Georgia Bar Association to inform them that he cheated on his exam and his career would be over. Or a visit to our boss to let him know about the deals he fucked up and meetings he missed due to his alcohol-soaked brain.

"He doesn't want you, Rylee." I tried not to flinch at his words, but he was really pushing my buttons. "You're going to throw your one chance away at real love for someone who will never reciprocate your feelings?"

I was shaking and knew it was time for me to get out of there.

I braced my palms on the table. "I had real love, Dom, with *him!*"

With that, I picked up his plate, which was loaded with grease and ketchup, dumped it on his lap, and marched out of the restaurant.

"Rylee, have a seat." Gary Rhys, the president of our company, smiled warmly at me.

"Thanks for meeting with me." I wiped my hands

down along my front and slipped into the chair opposite his. This was the same man who took a chance on an inexperienced kid fresh out of college and hired her.

He frowned at the paper in front of him. "I received a copy of your resignation letter from HR. I have to say, I wasn't expecting this."

Lucy and Stephanie tried to talk me out of it, but every time I thought about working with the same man who caused me so much misery, it killed me inside.

"Please know that this decision wasn't made lightly."

I had difficulty sleeping last night but woke up this morning knowing I had to do this for my mental health. I needed a fresh start. There were people already whispering about my confrontation with Dom in the restaurant. Some of my coworkers had already seen the pictures of him and me on Instagram. And people were talking about JP. I hated the attention and the gossip. I took pride in my job and didn't want this mess to follow me everywhere I went. And even though JP hurt me, I still wanted to protect his privacy.

"May I be frank with you?" He linked his hands together and rested them on the desk.

"Please do." I gave him a soft smile.

"I like you, Rylee, and you're one of the best event coordinators we've ever had. Your leaving will cost the company greatly, but I have to respect that you know what is best for you. Is there anything I can do to convince you to stay?"

Gary and I had developed a very good working relationship over the years. There was no doubt in my mind he would do anything to get me to stay, but that wasn't an option for me. I had to leave while I had leverage over Dom. Staying in a place where I had to deal with him wasn't feasible.

"You have been wonderful to me, Gary. Unfortunately, my reason for leaving is strictly personal. I'm going to miss working here."

The thought of this being the last time I'd be in this room hit me harder than I expected. My eyes got misty as I fought like hell to keep it together. I hadn't planned for so much change in my life. Losing my boyfriend and my job all in the same week left me wondering if I even had a future to be excited about.

He scooted forward and handed me a tissue. "I don't know everything that went down in your life, but I can see that you are heartbroken."

I should have been embarrassed by how emotional I was being, but after all I'd been through, I didn't have the energy to care anymore.

"Let's just say it's been a rough week."

He pulled on his tie. "Would offering you some paid time off entice you to stay?"

"I wish it were that simple." I wiped at the corner of my eyes. I had no plans. No other job offers. I was walking away from a job I loved. I kept telling myself I was young and still had options, yet it didn't make me feel any better.

He lowered his head in defeat. "I'm not going to hold you to the non-compete clause, and I'll make sure you get a reasonable severance package. One that will help get you through the next few months."

My eyes widened. "That's very generous of you."

He was making it so damn hard to walk away. But I had one goal in mind: to start a new life. I needed a fresh start, away from the drama, away from my ex, away from everything.

"I'd be happy to write you a letter of recommendation."

My hands were shaking, and my eyes were filled with

gratitude. "Thank you. I can't tell you enough about how much I enjoyed working here and all you've done for me over the years."

He stood from his chair and held his hand out. "If you ever change your mind, we will find a way to take you back."

If only JP felt the same way.

CHAPTER 29

JP

"You, my friend," Maverick's jaw was tight, "have some fucking groveling to do!"

"Great," I gritted out. He was the last person I needed to see standing on my doorstep. "I was hoping to clear the air with you before you talked to Rylee."

He shoved my shoulder and charged into my house. "I told you that if you ever hurt my sister that we were going to have problems."

It looked like my best friend hated my guts. "I get that you're mad at me and I expected you to take her side. And for what it's worth, I'm sorry this came between us."

He crossed his arms and glared. "That's it? Are you not sorry for the way you treated my sister?"

I didn't want to come across as an ass, so I gave him the best answer I could think of. "I'm sorry for how things ended. I was pissed and probably said some things I shouldn't have, but I think I have a right to be angry."

Maybe someday Maverick and I could at least be cordial toward each other.

"Listen, man, I've been in your shoes. I know how it

feels to be betrayed by someone you trusted, but my sister was loyal to you. She never betrayed you. That jackass she dated overheard a private moment between you two and decided to twist it around and make it sound like something it wasn't."

A private moment? What was he talking about?

When he saw the confusion on my face, he shook his head. "The day she left for Nashville; you guys were in her office having a conversation about Caroline. Ring a bell?"

I might not have remembered everything we said, but it was enough for Dom to draw conclusions and fill in the blanks.

My eyes slammed shut, and I tilted my head to the ceiling. What the hell did I do? I played right into his goddamned hands. That's what I did.

I pulled on my hair, feeling the panic tighten around my scalp. I stood there like an idiot, and with each second that passed, doubt started to trickle into my brain.

"I thought…" Scrubbing a hand over my face, I searched for words. "He told me…fuck."

I felt sick to my stomach. I said things to her that would haunt me for the rest of my miserable life. I should have listened to her. I should have believed in her.

"Yep, and she quit her job too, so way to go, asshole."

"She did what? Why would she do that?"

I had so many questions, but I was having difficulty processing this conversation.

"Because she didn't want to work with the man who destroyed her life."

God! I royally fucked up. Losing her was worse than losing the Super Bowl.

"I'm such an idiot. I blamed her for everything instead of believing her. I pushed her away instead of fighting for her." I turned to my best friend. "I know it doesn't matter now, but I love her, and I'm sorry that I hurt her."

I was rambling like an idiot because I was shell-shocked at learning the truth. A truth I should have known from the start. Instead, I was in the heat of the moment and allowed my emotions to override logic and common sense.

"Good, now get your shit together, take a fucking shower because you stink, and make things right."

My head whipped to his. "You want me to fight for her? After everything I said? You're okay with all that?"

He leveled me with a look. "I don't know every stupid thing you said, and it's probably better that I don't. What I do know is that she's in love with you and based on how miserable you look, I'd say the feeling is mutual."

I couldn't believe he was letting me off that easily. The fact that he hadn't beaten the shit out of me when he had every right to demonstrated what a great guy he was. I was lucky to have him as a friend. I should have been begging for his forgiveness, even though I didn't deserve it.

I looked at the floor in shame. "I do love her, Mav, more than I ever thought possible. But I lost her the second I pushed her away."

I'd been so beside myself that I couldn't think straight, and it cost me everything.

"You know, you're not the man I thought you were. I never took you for a coward."

My eyes shot to his. "How am I a coward?"

"Because you're too scared to fight for her."

"Is that what you think?"

He didn't know what the hell he was talking about. I loved that girl more than anything. I would do anything for her, but how was I supposed to win her back if she didn't want me? I knew Rylee better than anyone. She might have loved me, but I hurt her, and a simple apology just wouldn't cut it.

"JP, you allowed your fears and insecurities to lead you to a place of stupidity. Rylee may be my sister, but she is a good person. She deserves to be loved. She is that once-in-a-lifetime type of girl, and if you just let her slip through your fingers without even trying to salvage things, then you are a fool."

I hated the fact that what he said was true. And now that I knew how badly I messed up, I would do whatever it took to win her back.

"You're right." I sighed. "Any advice on how to get her back or convince her to forgive me?"

He laughed a full-on belly laugh. "Dude, you are on your own with that one. I was just giving you a little advice, but now that I know you're going to try to win her back, then I wish you all the luck in the world." He smirked. "You're going to need it."

———

I stared down at the last message I sent to Rylee.

> Please answer my calls. I know I treated you poorly, and I deserve the silent treatment, but I need you to hear me out. I love you, Rylee. So damn much. I'm sorry I made you doubt that. Please answer your phone.

There was a loud pounding at my door, and before I could lift myself off the couch, Rhett came strolling into my living room, holding a fast-food bag in his hands.

"What is all that?"

He pushed my leg off the table and set the food down. "Making sure you eat something."

"I'm not hungry," I grumbled.

"When's the last time you ate?" he asked, scattering a mixture of chicken nuggets, burgers, and fries in front of me.

"I'm not eating all that crap."

He walked into the kitchen to grab some beers from my fridge. "Yes, you are. You need to eat something."

He set the beer down, and I dragged a hand over my face. "Food isn't going to fix how I'm feeling."

"Okay." He sat down and rubbed his hands together. "Let's talk this out."

"I don't want to talk about this with you."

"Well, that's too bad." He kicked his feet up on my coffee table and leaned back. "I'm the only friend you got right now." He folded his hands behind his head. "That's what happens when you act like a dumbass, but lucky for you I'm not as easily turned off as some people."

I side-eyed him. "Yeah, I feel really lucky right now."

"You hurt her, man." He whistled. "Messed up big time."

I swallowed down a ball of regret. "I'm aware, but thanks for pointing that out."

"Did you try calling her?" Rhett asked while munching on a bag of pretzels like he didn't have a care in the world.

"She won't return my calls." I stood and started pacing back and forth in front of my couch.

"Maybe you should show up at her house or something."

"That's an awful idea, seeing that I got smacked last time I was there."

"Well, you were a dick, so I guess you had it coming."

I shook my head. I can't believe I called this dipshit over to keep me company.

"What do I do? How do I prove to her that I'm sorry?"

I spent all night racking my brain, thinking of ways to apologize. Somehow, someway, I would get her to forgive me, even if was the last thing I did on this earth.

He sighed. "Hell, if I know, man. But I think she needs convincing. You made her feel like shit and acted like an asshole." I narrowed my eyes at him as he continued with the insults. "The way you reacted was dumb and stupid."

I raked a hand through my hair. "God, do I regret opening that door to you."

"You don't have a lot of options right now, buddy, so suck it up. I'm one of the few friends you've got."

"You still haven't told me how to fix this, you jackass."

"I won't take that personally because I know you're only lashing out because you got your heart broken." He took a sip of his beer, and I rolled my eyes. "You need to acknowledge that you were wrong first, otherwise you'll never learn from your mistakes."

"I will gladly admit that I was wrong, but she won't let me get close enough to her to let me explain."

"Can you blame her? Don't get me wrong, I love the woman, like a sister, but she's a tough one. She's stubborn and defiant, I don't see her making things easy for you."

He walked over to my liquor cabinet and pulled out a bottle of Patron. I groaned because nothing good ever happened when we drank tequila.

"Seeing that you know Rylee so well, what do you suggest I do, genius?"

"You need something that screams 'romance.' Women love that stuff." He took a swig from the bottle and wiped his mouth. "You should write a poem and express your undying love to her."

I slumped my shoulders. "I fucked up big time. I'm not sure a poem is going to cut it."

Not to mention, it sounded childish and juvenile.

"Yes, you did. Now you have to unfuck things up." He scratched the side of his face. "First, you need to tell her that you are over Caroline."

I called the guys over last night and told them everything. It felt like a weight had been lifted off my chest. They were supportive and understanding. And once I was done, I wondered why I had waited for so long.

"It's not that easy." I pulled on my neck. "I'm not sure she'll believe me."

"JP." His tone turned serious. "What do you want?"

I swallowed hard. "What I want is Rylee."

When I was with her, I didn't feel so alone—the past few days had been a reminder of that. I hadn't slept or eaten, and I was as miserable as I'd ever been. All I've done is stare at my ceiling in the dark, letting my mind run through everything I shouldn't have done, and how I could have handled things differently.

"Then why are you wasting your time, sitting around getting shit-faced with me, when you should be telling Rylee how you feel?"

The only reason why he was here was because I was desperate. I was sick of being alone.

"What part of she won't talk to me, do you not understand?"

He rubbed his hands together; I could feel the wheels turning in his head. "I think it's time you start putting your thoughts into action."

I squinted my eyes at him. "I think you mean put a plan into action."

"I meant what I said."

I loved the guy, but trying to figure out how his brain worked was exhausting. Between the lack of sleep and the alcohol, I didn't have the mental energy to deal with him.

He kicked his feet up on my coffee table and leaned his

head back. "Let's look at this like a play action." He stood and swiped my iPad off the kitchen counter. "Now, first we need to determine if we are playing man to man or zone defense, because you have to know what you're up against in order to make a play."

I grabbed the bottle off the table and threw some back, hoping it would ease the ache in my chest. I've spent the last few days trying to get the look on her face to fade from my memory. I wanted to forget all the accusations I threw at her. She was pissed, hurt, angry, and I couldn't blame her. I ruined everything, just like I thought I would.

He took the bottle from my hand and took a huge gulp. "What's the last thing Coach says to us before every game?" he asked.

Sighing heavily, I leaned my head back on the couch. "You can't expect to throw a touchdown every single play."

"Exactly." He passed the tequila to me. I ran my fingertip along the rim, telling myself the last thing I needed in my system was more alcohol, but fuck, it was going down pretty damn smooth. So, I took another sip, hoping it would drown out the voices in my head. But the noise was too loud, and my heart was too heavy with regret.

Two beers later and half a bottle of tequila gone, Rhett jumped from my couch, proclaiming he had the best idea ever. We had been googling *ways to get your girl back* for the past hour, but all the suggestions online sounded stupid. I was ready to give up and call it a night.

"You need to woo her, sweep her off her feet. Remind her why she fell in love with you. Don't just apologize, show her."

Oddly, I think he was onto something. It should have concerned me that I was actually listening to him.

"Okay," I said, trying to think of some grand gesture to win her back.

"Yes!" He held his hand out. "Now let me see your phone."

"You're more shit-faced than I thought if you think I would allow you to text her."

He rolled his eyes. "I'm just going to write out a text, see how it sounds. If you don't like it, we tweak it until you're satisfied." He sat up straighter. "Actually, a poem expressing your undying love for her is more romantic."

Him and his damn poems.

Reluctantly, I handed him my phone. I figured things couldn't get any worse. He pulled up my last text exchange with her and hovered his thumb over the microphone button. "Okay, we are going to let SIRI do all the work because I don't trust my grammar right now."

"Roses are red, violets are blue. I'm so lost without you." He smiled like a proud student. "Nah, that's too childish." He looked off to the side and grinned. "I got a better one." He held the phone up to his face. "Baby, I was dumb, but I still like to cum, so if you forgive me, I'll drop to my knees and blow on your pussy like a sweet summer breeze."

"Give me the phone, you dumb idiot," I shouted, shooting my arm out, but he held it out of my reach.

"Would you rather me say, my dick is limp, I miss you so much that I jack off to pics of your tits?" He laughed. "Hold on, let me delete it." He hit a button and looked at me with panic in his eyes.

I snatched the phone out of his hands. "You fucking drunk moron, you just sent the text."

CHAPTER 30
RYLEE

I was scrolling through my phone when I heard the deep timbre of the male voice. "Hi."

Very slowly, my eyes traveled up to a pair of familiar green eyes. I nervously glanced around the bar. What on earth was happening?

"JP, what are you doing here?"

"I'm meeting you." He watched me cautiously.

I was beyond confused and damn near choked on my martini. "Um…no, you are not. I'm meeting someone about a potential job opportunity."

He was dressed in a blue and brown checkered dress shirt. His hair was styled to the side, and his beard was neatly trimmed. He looked good, like always, and I cursed myself for being unable to control my reaction to him.

It took me days to get out of bed. Simple things like taking a shower and getting dressed felt like a chore. After losing my job and my boyfriend in the same week, I had no motivation to leave my house. Until Kinley called and told me she had a friend, Jake Smith, who worked for the

University of Georgia. She said they were looking for someone to run their events.

I should have known she was lying. She didn't even go to the University of Georgia.

His grin was timid as he held his hand out. "I'm Jake, it's nice to meet you."

I reared back. "You tricked me?"

He at least had the decency to look embarrassed. We haven't talked since he ended things. He's tried to call and send me text messages, but I needed time. Time to process, time to grieve. Time to figure out my next steps. Things felt too raw, and I was too upset to talk to him. Not even the hilarious ones I received from Rhett were enough to weaken my resolve.

"You wouldn't talk to me or return my calls."

He was right because I knew just the sound of his voice would break me. And I was still pretty damn angry about everything he said and the way he made me feel. But seeing him up close made the ache in my chest worse because I was still in love with the idiot.

"So, you thought you would show up and accomplish what?"

He rested his hand on the edge of the bar. "I don't know. I didn't think this through, I just knew that I had to see you. Try to make things right and fix the mess I caused."

I didn't know what to make of his words; all I knew was that my body still craved him, and I was barely holding it together.

"I'm not sure that's possible."

He walked away from me. He stopped trying. He gave up without a fight.

His eyes dropped to the floor. "I'm so sorry about everything. For getting scared. For the things I said. I know it probably doesn't make sense to you, but I was scared of needing you and terrified of losing you."

Dark shadows tinted under his eyes, and the exhaustion was heavy on his face. He looked miserable, and my heart ached for him. All I wanted to do was comfort him, but I couldn't let him off that easily.

"You broke my heart." I swallowed hard, trying to fight off the tears.

"I broke mine too." His eyes held so much sadness. And for the first time, I saw the man who carried the weight of the world on his shoulders. Who struggled with himself and felt responsible for things that were out of his control.

I hated to think of him in pain, but he took things too far. He pushed my feelings aside when I begged him to believe me; he chose this ending, not me.

I stood taller, feeling a small amount of confidence return. "You showed up at my door, accused me of lying, of cheating on you, and basically stabbing you in the back. You didn't even give me the courtesy to explain or defend myself. Your mind was already made up, and now that you know the truth, I'm supposed to just forgive you and take you back?"

He scrubbed a hand over his beard. "I know there is no excuse for the way I acted. I regret every damn stupid thing I said. I'm not even going to ask for your forgiveness, because I'll never forgive myself. But I hope you'll at least give me a second chance to prove to you that I will never, ever doubt you again."

Tears pooled in my eyes. "I don't know what you want me to say. You made me feel like I didn't matter."

He pulled on the back of his neck. "That couldn't be any further from the truth. I didn't mean any of it. Once the words started flying from my mouth, I couldn't stop them. I would give anything to go back and not push you away."

"I would never betray your trust," I said, needing him to understand that.

"I didn't know that at the time and I should have."

I wiped at my cheeks. "Thank you for your honesty."

"Tell me what to do?" He stepped forward and cupped my cheek. Just a simple touch was going to be my undoing.

"I don't have all the answers. I don't know if we can move past this."

My heart was telling me to say yes but look where that got me.

I kept replaying the events over and over in my head; all I could see was his angry face and hear his hurtful words. And just thinking about it made me feel like I was right back in my living room again.

He wrapped his fingers around my wrist. "Rylee, I hate to ask this, but I need to know. Do you still love me?"

"As much as I don't want to, I do. I'm pretty sure I always will."

If he were any other man, I would have given up by now. I wouldn't be standing in an empty bar with tears rolling down my cheeks. Wait a minute. I glanced around, noticing the empty seats; even the bartender was gone.

"Did you…" I moved my head from side to side, noticing there wasn't a soul in sight.

"Yes." His forehead dropped to mine. "I had the owner close the bar down and paid him for his time. I needed you alone, without an audience."

We stood there, breathing each other in. I pressed my hands to his shoulders. "You went to a lot of trouble just to get me alone."

"You're worth it." His arms wrapped around me. "There is no one else in this world for me. You are the love of my life, and losing you was like losing the other half of my soul."

My jaw fell open at that proclamation, and it took me a minute to find my bearings. "Please don't say stuff like that to me, unless you mean it. My heart can't take much more."

He lifted my chin and stared into my eyes. "No truer words have ever been spoken."

I wasn't sure how many seconds passed, but his fingers splayed along my hips, pressing me closer. "Rylee, say something."

I licked my dry lips. "This feels like a dream. All I ever wanted was to be with you. I hoped that someday you would love me, and I was prepared to stay with you even if you didn't. Watching you walk away and take my heart with you was something I never want to experience again."

"You won't." He kissed a salty tear away as it trailed down to my chin. "You have my word."

I grabbed his arms, needing something to hold on to. "If I take you back, I can't lose you again. You have to promise me."

"Rylee, the first time I saw you walk onto the practice field, wearing a pair of short jean shorts and a tiny red crop top, I almost tripped during drills because my eyes were glued on you instead of the grass." He paused, taking a deep breath. "Just the sight of you literally almost knocked me over. I was so annoyed with myself because I never got distracted and you somehow knocked the wind right out of me. I felt something move across my chest, something I couldn't explain. Something I never felt before, not even with Caroline."

My bottom lip quivered, and those stupid traitorous tears wouldn't stop falling.

His smile was soft with understanding as he continued.

"I was so taken by you that it spooked me. I kept my distance for my own sanity, but the more I got to know you, the more I liked being around you."

"I don't know why you'd like me. I was kind of a brat to you." I laughed in between sobs.

His thumb caressed my jaw. "It started out as playful banter, and me trying to prove to myself that I could flirt and have fun but not touch. Until one night, we decided to take things further. One taste and one touch, and there was no going back for me. I've loved you for a while now, but I was scared to admit it. It felt like I was leaving her behind, and I wrestled with those emotions more than I cared to admit. But in order for me to be free to love you, I had to let her go." He drew in a breath and let it out slowly.

"I never asked you to leave her behind."

"I know." He pressed a kiss to my forehead. "But I thought you would leave me when you found out the truth. Instead, you stayed, and I knew that you were it for me. If I learned anything during our time apart, it's that if I can't have you, I don't want anyone else. A life with you is the only one I want. So, I'm here begging you for another chance and even though I don't deserve one, if you give me one, I will never give up on you again. I will never put anyone above you again."

"JP." I hiccupped through a sob.

He held his hand, stopping me from talking. "I'm almost done."

He reached over and handed me a paper napkin so I could wipe my eyes.

"Everything in life has a beginning and an end. I want you to be my ending. Until then, you are my present and my future and all I need. I promise never to doubt you again. I swear on my life that you will always come first."

Before he could finish, I dropped my face on his chest

as my tears soaked through his shirt. "Rylee," he kissed the top of my head, "I've made many mistakes in my life, but falling in love with you was never one of them. Please give me one more chance."

"You don't have to beg and I don't want a second chance. I want to start over."

"So, you forgive me?"

I smiled through the tears and pulled on his neck. "I'm not strong enough to stay away from you, and after that speech, I don't want to. I believe in you more than you believe in yourself. More importantly, I believe in us and as long as I believe, I know that somehow, we will find our way."

Our mouths met in a kiss, and everything in the world felt right. The kiss was soft and slow, and when our lips parted, I knew without a doubt that no matter where life took us, I was his, and he was mine forever.

"Come home with me?" he asked in between kisses.

"I can't."

His shoulders slumped forward.

I lifted his head to stare into his eyes. "Tilly is out of town, so I don't have anyone to take care of Oakley."

His body perked up at that. "Can I come to your place?"

My pulse sped up at the thought of being alone with him after all this time apart. "I would like that."

I grabbed my purse off the bar and slung it onto my shoulder. I was ready to get out of there.

"Good. We can pack up your things."

"You mean an overnight bag?"

"No, Rylee." He looked down and paused for a minute before lifting his head. "I want you to move in with me."

My eyes widened. "Excuse me?"

He reached for my hand and entwined our fingers. "I

know you think I'm moving too fast here, but it makes sense."

I just stared at him, blinking. "I'm a little caught off guard, considering less than thirty minutes ago we were still broken up."

"Before you turn me down, listen to me. I love you. You love me. You love my house and I think we could be very happy there. Honestly, the thought of having you there permanently feels right. Oakley would have more space to run around."

"You really want to live together?" My smile was so big I could barely speak.

"Without a doubt."

I chewed on my bottom lip, thinking it over. "Can I have the right side of the bed?"

He grinned. "If that's what it takes."

I tapped my lip. "Will you give up your half of the closet?"

He chuckled. "You can have the whole thing."

I grabbed on to his shirt and peered into his eyes. "Will you let me cook dinner one night a week?"

His face tightened like he was in physical pain. "Sure."

I patted his chest. "You got yourself a roommate."

EPILOGUE

The crowd at Westman Stadium was loud, making it difficult for the Arrows to call their offense. I practically grew up in football stadiums, and I don't remember being this anxious when Maverick played. I was no stranger to screaming fans, but watching JP play his heart out in the last game of his career was bittersweet. I wanted this win for him almost as badly as he did, but their chances of clinching the Super Bowl title were slowly slipping away. They were down by three points, with less than a minute remaining in the fourth quarter.

They ground it out all season but still managed to sweep through three playoff games to claim the NFC Championship. I'd hate to see them lose when they were so close.

"I can't believe people actually pay thousands of dollars to sit in these uncomfortable seats," Mike said next to me. I wanted to laugh because he wasn't wrong, but I couldn't care less about the seats because I'd been standing the entire time.

"You could have sat up in the suite with your mom and

dad," I shouted above the noise. Greg was slowly starting to reach out to JP on a more regular basis, but they still had a way to go. Greg and Vicky had since divorced and he was trying his best to win Jennie back, but I didn't see that happening anytime soon.

"Nah, it's safer down here." He laughed, offering me a piece of his pretzel, but I was too focused on the clock dwindling down to fifteen seconds.

"Where's the flag?" I yelled out when JP got tackled at the forty-nine-yard line.

"Here," he said, trying to hand me his beer as if it would somehow calm me down.

My hands were shaking, and my focus was on the field. "I don't think I can take much more of this."

"At least this is the last one." He squeezed my hand for moral support.

Thank goodness for that. I was sick of him getting hurt. I was sick of the bruises. If I was honest, this was ten times worse than watching my brother play. It brought me great relief to know he was done.

He considered playing for a couple more seasons but didn't want to risk it. His body had paid the price over the years, but thankfully, he was still healthy enough that we could enjoy the rest of our lives together.

My heart started to accelerate when I saw the team huddle and place their arms on each other's shoulders. They started spinning around in a circle and randomly broke from the huddle before running to their assigned positions. JP sprinted to the line, where he was able to line up in a single coverage. The ball snapped so fast that the defense couldn't make the proper adjustments.

Brent dropped back as his offensive line built a protective pocket for him to work with. He launched a fifty-five-yard pass that flew like a missile and landed perfectly over JP's right shoulder and into his waiting arms. He slipped out of the tackle with a powerful leap and ran with such speed with two of the fastest defensive linemen in the NFL on his heels that I was ready to have a heart attack. My guy was a beast as he crossed the goal line and rolled across the turf.

The refs threw their hands up in the air, calling it a touchdown, and all hell broke loose. Every single teammate on the field rushed over and lifted him in the air. I could practically hear his laugh as they all took turns passing him around. They would likely get fined for the theatrics, but it didn't look like they cared.

The refs blew the whistle, and they all ran back to the sidelines while the kicker lined up. The ball went sailing through the goalpost, making it official. They won by four points.

Everyone around me started high-fiving and banging on their seats. The stadium turned into a madhouse when they announced the Atlanta Arrows as the Super Bowl Champions. Blue and orange confetti rained down on the stadium as the entire team ran onto the field.

JP pulled off his helmet and searched me out in the stands. He knew exactly where my seat was. He reserved the entire row for both of our families and close friends. Everyone was here but Maverick and Kinley. Their second baby was due any day, so they didn't make the trip.

I had to squint to see his face, and I might not have been close enough, but I could feel his eyes smiling. He patted his heart three times and pointed to me. I blew him a kiss, and he crooked his finger and motioned to the field.

"I think he wants you down there," Mike yelled into my ear so I could hear him over the noise.

Without waiting another second, I pushed against the

crowd and made my way to the field. Two security guards greeted me.

"Are you Rylee?" the one with red hair asked.

"That's me."

A couple of his teammates jogged over and signaled for me to follow them onto the field. JP was talking to a reporter, so I waited for him to finish. It was probably a three-minute interview, but it might as well have been three hours.

As soon as the reporter walked away, I ran right into his arms. "You played an incredible game. I am so proud of you," I said as he hoisted me up so I could wrap my legs around his waist.

He squeezed my ass and brought his mouth to mine. "I couldn't have done it without you, Sunshine."

A tear slipped down my cheek. Cameras and people were everywhere, but he was all I could see.

"I love you so damn much," I shouted over the noise.

"Do you love me enough to marry me?"

"What did you just say?" I asked, feeling my heart start to race.

I was so caught off guard I didn't even notice Rhett come up behind him and slip something into his hand. I was having a hard time catching up to what the heck was happening.

JP slid me down his chest and got down on one knee. My blurry eyes stared in disbelief.

The entire stadium went quiet as the cameraman projected the image on every screen in the stadium. He held out his hand with a little black box in his palm. I looked down at the ring and gasped. The diamond ring glittered under the bright stadium lights. I did not see this proposal coming. We never even talked about marriage. I was always afraid to broach the subject because I didn't want him to get spooked. I was happy and content with the way things were. But this brought me a sense of peace I never knew I needed.

JP looked as nervous as I'd ever seen him. "I couldn't think of a better time and place to ask you this. I don't have an entire speech planned out. I just want you to know that you are the love of my life. You are the one I want by my side, no matter where life takes us after this. None of this means anything to me without you. When this is all over, the bright lights fade and the noise quiets down, you are all I will need. I love you, Rylee, with everything I have. You are my entire world. Will you marry me?"

Tears fell from my eyes. "Yes, of course, I will marry you."

"She said yes!" he shouted.

The stadium rang out in cheers, and he scooped me up into his arms and kissed me. The roar of the crowd had me laughing through my tears.

"I can't believe you just proposed on national television." I wiped at the moisture on my cheeks.

He grabbed my face. "Oh, you better believe it. I've got the digital proof to prove it." He wiped the rest of my tears that wouldn't seem to stop. "I love you, Rylee, and I can't wait until I can officially call you mine."

"I love you too." I pushed his damp hair off his forehead; his grin was wide as people ran up to congratulate him. "You are crazy, you know that?" I looked off to the side, where the team was waiting for him.

"I'm crazy for you, Sunshine."

I wiped at my lipstick on the corner of his mouth and playfully pushed him backward. "I think it's time you go collect that trophy, Mr. MVP, you earned it."

"That's not the only trophy I'm collecting today. I plan on coming right back to pick up my trophy wife when I'm done giving my interviews." He kissed me on the lips one last time, gave me a crooked smile, and walked away.

I looked off to the side where our families stood with huge grins and turned my gaze back to the man I loved with my whole heart. Finding true love doesn't happen for everyone, but I was thankful I found mine.

Thank you for reading. Want more from JP and Rylee? Get a glimpse into their future in this exclusive bonus epilogue.

You can download this fun, laugh out loud bonus scene here:
https://BookHip.com/GRKQLGV

(Already a newsletter Subscriber? Grab it HERE)

Up next is Fumbled Proposal (Rhett and Natalie's story). More details coming soon.

DO YOU WANT TO KEEP UP TO DATE ON ALL MY NEWS?

Join my exclusive mailing list, where you'll be the first to hear about new releases, sales and other book-related news.
To sign up
CLICK HERE
https://geni.us/sjonesnewsletter

LET'S CONNECT

Are you on Facebook? If you said yes, then I highly recommend joining my reader group. We play games, talk about books and life in general. It's a great place for me to get to know my readers on a more personal level. You can join here:

https://geni.us/izHU

Want to stay up to date on my new releases, sales and comings and goings? You can find all my social media links on my website here:

https://geni.us/sjonesauthor

———

THANK YOU

Thank you so much for reading. I know you have many other books to choose from, I am so grateful you took the time to read mine. If you enjoyed it and if you get a chance, I'd be so grateful if you could leave a review.

I can't wait to share more stories with you.

Love,

Sandy
Xoxo

ALSO BY S. JONES

Fumbled Love (Maverick & Kinley)

THE HARD SERIES

Hard to Love (Chase & Emily)

Hard to Stay (Brad & Lexi)

Hard to Leave (Jack & Chloe)

THE PROTECTIVE SERIES

Whatever It Takes (Quinn & Charlotte)

Whatever You Need (Marco &Amelia)

Whatever You Want (Logan & Ava)

ABOUT THE AUTHOR

S. Jones is a contemporary romance author from Upstate New York. She has a strong passion for writing and reading stories that will rip your heart out before it's put back together again.

If she's not buried in her writing cave, she's usually reading or planning out her next vacation.

She loves to travel to different places and spends all her free with her husband, and two college age children.

When the weather permits, you can find her outside walking her golden retriever, or enjoying a nice cocktail by the pool. She loves cooking and entertaining for her family and friends.

When she's not holding a glass of wine in one hand and her kindle in the other, she loves to hear from her readers at:

authorsjoneswrites@gmail.com

9 781737 088721